WHITE DEATH

Ken McClure

Most of the places and institutions mentioned in this story are real, but all the persons described are entirely fictitious. Any resemblance between characters in the story and any real persons, living or dead, is purely coincidental.

First published in Great Britain in 2009
First published in paperback in 2009 by
Polygon, an imprint of Birlinn Ltd
West Newington House
10 Newington Road
Edinburgh
EH9 1QS

www.birlinn.co.uk

ISBN: 978 1 84697 148 8

Copyright © Ken McClure, 2009

British Library Cataloguing-in-Publication Data
A catalogue record for this book is available
on request from the British Library

Typeset in Adobe Garamond by Palimpsest Book Production Limited,
Grangemouth, Stirlingshire
Printed and bound by CPI Cox & Wyman, Reading

If all the good people were clever,
And all clever people were good,
The world would be nicer than ever
We thought that it possibly could.

Dame Elizabeth Wordsworth
1840–1932
'Good and Clever'

PROLOGUE

Turnberry Hotel
Ayrshire
SCOTLAND
November 2004

'I just don't get it,' complained Sir Gerald Coates as he and his colleague Jeffrey Langley hurried from the helicopter to the nearby 4x4 that was to take them the short distance to the hotel. 'Why in God's name bring us all the way from London to Scotland on a night in the middle of bloody winter for a meeting about medicines procurement?'

'Someone obviously has a sense of the dramatic,' Langley replied sourly as the driver closed the doors with one hand and held on to his cap with the other while the helicopter pilot increased revs again and took off into the night.

'Rumour has it the PM himself was involved in calling it.'

'Rumour had it there were weapons of mass destruction in Iraq.'

Coates gave a wry smile. 'My source was better but I'm damned if I can see the point in coming all the way up here to discuss the cost of paracetamol, can you?'

'Not unless there's some showbiz angle we don't know about.'

'I can't say I'd call *this* show business.' Coates looked at the rain that was falling from the sky like stair rods, hammering on the roof of the car. 'And what was the point of giving us only three hours' notice?'

'No doubt all will be revealed,' said Langley as they reached the long, white frontage of the hotel. 'Ye gods, what's this all about?'

The Range Rover drew to a halt as its headlights picked out two armed soldiers in waterproof capes signalling them to stop. The driver lowered his window and said, 'Sir Gerald Coates and Mr Jeffrey Langley.'

'ID please, gentlemen,' said one of the soldiers, shining his torch at the two men in the back while water dripped from his helmet.

Both men reached inside their overcoats, produced what was required and the soldiers waved them on.

'What in God's name . . .' said Coates as they slowly passed rows of official vehicles interspersed with military and police cars. 'I'd say someone's sense of the dramatic is in danger of going off the scale.'

Langley was about to reply when their vehicle passed a long, black limousine parked at the main entrance to the hotel. A Stars and Stripes pennant hung wet and limp from the staff on the nose of the vehicle. 'Ah,' he said.

'That would explain it,' agreed Coates. 'We're only thirty minutes from Prestwick Airport.'

'And the wide, blue Atlantic . . .'

'. . . that divides our two great nations. Well, well, well . . .'

'Curiouser and curiouser.'

The two men got out and entered the hotel after showing ID again. They exchanged a glance, noting the two Royal Marines, present on the door.

'Thank you, gentlemen, please follow me,' said the soldier who had been detailed to look after them.

Coates and Langley were relieved of their overcoats and given a few minutes to freshen up in the welcome calm and warmth of the washroom to the muted strains of Vivaldi before being shown into the room where the meeting was due to take place. There were about twenty people present – mostly men in dark suits although there were three women and two senior ranking military officers in uniform. They were seated just below the top table, which was currently unoccupied despite having place settings – a carafe of water and a note pad – for six.

Coates and Langley, who were seated halfway down one side, looked for familiar faces. They recognised a number of senior people from the Home Office and the Ministry of Defence and nodded when their eyes met. The man to Langley's left was a consultant from the London School of Hygiene and Tropical Medicine, he read on the place card. 'Any idea what this is all about?' he asked in a friendly but mock-conspiratorial manner.

'I was just about to ask you that,' replied the man. 'I haven't the faintest idea.'

Coates got a similar response from the woman to his right, Dr Linda Meyer from the Center for Disease Control, Atlanta, Georgia. 'One minute I was eating pasta with my family and talking about going bowling, the next I was packing for a trip across the Atlantic to wherever the hell it is we are right now.'

'You're in Ayrshire on the southwest coast of Scotland,' said Coates.

'Thank you,' replied Meyer in a tone that suggested she really knew that much; she'd just been making a point.

The conversation paused as a Royal Navy officer came into the room and approached one of the men sitting at the other end of the table. He whispered something in the man's ear and the man rose to accompany the officer out of the room.

'I know him,' whispered Linda Meyer.

'I'm afraid I don't,' confessed Coates.

'Homeland Security.'

'Ah, interesting.'

'And you are?' asked Meyer, noting that Coates' place card gave only his name.

'I'm so sorry,' said Coates. 'You could say I was "homeland security" too. Albeit a much smaller homeland,' he added in self-deprecating fashion. Coates and Langley were members of a special think-tank charged with advising the government on health matters linked to security issues.

'Ladies and gentlemen, thank you for coming. I think we're just about ready to begin,' said the young man who took the microphone while the top table filled up. 'This meeting has been convened at the specific request of both the Prime Minister and the President of the United States.'

He paused to let the murmur die down. 'And so, without any more ado, I'll hand you over now to Mr Simon Maltby, Secretary of State at the Home Office, who will tell you more.'

Maltby welcomed everyone and introduced those sitting on either side of him. He apologised for the short notice given, particularly to 'our American friends'. 'But, as I'm sure you'll come to realise, what we have to discuss here tonight is of enormous importance to us all. Rather than use the more normal channels of government to disseminate information, the Prime Minister and the President decided to get all the key players together so that they might be told jointly about the problem that besets us. Mr Malcolm Williams, a specialist in strategic planning with MI5, will now fill you in on some background details.'

A tall, painfully thin man, who looked as if he might have been more at home in an academic common room, stood up and cleared his throat. 'Ladies and gentlemen, many people believe that the biggest threat facing civilised society today stems from the rogue proliferation of nuclear weapons and terrorist bomb attacks. While not wishing to diminish these problems, it does not. It comes, as it has so often in the past, from disease. Throughout our history mankind has been at war with the microbial world. On several occasions we've come perilously close to losing that war as when great plagues swept the planet – smallpox in ancient Egypt, bubonic plague in fourteenth-century Europe, pandemic 'flu in the early years of the twentieth century – but in the end, we survived and prevailed. We survived because it was a straight fight, us against them, and we were the ones with brains. We had the capacity to study our enemy and design counter-strategies based on our knowledge of it. The microbes, of course, did not have the benefit of intellect.

'This, I'm sorry to say, is no longer the case. Those who would destroy our society have teamed up with the microbial world to present perhaps the biggest challenge we have ever faced – biological terrorism. The possibility of biological weapons being used against us has been growing ever more likely and now has the potential to be catastrophic. AIDS, pandemic 'flu, tuberculosis, plague, anthrax, botulism, smallpox are all out there along with a host of others. Many have been genetically altered to enhance their killing capacity – disease enhanced by human malice, weaponised microbes.

'These agents are cheap and easy to obtain and their culturing and growth is well within the scope of the average hospital lab technician. A garage in the suburbs could harbour enough biological mayhem to wipe out an entire city. Keeping tabs on nuclear weapon facilities is child's play in comparison to monitoring garden sheds. We cannot hope to detect and head off every threat, so where does that leave us?'

Williams looked up from his notes and paused for a moment before saying, 'We have to take action *before* the threat becomes reality. Acquired immunity is the key to our survival in this war and, in practical terms, that means vaccination. We need vaccines to protect our people against these agents and we need them quickly but the fact is – and this is the reason you are here – we either do not have these vaccines or we do not have the capacity to produce them in the quantities required.'

Williams looked around the room. 'I can see you are all thinking we just step up research and production facilities and everything will be fine. If only it were that simple. Vaccine development and production in western civilisation is the province of the pharmaceutical industry and, rather than increase development and production because of the threat . . . they are currently scaling it down.'

This time a hubbub broke out in the room and Williams had to wait until it had subsided. 'Top level talks in the past week between the UK and US governments and major pharmaceutical companies on both sides of the Atlantic have broken down without agreement. Even personal appeals from the Prime Minister and the President of the United States have failed to convince the industry that their vaccine programmes should be accelerated and expanded as a matter of extreme urgency. In short, they have declined to cooperate.'

'But why?'

'This is where I'm going to hand you over to my American colleague, Dr Milton Seagate from the US Defense Department. Dr Seagate is their chief analyst on health matters. He is also an ex-vice president of Schaer Sachs Pharmaceuticals.'

Seagate was a full head shorter than Williams, stocky and short-changed in the neck department. He tugged at the edges of his jacket, pulling them together in an unsuccessful effort to conceal a bulging waistline, but when he spoke the clown image gave way to a sharp, articulate delivery. 'I believe you British might refer to my position as poacher turned gamekeeper.'

Polite laughter.

'While it's certainly true that I can see both sides of the argument, I am frankly of the opinion – in my gamekeeper role – that we have only ourselves to blame. Chickens are coming home to roost at an alarming rate. Thirty years ago vaccine production was a welcome and lucrative pursuit for the pharmaceutical industry. There was healthy competition among companies for supply contracts and money to be made but over the last ten years the situation has changed dramatically. Successive governments have demanded compliance with an ever-growing raft of rules and regulations. On top of that, it has become fashionable for politicians from all sides to attack pharmaceutical companies. The more cynical among us might suggest that this be for self-publicising ends, but heaven forfend.'

There was muted laughter.

'Whatever the motivation, there is no doubting the damage these people have done. Senator Hillary Clinton's "Vaccines for Children Program", which introduced the prospect of a freeze on prices and the introduction of bulk purchase contracts, may have won her a round of applause from the American electorate but the end result for the drug industry was a whole bunch of vaccine producers throwing in the towel and deciding to call it a day. Senator Charles Schumer calling for government seizure of antibiotic patents from drug companies didn't exactly build bridges either . . . Currently, he's calling for the seizure of Tamiflu patents so that the US government can make its own arrangements for fighting pandemic 'flu. Can you really blame the drug companies for not wanting to play ball with politicians in an atmosphere like this?

'Such companies have to deal with regulatory bodies who demand ever higher standards in the realm of safety testing before they will even consider letting products near the market place while regulatory bodies introduce ever tighter restrictions . . . and all because the public will accept nothing less than one hundred per cent safety where medicines are concerned.'

'Quite right too,' said someone out loud. It drew murmurs of agreement.

Seagate paused. 'Let me tell you a story. Some years ago a vaccine was introduced against rotavirus. It unfortunately caused severe side-effects in something like 150 children worldwide. The press, of course, concentrated on these cases rather than the millions of other children the vaccine had protected with the result that, when a new vaccine against rotavirus came up for licensing some time later, the Food and Drug Administration (FDA) demanded that it be tested on a minimum of 60,000 individuals over a period of ten years before they would grant a full licence. A reasonable estimate would be that six million children a year died in the interim . . . in order to make sure that another 150 wouldn't suffer side-effects. Still seem like a good deal?'

There was silence in the room.

'There is no such thing as a one hundred per cent safe vaccine, ladies and gentlemen, but Joe Public's refusal to accept that, along with the continual assertions by politicians that pharmaceutical companies are fuelled only by greed and self-interest, has led to the situation we now find ourselves in. There are now only a tiny handful of companies left with the will and the expensive, sophisticated set-ups necessary to operate in such a restrictive environment and even these are being squeezed because of the increasing threat of legal action against them from an ever more litigious society. No one in the business wants to get involved in vaccine production any more, let alone engage in the hugely expensive development of new ones . . . just when we need them most.'

'But surely, if push came to shove, governments *could* take over the business of vaccine production for the vaccines we already have?' suggested Linda Meyer. 'I'm thinking of smallpox and tuberculosis.'

'Forget it, Doctor. Vaccine production is a highly sophisticated business demanding specialised facilities and the knowledge and expertise that is only available in companies that have been doing it for many years. Smallpox vaccine production was run down in the aftermath of the disease being declared extinct by the World Health Organisation. We didn't know at the time that the old USSR was full of labs stocking up with the virus which, in worst case scenario, is now being made available to terrorist groups. God knows what modifications have been made to the virus by genetic engineers. Likewise, there has been no general call for vaccination against tuberculosis for many years but the disease is making a big comeback and drug-resistant strains are becoming increasingly common. We need vaccines against AIDS and pandemic 'flu but there is no concerted effort being made to develop them. We're running out of time, ladies and gentlemen. We need vaccines and we need them now.'

Seagate sat down.

Maltby thanked Williams and Seagate. 'I think you can now see the problem, ladies and gentlemen. We desperately need new vaccines but nobody wants to make them. This is an impasse we have to break. Current intelligence suggests that if we don't come up with new vaccines against plague, anthrax, botulism and tuberculosis very soon, we can say goodbye to western civilisation. The Prime Minister and the President have done their level best over the past few weeks to lean on the big players in the pharmaceutical industry and persuade them to step up their development programme, but without success. These people have decided that their shareholders come first, that there is no point in investing huge sums in developing vaccines when they're just going to get bogged down in years of trials and testing with the added "bonus" of lawyers breathing down their necks all the time. This is why we summoned you here. We need to find a way out of this mess.'

'Couldn't you try a softer approach?' asked a woman whose place card proclaimed her to be a senior adviser in the Department of Health.

'We've tried schmoozing them,' said the American sitting to the right of Maltby. He was George Zimmerman, Deputy Secretary at the US Department of the Interior. He had an air of aggression about him that Coates felt might warrant the euphemistic epithet, 'does not suffer fools gladly'.

'We've mooted tax breaks and grant incentivisation but maybe these guys are making too much money already. They're not interested. It's a no go.'

'I was thinking about a more . . . relaxed environment for the companies to operate in . . .' suggested the woman.

'If you mean relaxing the rules and regulations about trials and tests, the FDA won't have it. The public won't have it. There's already a great big spotlight shining on anything to do with drug safety. Committing political suicide isn't going to help anyone. Our anthrax vaccine is a case in point. We've got the goddamn vaccine but we can't use it to protect our boys because of some goddamned court room argument that's been going on for years.'

'There are some genuine concerns about the safety of that particular vaccine, Mr Secretary,' said a silver-haired man wearing the uniform of a colonel in the British army.

'Genuine concerns aren't going to save your ass when the anthrax bug starts to fly, Colonel.'

'We have to strike a balance,' interjected Maltby quickly, trying to defuse the situation. 'Look,' he appealed to the room, showing the backs of his hands to the audience with raised thumbs, 'we're all in favour of sensible precautions but frankly, there comes a point when too much adherence to safety considerations is going to stop us getting out of bed in the morning. The public demands one hundred per cent safety when it comes to vaccines but they can't have it . . . It's not possible.'

'What would an acceptable level of safety be, Minister?' asked the colonel.

Maltby shrugged his shoulders and adopted a disarming smile as if he'd been asked something he couldn't possibly answer.

Zimmerman was not so reticent. 'If certain death is facing you, Colonel, anything with a better than fifty per cent chance of saving you is worth grabbing.'

Maltby didn't disagree but looked as if he wished Zimmerman hadn't quite put it that way.

'I'm sorry, gentlemen,' said Linda Meyer. 'Maybe I'm missing something here but I'm really not clear about what it is you're asking us to do . . .'

Maltby looked to Zimmerman who signalled with a nod that he should continue. 'You people here are the brightest and best we have when it comes to health and security matters . . . on both sides of the pond. We need you to use your ingenuity and initiative to come up with answers. We need vaccines against the bacteria and viruses that threaten our security and we need them fast. Generous funding will be made available to support the best ideas and it will be channelled . . . discreetly . . . and with a minimum of bureaucracy.'

'So you want us to succeed in persuading the drug companies

to cooperate where you have failed?' asked the woman from the Department of Health.

'That would be one way,' replied Maltby. 'But maybe there are others. Who knows? We're calling for initiative from the best minds we have.'

'God, I need a drink,' said Coates as he and Langley made their way to the bar. 'What d'you make of all that?'

A waiter materialised at their table and Coates ordered two large gin and tonics.

'Rock and hard place spring to mind,' said Langley. 'But let's be honest, this is a situation that's been waiting to happen. Public obsession with safety is grinding everything to a halt in the UK. Councils can't put up a bloody Christmas tree without Health and Safety getting involved and lawyers getting all excited about the prospects. Kids aren't allowed out on bicycles unless they're encased in carbon fibre.'

'We must make grazed knees a thing of the past,' intoned Coates.

'So how do we convince the boffins that they should spend time and money developing new vaccines for an ungrateful public who'll require a public debate on *Newsnight* and a consultation with their solicitor before they'll even consider taking them?'

Coates ran his finger lightly round the rim of his glass. 'Well, Maltby did say that money wouldn't be a problem . . . That's a big plus.'

'But the American pointed out that the pharmaceutical companies are already awash with cash.'

'The *big* ones are . . .'

'Would small ones have the wherewithal?' asked Langley, picking up on Coates' nuance.

'They may not have the wherewithal but they do have the brains,' countered Coates thoughtfully. 'Some of the best biological scientists of our generation are to be found in small biotech companies. As I see it, there are three facets to the problem, design of new vaccines, testing them and finally manufacturing them on a scale large enough to protect an entire population. Let's take it one step at a time. If you don't have a vaccine, you don't have anything to test or manufacture.'

'So if I understand you correctly, you propose using government cash to help small biotech companies come up with new ones?'

'Not quite,' replied Coates as if he were still thinking it through. 'We couldn't possibly fund hundreds of small companies, knowing that most of them would fail anyway.'

'Well, they're certainly not going to do it themselves and the City isn't going to touch investing in vaccines with a bargepole.'

'I was thinking more along the lines . . . of a prize, a prize for success.'

Langley's eyes opened wide. 'You know, you may have something there. Everyone loves prizes these days. There seem to be prizes for everything. I sometimes think it can only be a matter of time before we see Wogan presenting prizes at the glittering binmen's awards . . . The nominations for disposal of garden refuse are . . .'

'We'd have to do it discreetly because we wouldn't want to antagonise the big companies any more than we have already but, if the stakes were high enough, I reckon we might tempt quite a few smaller concerns to put their financial toes in the water and broaden their development base. What d'you think?'

Langley's response was positive. 'It would have the added attraction of limiting the entrants to those who really thought they could do it and more than that, to those who could persuade their bosses and backers that they could. Brilliant! We'd attract the brightest and best without even having to fund them unless they were successful. I think I'm going to buy you another very large drink.'

ONE

Meeting of the Special Policies and Strategies Group
Downing Street
LONDON
February 2006

There was an informal feel to the SPS group meeting in Downing Street as indeed there always was when Oliver Noones was in the chair. He favoured the gentleman's club approach to the exchange of ideas despite the fact that two of the six people present were women. It was not the function of the group to formulate policy: this would come further down the line. Rather, it was their brief to consider all aspects of life in the UK and discuss possible courses of action without reference to political dogma.

'Frankly, ladies and gentlemen, Her Majesty's Government could do with some good news from you. In fact, if truth be told, HMG would welcome some good news from anyone right now such is the valley of darkness we currently find ourselves in. Trevor, Susan, I don't suppose you've come up with an exit strategy from Iraq that leaves us looking good?'

Professors Trevor Godman and Susan Murray smiled but treated the question as rhetorical.

'I feared as much. What are your conclusions on that benighted place, dare I ask?'

'Iraq is a complete disaster,' said Godman. 'Public opinion is wholly against it and can't be turned round but we can't pull out unilaterally. If we do, it will all have been for nothing and we can kiss the special relationship goodbye.'

'Something the American Right are keen to do anyway,' added Susan Murray. 'But we must make it clear to the Americans that we will not be drawn into committing any more troops. Apart from anything else, we're overstretched as it is, so if they want to push up the ante and commit more soldiers, that's up to them.'

'It would also be a good idea,' continued Godman, 'if pressure were brought to bear on George W to back-pedal on the "war against terror" rhetoric. Nobody's buying it any more and it's stopping any meaningful dialogue opening up between us and Syria and Iran. Improving relations with these countries is vital in stopping the flow of weapons to subversives in Iraq.'

'Thank you for that,' said Noones. 'Any thoughts on the state of play in Afghanistan?'

'Only that no invading force has ever emerged from Afghanistan with heads held high,' said Susan Murray.

'Rudyard Kipling could have told HMG that,' added Godman.

'Maybe I'll refrain from passing that on,' said Noones with a wry smile. 'And now to matters domestic.' He turned his attention to another couple at the table. 'Charles, Miriam, HMG is becoming more and more concerned about young people being perceived as rude, lazy and shiftless these days and how we deal with the problem is turning out to be something of a political football at the moment. As one paper put it, "Can there be any more dispiriting phrase in the English language than 'local youths'?"'

Miriam Carlyle, chair of the educational psychology unit at

Birmingham University, adopted a pained expression and said, 'HMG has only itself to blame. An entire generation has been brought up to believe that they are untapped reservoirs of talent and potential just waiting to be discovered – no losers, only winners. If they have their way we're going to finish up with a nation of TV presenters . . . with nothing to present because anyone with any real talent and ability will have been declared elitist and forced into feigning mediocrity in order to fit in.'

'I think we all recognise the problem but what do we do about it?'

Charles Motram, Miriam's counterpart at the University of Sussex, said, 'It's our considered view that it's already too late for the sixteen and overs. The die is cast in their case. They're going to have to make lots of unpleasant discoveries for themselves, but it might just be possible to do something about those just becoming teenagers. It's an old enough idea but we feel that summer camps would help promote an environment where the importance of self-discipline and self-reliance could be nurtured.'

'Boot camps?'

'No, definitely not. There should be no suggestion of punishment. We are thinking more along the lines of summer schools in places like the Welsh Mountains, the Lake District, the Scottish Highlands where teamwork can be encouraged and kids can see for themselves the value of getting along with each other, relying on their team-mates in tough situations, earning respect instead of demanding it.'

'Sorry, but I don't see how this differs from similar schemes that have gone before,' said Noones.

'The difference is that HMG pays for it.'

'Why?' asked a surprised Noones.

'What parent of a thirteen-year-old these days is going to say

17

"no" to the chance of getting rid of their offspring for a couple of weeks when no charge is involved? They'd get a break from the relentless demands for money and gadgetry, the kids would gain some notion of self-respect and the rules of social interaction, and HMG might win back a lost generation. We see this as win-win all round.'

'An intriguing notion. Thank you, Charles and you too, Miriam. I'll certainly pass on your thoughts. And now, Gerald,' said Noones, turning to Sir Gerald Coates, 'you are going to make my day by telling me one of your little biotech companies has come up with a vaccine against bird 'flu?'

'I'm afraid not,' confessed Coates. 'The problem remains that while the form of the virus that will pass from human to human does not yet exist, it remains impossible to design a vaccine against it. It's quite possible to design one against the H5N1 strain but there's no guarantee that it will be effective against a mutant variant of it. We have had significant success, however, with another vaccine.'

Coates paused to enjoy the moment and the expression that appeared on Noones' face. 'One of the companies we tempted with the prospect of filthy lucre has come up trumps. In fact, we are rapidly approaching stage two which will involve setting up testing regimens. That's something I'd like to speak to you about later, if that's all right?'

'By all means. It's wonderful to hear something positive for a change.'

The meeting broke up shortly afterwards with Jeffrey Langley asking Coates if he wanted him to stay.

'No point in both of us being here,' replied Coates.

'Remember to ask about the cash,' said Langley.

'What was that about cash?' asked Oliver Noones as he returned from seeing the others to the door.

'The biotech company I was talking about want to know just when they will be eligible for the prize money. Only natural, I suppose. They've invested quite a bit so far.'

'Why don't we go along to my office? I'll break out the Amontillado and you can tell me all about it.'

Twenty minutes into the conversation, Noones got up to replenish their glasses and said, 'Well, I must say it all sounds absolutely splendid, just the sort of thing we've been hoping for. What was that last point you said I should stress to the Cabinet?'

'It's not a live vaccine and apparently that's a big plus when it comes to safety concerns.'

'I'm afraid you've lost me there. What does "not a live vaccine" mean in this context exactly?'

'Vaccines are usually live viruses themselves but they have been attenuated or disabled in some way so that they won't give rise to disease but will still stimulate the production of antibodies in the recipient which will protect him or her against the real thing. For instance, vaccinia is a live virus that will give people protection against smallpox. The trouble is that although most of us don't suffer any adverse reaction to being infected with vaccinia, every now and then some poor soul does. They develop a condition called disseminated vaccinia and that's almost as bad as smallpox itself.'

'I see. No such thing as an altogether safe vaccine . . .'

'Exactly. That's why it's better to use a non-live vaccine if at all possible.'

'Got you,' said Noones. 'And this is one. I'm sure the powers-that-be will be delighted.'

Coates circled the glass in his hand betraying a little hesitation when he said, 'Now that we have the vaccine . . . it will have to be tested.'

'What does that entail?'

'Testing on animals in the first instance where the official hurdles are low and then on humans where they are becoming practically insurmountable . . .'

'Perhaps in the normal course of events . . .' said Noones thoughtfully. 'Something tells me that it when it comes to a contest between national security and public paranoia, someone in government is going to have to make what they delight in calling . . . a tough choice . . . a difficult decision. Only this time . . . it's going to be for real. Leave it with me.'

'You won't forget to enquire about the money?'

'I'll be in touch.'

St Clair Genomics
CAMBRIDGE

'Well, Alan, all ready to give your presentation?' asked Phillip St Clair.

'As ready as I'll ever be,' replied the young post-doctoral scientist who for the first time since an aunt's funeral some eighteen months before was wearing a collar and tie instead of a T-shirt. He was about to present his research to the financial backers of St Clair Genomics – a consortium of people who had been persuaded to invest heavily in an exciting new aspect of molecular biology by the founder of the company, Phillip St Clair.

Some five years had passed without the money men seeing anything like the return they had imagined at the outset, but they had persevered, aware that this was the case for most who had invested in a science that had promised much but, to date, had delivered little. Genetic engineering had not turned out to be the golden goose many had thought it might be and the situation wasn't being helped by the government who had applied strict rules and regulations at every turn in order to appease a public suspicious of anything to do with gene alteration.

It had therefore been something of a major triumph for St Clair to convince his backers to sink even more money into the company in order that Alan, one of his six researchers, could develop his ideas about a new vaccine in the hope of winning government approval and a substantial monetary prize for the company. He was under no illusion, however, that this might be the last gamble the backers would take on his company.

'They're here,' announced Vicky Reid, St Clair's secretary, appearing in the doorway with an excited look on her face.

'Good show,' said St Clair. 'Good luck, Alan.'

Alan was left alone to carry out a last check on the Power-Point slides he planned to use in the presentation. This was a big moment in his career and he knew it. Nothing could be left to chance.

Four extremely well-dressed men were shown into the small seminar room where Alan awaited them. He could smell the expensive leather of their briefcases and the subtle tones of their aftershave as they passed in front of him. It was Vicky who ushered them in, her face wreathed in smiles. St Clair brought up the rear.

'Would you gentlemen care for coffee?' asked Vicky.

'I think we're fine,' replied Ruben Van Cleef, director of venture investment at Edelman's Bank.

Vicky smiled and withdrew and, to Alan's dismay, St Clair said, 'If you'd just excuse me too for a few minutes, I'll leave you in Alan's capable hands.'

Alan suddenly felt very much alone as he faced the four unsmiling men in front of him. 'Perhaps I should just start?' he ventured.

He took the four blank stares as a yes. 'I think you probably know the basics of what I've been doing,' he began, construing the continuing blank stares as a maybe. 'Instead of searching for weakened or attenuated strains of virulent organisms, I've been investigating the possibility of altering their genome so that they are no longer viable but can still give rise to an immune response in people.'

'Their "genome" is their DNA, is that right?' asked Van Cleef.

''Yes, or RNA in some cases. Some viruses have RNA as their genetic material instead . . .'

'Whatever,' said Van Cleef with a dismissive hand gesture. 'So you damage the bug so it can no longer kill people and then inject it into them so they'll make antibodies against the real bug which will?'

'That's it in a nutshell,' agreed Alan.

'So how has it been going?' asked another of the investors.

Alan felt flustered. He had prepared a whole seminar about what he'd been doing and the pitfalls he'd encountered along the way. He'd planned on giving that before addressing such questions. His discomfort, however, was short-lived.

'I think I can answer that,' said St Clair, coming back into the room carrying an ice bucket with champagne in it. Vicky trooped along behind with a tray of glasses.

'First let me apologise for this little deception but I know more than you gentlemen do, including you, Alan. The answer to your question is that it's been going very well indeed . . . The government has agreed to award its first vaccine development prize to our company for Alan's vaccine.'

Smiles broke out all round and the buzz of congratulations filled the room. Alan sank into a chair to close his eyes for a moment as if thanking the Almighty.

'It's early days,' continued St Clair. 'But our man in Whitehall assures me that the sum of four million pounds will be paid to the company in the next few weeks with the remaining eighteen million to be paid after successful trials.'

Alan was showered in congratulations and praise while St Clair concentrated on opening the champagne. 'Apart from the bonus of the prize money,' he said before popping the cork, 'the rights to the vaccine will remain ours and a very favourable licensing contract will be drawn up between ourselves and the government once all the safety tests have been completed.'

'Is that likely to be a problem?' asked one of the backers.

'It's more time-consuming than problematical,' replied St Clair. 'That's largely why we've stayed away from anything to do with vaccines in the past: the paperwork is a nightmare. It can take years for products to reach the marketplace.'

'So what's different this time?' asked Van Cleef.

'Well, nothing that I know of,' replied St Clair, appearing slightly embarrassed at the question. 'But I am assured by our friends in high places that the West's perceived urgent need for new vaccines to protect what they see as a vulnerable population will be taken into account and, to use their phrase, accommodations made.'

'Let's hope that isn't just empty talk,' said another of the backers, Leo Grossman of Lieberman International. 'Taking on Health and Safety in this country is not for the faint-hearted. If it was up to them, you wouldn't be popping champagne corks right now without us wearing crash helmets and safety visors.'

Everyone laughed.

'On the other hand, vaccines have to be tested,' St Clair reminded them.

There were nods of agreement.

'But we can do without a bunch of bureaucrats putting

obstacles in the way just to guard their own backsides,' said yet another of the backers, Morton Lang of merchant bankers, Field and Syme.

'That sums it up nicely,' smiled St Clair.

'I would guess that you folks have already carried out some kind of safety evaluation?' asked Grossman. 'Am I right?'

'Of course,' replied Alan. 'Although there are limits to what we can do in the lab, we've done preliminary tests to ensure that the vaccine will not actually cause any illness or disease in lab animals but will promote good levels of antibodies. Lots more tests to do, of course, before we finally test on humans but things are looking good.'

'I'd agree with that, young man,' said the one backer who hadn't as yet spoken but had been taking everything in. He was Marcus Rose of European Venture Capital, the principal investor in the St Clair company, a tall, distinguished man, wearing an old Etonian tie and speaking with an accent that confirmed the source of his education. 'Well done.'

'Yes, well done,' echoed the others.

Turning to Phillip St Clair, Rose said, 'I think you should insist to the government, St Clair, that Alan's baby be named after him. This young man deserves his place in history.'

'Hear, hear!' murmured the others, raising their glasses.

TWO

Carlisle Royal Infirmary
March 2007

'Dan? It's Keith, he's been taken ill. He's really bad. Can you come?' Marion Taylor's voice broke and she gave in to sobs.

'I'll be there in thirty minutes, love. Hang on.'

Dan Taylor descended from the scaffolding he had been working on like a man possessed. He ran across the building site to his van, shouting to his foreman on the way. 'The lad's poorly; got to go.' He threw his hard hat in the back of the van and cursed as it took him three attempts to start the engine. When it finally caught, the wheels sent up a cloud of sand and gravel as they scrabbled to find grip on the loose surface, causing workmen crossing the site to seek protection for their faces behind hands and elbows.

'Bloody loony,' mouthed one.

'It's Dan Taylor. His kid's been taken bad.'

'No reason to have my bloody eye out.'

True to his word, Taylor was at the hospital in thirty minutes having contravened most of the Highway Code on the way and collected the flashes of at least two speed cameras to mark his passing. He compounded his list of offences by parking on a double yellow line outside A&E and rushing inside to ask where his son was, drumming his fingers impatiently on the desk while he waited for the answer.

He found his wife sitting in the corridor just inside the door of the ward. She was holding a wad of tissues to her face. He sat down beside her and put his arm around her shoulders. 'So, what happened, love?'

'He came home from school at lunchtime, saying that he wasn't feeling well.

'I thought he was having me on at first and I half expected him to say he was feeling better after half an hour and asking if he could go down to the arcade but I was wrong. He was sick a couple of times and his temperature seemed way up so I put him to bed. Things just seemed to get worse though. He was sick again and then he started talking nonsense. I was frightened. I couldn't get any sense out of him, then he tried to go to the bathroom but he fell flat on the floor when he came out and I had to help him back into bed. I called the doctor and some silly cow in Reception told me I should bring him in. Can you believe it? I gave her a piece of my mind and told her I'd be writing to my MP if she didn't pull her finger out and tell the doctor it was an emergency. When he got to the house, he just took one look at him and called for an ambulance. I phoned you as soon as we got to the hospital.'

'So what's wrong with him?'

'The doctor didn't say, just that the hospital would have to carry out tests.'

'Was this our doctor or the hospital one?'

'Ours. No one here's come to speak to me yet.'

Taylor shook his head. 'Surely it can't be rejection after all this time. He's been right as rain for the past year.'

Keith Taylor had been the recipient of a bone marrow transplant nearly a year before after contracting leukaemia. It had been touch and go at the time but he had made a good recovery and seemed to be in every sense a normal thirteen-year-old.

He was perhaps more susceptible to minor ailments than his peers – because of the immuno-suppressant drugs he had to take to stop his body rejecting the transplant – but his energy levels were more than a match for his pals and he was a willing participant in the scrapes they got themselves into.

'The doctor didn't think it was rejection either. He thought it looked like some kind of an infection.'

A young doctor appeared in front of them, white coat flapping open, stethoscope slung round his neck and pushing a wayward flop of fair hair back from his forehead. 'Mr and Mrs Taylor? I'm Dr Tidyman. I'm afraid your son's very ill. We've had to put him on a ventilator and transfer him to intensive care while we try to establish just what's wrong.'

Marion Taylor found this too much. She broke down in tears. 'Oh dear God.'

'Have you no idea at all what's wrong with him?' asked Dan.

'I'm afraid not at the moment. We're waiting for information and data to come back from the lab.'

'You know he had a bone marrow transplant last year?'

'We're aware of that but, if it's any comfort, we don't think that's anything to do with his current problem.'

'The leukaemia's not come back?'

'No, nothing like that. He seems to have picked up some kind of infection that appears to be coursing through his body. Hopefully the lab'll be able to tell us just what's causing it and we can start fighting it.'

Taylor felt a strange conflict of emotions inside him – relief that the leukaemia hadn't returned but quickly followed by fear about the infection. 'This ventilator thing you mentioned . . . ?'

'It's a machine that's doing Keith's breathing for him. We'll keep him on it until he is strong enough to take over again for himself.'

'Can we see him?'

'Of course, but I have to warn you that people often find it distressing to see wires and tubes seemingly coming out of just about everywhere in their loved ones but try to remember that it's for Keith's own good. We have to know what's going on inside his body. This is why we monitor everything we can electronically.'

Dan Taylor nodded and helped his wife to her feet. He kept his arm round her shoulders as they followed the doctor to a small room with a large viewing window into the Intensive Care suite. He gave her a squeeze as they looked at their son lying motionless and unaware while the ventilator clicked and hissed and the monitors beeped their messages. Green spikes chased each other across an oscilloscope, encouraging Dan to think positive thoughts. He'd seen enough TV medical dramas to know that spikes were good. Flat lines were not.

'I want to hold his hand,' murmured Marion.

Dan Taylor looked at the doctor who shook his head apologetically. 'It's for Keith's own good that we keep everyone outside right now. We don't want him having to cope with any more infection.'

'When will you get the lab results, Doctor?'

'We should start getting the first within the hour.'

'We'll wait . . . Can we stay here?'

'Of course. I'll get you a couple of chairs.'

Dan and Marion sat, holding hands in silent vigil, on moulded plastic chairs for at least thirty minutes before either spoke. Marion said, 'Look at the skin on his face . . . It looks . . . strange.'

'I suppose it's the infection, love,' said Dan, but he saw what she meant. The skin on what they could see of Keith's face behind the mask and tubes seemed to have an unhealthy pallor.

The doctor returned with a clipboard in his hand. 'Good news and bad news I'm afraid.'

'For God's sake, tell us the good,' said Marion as if approaching the end of her tether.

'There's no suggestion that the leukaemia has returned and we've ruled out meningitis which was a major concern at the outset.'

'And the bad?' asked Dan.

'We still don't know what's causing the infection. The lab has drawn a blank so far but let me say quickly that that's just from examination of direct specimens. The chances are that they'll have a much better idea in the morning when the overnight cultures have grown up.'

'Sorry?'

'Sometimes there are too few bacteria to find when we look at samples directly under the microscope,' explained Tidyman. 'So we spread them on artificial culture media and leave the bugs to grow and divide overnight in an incubator.'

'So we wait,' said Dan with a sigh in his voice.

'I'm afraid so,' said Tidyman sympathetically.

'Doctor, have you seen his skin?' asked Marion.

Tidyman took a deep breath as if contemplating a question he'd rather not have had put to him. 'Yes,' he said. 'It's giving us cause for concern and the nurses have been asked to keep an eye on the problem. It's probably just some kind of reaction to the infection but they'll apply moisturiser at intervals throughout the night . . . I know the suggestion won't be welcome but there really is nothing you can do here. Why don't you both go home and try to get some rest. We'll call you if there's any change and be assured, our nurses will take great care of your son.'

'Thank you, Doctor,' said Dan, 'I think we will.' He steered

Marion towards the door. 'Mind and call us if anything changes? . . . We won't be sleeping.'

Dan and Marion were back at hospital before nine next morning leaving a sleepless night behind them and half-eaten sandwiches and half-drunk cups of tea all over the house. It had seemed that making tea and sandwiches for each other was therapeutic but eating and drinking them wasn't. They were met by a new doctor when they got to the IC suite.

'You've just missed Dr Tidyman; he's just gone off duty. I'm Dr Merry.'

Dan looked at the slip of a girl in front of him with Dr Jane Merry on her name badge, dark hair tied back with a lilac ribbon, tight matching sweater emphasising young breasts and a pencil slim skirt and dark stockings worn in deference to the notion of power dressing. Christ, thought Dan, she looks fourteen years old. Her gaze and confident voice however assured him that she wasn't. 'How is he this morning, Doctor?' he asked.

'Not much change I'm afraid. We're expecting the lab culture reports within the next thirty minutes,' she said. 'Why don't you both go along to the machine and grab some coffee and I'll come and find you. I'm sure you didn't get much sleep last night.'

Marion warmed to the solicitous comment and smiled. 'Thank you, Doctor, C'mon Dan. Let's do that.'

They were on their second coffee, sitting by the machine, when Dan saw the young doctor coming towards them. There was something in her walk that suggested immediately to him that all was not well – that and the fact that she wasn't alone.

'Hello again,' said Jane Merry. 'This is Dr Trevor Sands, my boss,' she said with a weak attempt at humour. 'We've got the lab results. Dr Sands thought we'd be more comfortable in his office.'

Dan and Marion nodded to Sands and got up to follow the other two without comment although alarm bells were ringing in their heads.

At least, he looks like a doctor, thought Dan, appraising the middle-aged man across the desk from them who was smartly dressed and wearing a college tie. He also found the wedding ring, short conventional haircut, and golf club calendar on the desk reassuring. 'Any further forward, Doctor?'

Sands folded his hands on the desk in front of him and said, 'I'm afraid the lab has failed to find the cause of your son's infection. Their tests for bacteria and viruses have all proved negative . . . so far.'

'But how can that be?' protested Dan. 'If he's clearly got an infection how come the lab says he hasn't?'

'I have to say it comes as a bit of a surprise to us too,' said Sands. 'We felt sure that they'd find the cause if for no other reason than because the infection is at an advanced stage and has spread throughout Keith's body. But, having said that, there's still time for them to come up with the answer. Some bugs take a longer time to grow up in culture than others.'

'And in the meantime?' said Dan, a hint of exasperation creeping into his voice.

Sands made a defensive gesture with the palm of his hand and said, 'Rest assured it's not a case of us doing nothing until we hear back from the lab. Your son is being given a course of broad spectrum antibiotics as we speak.' He saw the blank look on Dan's and Marion's faces and added, 'Broad spectrum in the sense that these antibiotics are capable of killing a wide range of bacteria. There's a good chance that one of them will be the culprit causing Keith's infection.'

'So we wait.'

'There's nothing else for it, I'm afraid. I promise you we'll call you if there's any change in your son's condition.'

Dan and Marion got up to leave. 'Could I just see him once more before we go?' asked Marion.

Dan and Marion stood looking through the viewing window with Jane Merry standing between them. 'His skin,' said Marion. 'It's getting worse.'

'I'll mention it to the nurses again,' said Jane Merry.

Night Nurse Evelyn Holmes glanced up at the clock and saw that it was time to sponge down Keith Taylor. She had all the other information about his condition on the monitors in front of her on the desk nicknamed 'The Enterprise' by the staff due to its similarity to the flight deck of the famous starship. Sponging a patient's skin and applying lanolin required the human touch.

'There we are, my lovely,' she cooed as she gently cleaned the skin of her unconscious patient, thinking to herself that Keith Taylor was round about the same age as her eldest boy who, at three in the morning, would be sound asleep in his bedroom and completely oblivious of the fight that her charge, Keith Taylor, was engaged in.

'You are in a bit of a mess . . . aren't you,' she whispered as she patted Keith's neck and face dry before starting to apply the cream. 'But you're young . . . you can fight this thing . . . In a few months' time . . . you won't even remember any of this . . . Oh, Jesus Christ!'

The nurse recoiled in horror and felt her blood run cold as part of Keith Taylor's cheek started to come away in her hand as she applied the cream. One minute she was making gentle circling motions with the tips of her gloved fingers, the next a hollow furrow had opened up under Keith Taylor's left eye and blood welled up in the trough as the skin gave way and a portion of flesh doubled over to hang limply on Keith's lower cheek like some giant, hellish, teardrop.

Trevor Sands, called from his bed by an anxious duty doctor, had lost all semblance of urbanity. Sweat was trickling down his nose as he listened to Evelyn Holmes' account of what had happened while he examined Keith Taylor for himself. 'Ye gods, his skin is like tissue paper,' he complained as his gloved hands probed gently. He took the bridge of Keith's nose between his thumb and left forefinger while he tried to restore the loose flap of flesh to its rightful place but felt a hollow appear in his stomach when he felt movement between his fingertips.

'Something wrong?' asked the duty doctor.

Sands looked at him, his eyes filled with disbelief. 'The bridge of his nose . . . it's collapsed . . .'

Evelyn Holmes put her gloved hands to her mouth. She was unable to stop herself from saying, 'He's falling to bits.'

The corner of Keith's mouth was next to go causing the ventilator tube to hang at a crazy angle and deepening the living nightmare of all those around him. No one wanted to touch the patient so it was left to Sands, as the senior medic present, to try to reposition the tube but what he feared might happen did happen as Keith Taylor's insides proved as fragile as the rest of him and his trachea collapsed. 'It's hopeless,' he said.

Keith Taylor died shortly after 4 a.m., before his parents could be summoned. Sands was waiting for them when they did arrive and invited them into his office. 'I'm so sorry,' he said. 'I'm afraid it was all very sudden. It took us completely by surprise.'

Dan Taylor looked at the man sitting behind the desk and thought how different he looked from the last time he'd seen him. This man was wearing a sweat-stained T-shirt and needed a shave. He was wringing his hands in front of him as he spoke. Taylor closed his eyes as Sands said, 'We did everything we could.' He'd somehow known the man was going to say that and it left him cold. 'What happened?' he asked in a voice he scarcely recognised himself.

'We won't know for sure until . . .' Sands paused as he realised he was about to mention the post mortem that would have to take place and changed his mind. This wasn't the time . . . 'We don't have all the lab results back yet but it now seems pretty certain at this stage that your son died of something we call necrotising fasciitis.'

Marion Taylor looked blankly over the top of the wad of tissues she held to her mouth, Dan shook his head slightly.

'The papers often refer to it as the flesh-eating bug,' said Sands, letting his voice fall to a whisper in deference to the images he knew he was conjuring up and causing Dan to close his eyes again.

'And what causes that?' asked Dan, clearing his throat and trying to sound controlled when, in reality, his heart was breaking.

'It's a rare condition, usually caused by a bacterium called streptococcus,' said Sands. 'It's a strange bug because it can cause so many different conditions, ranging from sore throats to scarlet fever and unfortunately, on rare occasions, to necrotising fasciitis. We really don't know why its behaviour can change so dramatically. But other bugs can also cause the condition, staphylococcus, clostridium, vibrio and a number of others. We're not at all sure what triggers it off.'

'And these drugs you were giving Keith . . . ?'

'In theory, they should have dealt with streptococcus, and I would have thought most of the others,' said Sands. 'But obviously, on this occasion, they didn't. Hopefully the lab will be able to tell us why not.'

'I want to see my son,' said Marion Taylor in an unexpectedly firm voice.

Sands moved uncomfortably in his chair. 'Mrs Taylor . . . I really don't think that's a good idea . . .'

'I want to see him.'

Sands looked to Dan Taylor for support before saying, 'Keith underwent a great deal of trauma before he died although I can assure you he felt no pain. He never regained consciousness. I honestly think it would be better if you just remembered Keith the way he was.'

Dan Taylor got up and put his arms round his wife while maintaining eye contact with Sands. 'The doctor's right, love. Let's just remember our lad the way he was, not as the victim of some . . .' He searched for inspiration. 'Bastard disease.'

The words 'flesh-eating' were still going round and round inside his head. He was praying that Marion wouldn't stick to her guns. She looked up at him and finally acquiesced with a small nod.

'Bloody bizarre,' muttered pathologist Simon Monkton. 'How come the lab can't grow anything when he's absolutely riddled?'

'I think they're quite embarrassed about that too,' replied Sands, who had chosen to be present at the post mortem on Keith Taylor. 'I spoke to the consultant bacteriologist earlier. He was very apologetic.'

Monkton gave Sands a look that suggested apologies were less than useful.

'You are sure it was necrotising fasciitis?' asked Sands.

'What else could it be?' replied Monkton. 'It's practically eaten the poor kid alive.'

'So that's what you will be putting down as cause of death on the death certificate?'

Monkton paused in what he was doing and looked at Sands over his half-moon specs. 'Of course. Why do you ask?'

'The boy's GP told me that Keith Taylor was part of a monitoring study being carried out by the Department of Health. He is obliged to inform them immediately about any health issues that crop up.'

'Health issues?' snorted Monkton. 'I suppose you could say dying of necrotising fasciitis was a *health issue that cropped up* ... poor kid. I take it you are absolutely sure he wasn't taking any antibiotics when he became ill?'

'That was the first thing I thought of when the lab failed to grow anything from his specimens but his GP and his family assure me that he was taking nothing apart from his usual immuno-suppressant drugs.'

'Ironically, I suppose that's probably why the infection ripped through him so fast,' said Monkton. 'The drugs would severely compromise his natural defences. I take it the suppressants were stopped as soon as he was admitted?'

'Of course.'

'Well, that's it then,' said Monkton, stripping off his gloves and dropping them in a pedal bin he opened with his foot. 'When God throws a curve ball ... you're out.'

'His parents are coming in later to be told the findings of the PM.'

'Something no parents should ever have to do,' said Monkton. 'I don't envy you dealing with the living.'

'Horses for courses,' said Sands. 'I can't say I envy you your job either.' He was looking down at the open cadaver of Keith Taylor.

THREE

EDINBURGH
March 2007

'I don't want to go to school.'

Virginia Lyons glanced at the kitchen clock on the wall. 'Look, Trish, you have to go. There's nothing wrong with you. Why have you started doing this to me? You've always liked school, you know you have.'

'Don't want to go,' mumbled her daughter, looking down at the floor.

'Forget the "don't want to go" nonsense. There has to be a reason. Tell me.'

'Just don't want to, all right?'

Virginia stayed silent for a moment to let the spark of anger in her daughter die down. 'Are you being bullied?' she asked. 'Is that it? Just tell me if you are because I'm not having that. I'll go straight to the head teacher about it. We'll nip this in the bud.'

Trish shook her head silently, still staring studiously down at the floor.

'Then what?'

Silence.

Virginia looked at the clock again and felt her stomach tighten. She was going to be late for work again and, as a divorced single mother, she needed the job even if it was only as a filing clerk in an estate agent's office. It was a busy office. 'Please Trish, tell me.' She tried to make eye contact by taking Trish's hands in hers and pulling her to her feet.

'They've started calling me Patch in the gym class.'

'Patch? And this is what this is all about?' exclaimed Virginia. 'Some silly children calling you some silly nickname?'

'I don't like it. I want it to go away.'

Virginia back-pedalled on derision when she saw the tears start to run down her daughter's face. In recent months Trish had developed a patch of white skin on her right shoulder which ran nearly all the way down her right arm. Since she was dark haired and sallow skinned, it was very noticeable. The doctor had said it was really nothing to worry about and probably the result of hormonal changes in her body – she had just turned thirteen. He was confident that, given time, the discolouration would disappear of its own accord but it had been three months now without much change if any.

'Look, if it will make you any happier, we'll go back to the doctor and tell him there's been no improvement.'

Trish nodded. 'Yes please, Mum.'

'You go off to school now and ignore these ignorant people. I'll call the doctor before I leave for work and try for an evening appointment. Okay?'

Trish nodded and kissed her mother goodbye.

'I'm not sure what you want me to do,' said Dr James Gault when Trish and her mother told him the rash wasn't getting any better. He sounded irritable. 'It's not technically a rash,' he corrected. 'It's just an area of skin discolouration and most probably psychological in origin.'

'Whatever it is, it's showing no signs of going away and some of her class-mates have started calling her names and it's very upsetting.'

Gault shrugged. 'It's absolutely harmless and what's a little name calling. Sticks and stones, eh Trish?'

Trish stared resolutely at the floor.

Virginia felt a wave of exasperation sweep over her at what she felt was Gault's lack of sensitivity. 'It's not harmless if it's making her so unhappy,' she pointed out. 'It's only a matter of time before it begins to affect her school work. School kids can be very cruel.'

'I'm reluctant to refer her to a skin clinic when it's clearly just a harmless and almost certainly temporary loss of pigment. Frankly it would be a waste of time and resources.'

'Then I'd like a second opinion,' said Virginia.

Gault looked as if he might be thinking about arguing but then he changed his mind and conceded. 'Very well,' he sighed. 'I'll see if one of my colleagues will take a look at her but I'm sure they'll tell you the exact same thing. It's impossible to predict how long these things will take to go away. The more you make of them the more likely they are to persist.'

'Tell that to her class-mates,' countered Virginia.

Gault excused himself, leaving Virginia and Trish alone in his surgery. Although he was probably gone for less than two minutes, Virginia found the seconds passing like hours as she and Trish sat in silence. Both were unhappy, Virginia because she hated coming into any kind of conflict with authority and Trish because it seemed that nothing could be done to help her.

Gault returned and said, 'Our Dr Haldane will see you after his next patient . . . if you'd care to wait in the waiting room . . .'

Virginia found Gault's manner was now even more curt and decidedly distant but this was not unexpected. He was clearly taking her request as a personal slur. Gault held the door while she ushered Trish out first. She neither made eye contact with him nor said anything.

Scott Haldane beamed broadly when Virginia and Trish entered and Trish took to him immediately. He was young, broad-shouldered and wearing a smile that suggested openness. 'Hi, how are you doing?' he asked Trish.

'All right,' she mumbled.

'All right apart from the patch on your arm, eh? Let's have a look at it, shall we?'

Trish managed a nod and the suggestion of a smile. She took off her blazer and cardigan before slipping off one sleeve of her blouse and holding out her arm for inspection.

'How long have you had this, Trish?' asked Haldane, closely examining the area of white skin running up Trish's arm.

'Just over three months,' said Virginia.

'Thirteen weeks,' said Trish.

Haldane smiled. 'You're the one counting the days,' he said to Trish as if it was a secret between them. 'Any pain or tenderness?'

Trish shook her head.

'Good. How about itching, scaliness?'

Another shake of the head.

'Good show. So it's just that it's a bit of a nuisance that's a bit slow to go away eh?'

'A bit?' exclaimed Trish with such vehemence that both Haldane and Virginia smiled.

'Have you been abroad in the last year, Trish?'

'I've never been abroad,' said Trish.

'That's not strictly true,' said Virginia. 'Although you were too young to remember, your dad and I took you with us to Greece when you were two.'

'Before you broke up,' said Trish.

'And when was that?' asked Haldane cautiously.

'The break-up or the holiday?'

'The break-up.'

'Three years ago.'

'And three months,' added Trish.

Haldane looked thoughtful.

'She still sees her dad regularly,' said Virginia, figuring out which road the doctor was about to travel down. 'We all get on.'

Haldane nodded.

'Why did you ask if Trish had been abroad?'

'Just a routine question.'

Virginia seemed unconvinced and didn't hide the fact. The question lingered in her eyes. Haldane, however, diverted his gaze and got up from his seat. He brought out a sterile stylet from a small chest of shallow drawers sitting by the wash-hand basin and removed its wrapping. 'Trish, I'm going to give your skin a little prick here and there. I want you to tell me what you feel.'

'Dr Gault didn't do this,' said Virginia, a comment that Haldane ignored as he moved the sharp point around the area of discolouration on Trish's arm.

'Not sore,' said Trish. 'Not sore . . . not sore . . . not sore.'

'Good. Let's try your other arm.'

Trish removed her blouse completely and placed her other arm on the table while Haldane fetched a new stylet. 'Here we go again. Tell me what you feel.'

'A bit sore . . . Ouch! . . . Ouch!'

'Sorry, Trish,' said Haldane, 'I was a bit too heavy handed there. Sorry. Okay, you can put your blouse back on. I think maybe we should refer you to a specialist skin clinic, just to see what they say.'

'What do *you* think it is?' asked Virginia anxiously.

'In all probability the chances are that it's exactly what Dr Gault thinks it is – just one of these unfortunate reactions we see now and then resulting from some kind of emotional stress – but there's no harm in being absolutely sure and, as it's clearly causing Trish some anxiety, the clinic may be able to suggest some treatment to speed up things – UV light or something like that. I'll have a chat with Dr Gault after surgery's over and we'll get things moving on the referral front.'

'Thank you so much, Doctor,' said Virginia. 'I didn't mean to cause trouble. I just want the best for Trish.'

'Nothing wrong with that, Mrs Lyons.'

'How did you get on with the over-protective mother?' asked James Gault, putting his head round the door of Haldane's office when the last patient from evening surgery had gone.

Haldane smiled. 'She's not so bad,' he said. 'Her kid's having a hard time at school and she feels helpless. Perfectly understandable.'

'Fine, but you have to remember we're not social workers,' said Gault. 'What did you think of the child's skin problem?'

'I think you're probably right but all the same I'd like to refer her to the skin clinic just to be on the safe side. There were certain unusual aspects that I'd like checked out.'

'What aspects?'

'It's probably just an over-active imagination on my part,' smiled Haldane, getting up from his chair and giving his colleague a reassuring touch on his upper arm.

'Well, if you really feel you must,' said Gault, sounding slightly miffed. 'Perhaps in the circumstances you'd care to do the paperwork?'

'Of course. Remind me, who's the main man at the skin clinic?'

'Ray McFarlane. He's the kind of chap who won't thank you for wasting his time.'

April 2007

'Look, I'm sorry, Trish, I just don't know what more we can do,' said Virginia Lyons as they came out from morning surgery after getting the results from the skin clinic. 'The specialist agrees with the other doctors. He says it's something called vitiligo. It's nothing serious and it'll go away in its own good time. Unfortunately, there's nothing they can do to speed it up so you'll just have to persevere until it does. I know you hate it, sweetie, but hang on in there, huh? Let's just be grateful it isn't something more serious.'

'You don't know what it's like,' mumbled Trish.

Virginia looked at her daughter with a lump in her throat. She hated seeing her so unhappy. 'I could write and ask Miss Neilson if you could be excused gym classes until it clears up?'

Trish nodded.

'When's your next class?'

'Tomorrow.'

'I'll do it tonight. You can take the letter with you in the morning.'

Virginia came home next evening to find Trish sitting at the kitchen table in tears. Her shoulders were heaving, her head resting on folded arms. Wrapping her arms round her made matters worse for a few moments until cuddles and soothing words finally did their job and she was able to get some sense from her daughter.

'They made me do gym.'

'What?' exclaimed Virginia. 'But what about the letter I gave you?'

'Miss Neilson said there was nothing physically wrong with me so I'd need a letter from a doctor before I could be excused. Everyone was laughing at me.'

'Give me strength,' murmured Virginia, entertaining notions of flattening Miss Neilson with a hockey stick. 'All right,' she said. 'If it's a letter from a doctor they want, a letter from a doctor is what they'll get. I'll go round to the surgery first thing in the morning. When's your next gym class?'

'Friday.'

'Plenty of time.'

'Frankly, Mrs Lyons, I'm inclined to agree with the school. There is no physical reason why your daughter shouldn't take part in gym classes,' said James Gault in response to Virginia's request. 'I'm very reluctant to take sides in this sort of thing.'

Virginia took a deep breath. 'It's not really a physical reason we're discussing here, Doctor.'

'Ah, we're moving into the realms of popular psychiatry, are we? Underlying psychological issues and all that?'

'No, we are bloody not,' replied Virginia, her patience coming to an abrupt end. 'We are attempting to move into the realms of common sense but obviously failing. Kids don't see things the way adults do.'

Gault seemed shaken at the outburst. He paled and swallowed before digging in and saying, 'I have no intention of referring your daughter to a child psychiatrist over a little bit of skin discolouration.'

'But that's the whole point. Trish doesn't see it as *a little bit of skin discolouration*. It's making her whole life a misery. I'm not asking you to refer her anywhere. I'm asking you to write a simple bloody letter which anyone with a modicum of imagination would understand the need for ... but not, apparently, you.'

Gault swallowed again. 'I think we may have come to the point where a change of doctor ...'

'Would be most welcome,' completed Virginia.

'I'll get the forms,' said Gault, getting up.

'That's going to take time. Trish needs help now. I'd like to transfer within the practice to Dr Haldane; Trish seemed to like him.'

Gault looked as if he had just encountered a nasty smell under his nose. He took his time replying and Virginia surmised he was weighing up the pros and cons of full-scale confrontation as the alternative to giving in to her request. She decided to push him. 'Then we could call this just a clash of personalities and there would be no need for me to write a letter of complaint to the relevant authorities about what I see as your complete lack of sensitivity towards my daughter.'

'I'd have to sound out Dr Haldane about such a change.'

'Then please do.'

Virginia remained seated in Gault's surgery. She could feel a nervous tremor in her fingers. She stared out the window behind his empty swivel chair, watching birds come and go in the branches of a tree in the garden – the one she could see above the frosted lower pane. A group of children passed by on the pavement and, in the silence of the room, she could hear their laughter. She wanted Trish to be like that, carefree and happy, but it was getting to the point where she couldn't remember the last time she'd heard her laugh and it was all very reminiscent of the trauma she'd undergone at the time of the divorce. She and Andrew had done their best to shield her from unpleasantness but a split was a split whatever way you looked at it from a child's angle. There had to come a point where it seemed logical for the child to ask, 'If you still like each other so much, why are you breaking up?'

Gault returned and stood holding the door for her. 'Dr Haldane will speak to you when he can. Perhaps you'd care to wait in the waiting room?'

Virginia had thumbed her way through three long out-of-date copies of *Scottish Field* before Haldane was free to see her. He welcomed her with the same broad smile she'd remembered from the time before. 'I'm so sorry about this,' she began. 'I know this must be causing you all sorts of problems but I'm so worried about Trish and Dr Gault doesn't seem to take me seriously. I'm at my wits' end.' She told Haldane about the school forcing Trish to take gym classes when she was so self-conscious about her skin disorder. 'They call her names like "Patch" and I know it seems trivial but it's not to her and it's what goes on in her head that really matters, don't you think?'

Haldane smiled and said, 'It's all right, you don't have to make out the case to me. People like to pretend that kids are just mini adults but they're not. They follow the rules of the jungle until they're taught differently. I take it you'd like some kind of official letter for the school?'

'Yes please,' said Virginia with real gratitude in her voice.

'Do you think that will be enough or do you think Trish might need some sort of counselling or . . .'

'No, really, I think the letter will be enough. If she doesn't have to expose her "difference" in public, I think she'll soon start to be seen as one of the herd again and when that happens, who knows, the damn thing might start to fade and we can all get back to normal.'

'Has Trish noticed any change in the rash since I last saw her?'

'Dr Gault said it wasn't a rash,' said Virginia.

'And technically it isn't,' said Haldane with a smile that conveyed to Virginia some sympathy with her views on James Gault.

'She hasn't mentioned anything. Fading, you mean?'

'No . . . just anything.'

Virginia shook her head.

'If she does, let me know, will you?'

Virginia waited again in the waiting room while Haldane wrote the letter and finally delivered it to her in a sealed envelope marked, 'To Whom It May Concern'. She left the surgery with a lightness in her step. She was going to be late for work again but she had the letter and Trish would be pleased. They could have an evening free of fretting and angst. She started planning a surprise trip to the Dominion, their local cinema. They might even have a burger afterwards – if only to spite the medical profession.

May 2007

'What's up?' Virginia asked Trish in response to her silence.

'It's not getting better,' said Trish.

'The doctors did say it might take some time.'

'Mum, they've no idea what it is let alone how long it's going to take to clear up.'

'But they said it was vitiligo.'

'I looked it up on the net. They've given it a name but they've no idea what it is or what causes it.'

'You don't want to believe everything you read on the net, love. It's full of half truths and downright lies.'

Virginia could see that she was not getting through to Trish who seemed to be on a worrying downward spiral.

'I think it's getting worse . . .'

Virginia was alarmed. 'You mean it's spreading?'

'Spreading . . . and changing . . . my skin feels funny . . .'

'Let me see.'

Virginia examined Trish's arm but couldn't see anything different. She didn't want to say this to Trish so she said, 'Dr Haldane said we should get back in touch if you noticed any changes. I'll make an appointment first thing in the morning.'

Virginia couldn't get an appointment for Trish until the evening surgery session. She hoped to get away sharp from work but it was ten past five before she was finished and she was out of breath from the run home from the bus stop when she opened the front door. 'Trish, I'm home. Did you think I'd got lost?'

There was no answer. 'Trish? Are you in?'

Virginia was puzzled. She had expected to find Trish ready and waiting to go round to the surgery. She looked in the living room and then Trish's bedroom before realising that she could hear a gas burner on in the kitchen. 'Trish?' she said, pushing open the door.

Trish was on the floor. She was sitting at a strange angle with her back propped up against one of the cupboards. Her arm was bare and livid flesh was peeling off it from where she had obviously suffered severe burns. The gas flames from a front burner on the hob and the pot lying on its side on the floor beside her told a horrifying tale of boiling water.

Virginia's throat went into spasm and for a moment she couldn't speak as she fell to her knees beside Trish, her mind a whirlpool of shock and terror. 'Oh my God, Trish . . . oh my God . . . Trish, speak to me . . .'

Trish appeared to be in shock. She was staring unseeingly into the middle distance with glazed eyes. She seemed frighteningly calm when Virginia expected her to be writhing in pain. 'I didn't feel . . .'

Virginia completed the sentence in her head . . . *I didn't feel I could stand it any more* . . . Her daughter had tried to burn the rash off with boiling water . . . She got up and punched three nines into the kitchen phone on the wall with a shaking forefinger and without taking her eyes off her daughter. She almost screamed her request for an ambulance but the calm voice of the operator talked her into giving all relevant information.

Virginia was only vaguely aware of well-meaning neighbours asking what was wrong as she followed the stretcher bearing her daughter downstairs to the ambulance. 'An accident . . .' she murmured. 'Trish has had an accident . . .'

Virginia was an hour into her vigil at Trish's bedside when she became aware of someone appearing at her shoulder. She glanced up and saw that it was Scott Haldane.

'How is she?' he asked.

'Sleeping. They sedated her. They're not sure yet about her arm . . . how did you know?'

'When you didn't turn up at the surgery I popped round to see what was wrong. The neighbours told me about the accident.'

'Accident?' murmured Virginia bitterly.

Haldane felt his blood run cold. 'What are you saying?' he whispered hoarsely.

Virginia didn't take her eyes from her sleeping daughter. 'Trish decided to treat the rash in her own way . . .'

Haldane shook his head in horror. 'No,' he protested. 'Trish is a perfectly level-headed girl. She was upset but she wouldn't do anything like that . . .'

'It's what she said,' interrupted Virginia.

Haldane shook his head. 'Tell me exactly what she said.'

'She said she didn't feel she could go on.'

Haldane shook his head again as if unwilling to believe what he was hearing and then a thought seemed to occur to him. 'Tell me again,' he said. 'Her precise words, nothing else.'

Virginia looked at him as if he were making some kind of a mountain out of a molehill but rather than argue she took the easiest course of action and said, 'She said, "I didn't feel . . ." She didn't have to say any more. I knew what she meant. I'm her mother.' She looked up at Haldane and saw the questioning look on his face. 'What is it?'

Haldane behaved as if he hadn't heard her. He gave her a preoccupied look and mumbled something about having to go.

FOUR

Dr Steven Dunbar opened his eyes at the ring of the alarm and let out a groan. He could have done with another hour in bed but he had to be at the Home Office by ten. Normally, a summons to the Home Office with the prospect of a new case to investigate would have had him fired with enthusiasm and champing at the bit but a slight over-indulgence in gin and tonic the night before had taken the edge off this and left him with a nasty headache instead. He made some strong black coffee and used it to wash down three aspirins before taking a shower and lingering longer than usual in the soothing spray before he revisited his problem.

Steven's problem was Jenny, his nine-year-old daughter, and her new-found skill in manipulating grown-ups.

Steven's wife Lisa had died of a brain tumour many years before and since that time Jenny had lived with his sister-in-law Sue and her solicitor husband Richard in the Dumfriesshire village of Glenvane in Scotland. She had been brought up as one of their family along with their own two children, Robin and Mary, with Steven making a point of visiting as often as he could – usually every second weekend, at least for a week in

51

the summer and with special efforts being made at birthday time and Christmas.

In the early years, Steven had seen the arrangement as being temporary – he just needed time to get back on his feet after the nightmare of losing Lisa – but as time had gone on, reality had struck home and he had come to accept that there was no way he could do the job he did and bring up a daughter on his own. Apart from that Jenny was happy and settled with Sue and Richard and their family and they had quickly come to love her as one of their own.

Sue had been very close to Lisa and often remarked that she could see so much of her sister in Jenny as she grew up. Steven had noticed this too and it could bring a lump to his throat. The thought that Lisa lived on in Jenny gave him something to cling to in dark moments when he found himself dwelling on his loss – something that still happened from time to time, even after all these years.

Usually, something simple would trigger it off, seeing a family walking by the Embankment on a sunny afternoon, opening the door to his apartment on a winter's evening and finding nothing there but darkness and silence. These incidents, however, were few and far between these days but when they did happen, Steven had to remind himself that he didn't have a lifestyle that permitted the playing of happy families on anything approaching a regular basis. He had a job that was demanding, unpredictable and occasionally downright dangerous. He didn't know where he would be from one day to the next and, on more than one occasion over the years, he'd come within an ace of losing his life.

He had met Lisa on his first big investigation for Sci-Med after having been sent to a hospital in Glasgow where she had been one of the nurses. That particular assignment had brought both of them into danger although they had seen this as the exception rather than the rule with neither suspecting that the job would be any kind of impediment to married life. Now with the benefit of hindsight, he had to admit that there had been several more 'exceptions to the rule' over the years, perhaps too many for him even to consider inviting another woman to share his life without him having to give up the job.

This did not mean that female company had been absent from his life during his widower years. A number of women had appeared on the scene like shooting stars, bringing love back into his life, but, for one reason or another, these relationships – and a couple of them had been very special – had all proved ill-fated before the need for the final hurdle to be crossed. Could he give up the job? He wasn't at all sure.

Jenny's latest ploy had been to play off Sue and Richard against him. If Sue had occasion to discipline her she would react by pointing out that she didn't have the right; she wasn't her real mother and that she wanted to go and live in London with her father. When Steven told her that this was not possible she had accused him of not really loving her and abandoning her in Scotland. Sue and Richard were very understanding about Jenny's behaviour and recognised it for what it was – childish tantrums – as did Steven. Jenny could not have had any more loving parents than Sue and Richard and she loved them too except when she was having one of her moments.

Despite this, Steven still felt bad about the whole thing. Perhaps it was guilt over never having really tried to find the kind of job that would have permitted him to bring up a daughter or perhaps it was hearing the accusations that Jenny had levelled at him about not loving her, but he had felt bad enough to climb into the bottle on the previous evening. But today was another day and he had to get his act together before he went to see John Macmillan at the Home Office.

Steven had been born and brought up in the Lake District, in the small village of Glenridding on Ullswater where he had had an idyllic childhood. Being raised in the shadow of the Cumbrian mountains had fostered in him a great love of the outdoors. He had done well at school which had encouraged parents and teachers to push him towards medicine and he had duly complied by studying medicine although his heart had never been in it. After qualifying and doing his registration year, he had stopped pretending and admitted to his nearest and dearest that this was not the career for him. He had bitten the bullet and informed his family that he was joining the army.

Army life had suited Steven down to the ground. A naturally strong and athletic man, he had taken to it like a duck to water, serving first with the Parachute Regiment and then on secondment to Special Forces where his medical skills were put to good use, ensuring over the years that he had become an expert in field medicine with his skills honed in the deserts of the Middle East and the jungles of South America.

The operational life of a Special Forces soldier, however, has a lifespan not much longer than that of a professional footballer and Steven had recognised this as he approached his mid-thirties. Time for him was running out and the bleak prospect of a return to civilian life was looming on the horizon. The few options he could see had not seemed attractive. The medical career train had long passed him by and demand for his specialist skills in wound treatment and bullet removal under field conditions was not going to be great in civvy street. He saw himself becoming an in-house medic for some large insurance company or working in a liaison role in the pharmaceutical industry, but neither appealed to someone who had always known and craved adventure.

He was saved from the humdrum, however, by John Macmillan

who ran a small, elite unit at the Home Office called the Sci-Med Inspectorate. This comprised a small body of medical/scientific specialist investigators who would look into the possibility of crime in areas where the police lacked expertise. Steven was taken on board as a medical investigator and had found his niche in an organisation that only recruited the best. It was a pre-condition that Sci-Med investigators had to have had other careers in which they had demonstrated resourcefulness and initiative on top of professional expertise and above all, in John Macmillan's estimation, be blessed with a great deal of plain common sense.

Macmillan took the view that no man knew how he would react in times of great personal danger until he was actually placed in that situation and tested. Very few ever were in the course of 'normal' jobs. Paint-ball wars and building bridges over imaginary rivers on company weekends was fine for salesmen but not for Sci-Med people. Heroics on the rugby pitch were one thing but continuing to fight on when the man beside you has just been cut in half by automatic weapon fire was quite another. Steven had been tested for real and had come through with flying colours. He had become one of Sci-Med's top investigators.

Steven still didn't feel too well but there were no outward signs of this as he dressed in dark blue suit, light blue shirt and Parachute Regiment tie and checked his appearance in the mirror, making sure his dark hair wasn't standing up. Macmillan did not like sloppiness. He checked his watch and set off for the Home Office.

As he climbed the stairs he knew that the first thing Jean Roberts, Macmillan's secretary, would ask about would be Jenny and so it proved.

'She's growing into quite the little madam,' replied Steven.

'Ah,' said Jean. 'Getting to that age?'

Steven nodded. 'How's the choir doing?' he asked, wanting to change the subject and knowing that Jean's membership of the South London Bach choir was one of the cornerstones of her life.

'Busy, busy, busy,' replied Jean. 'One concert every week for the last three weeks and we have a ten-day tour coming up in two months' time.'

'That should keep you out of mischief.'

'Who's keeping who out of mischief?' asked John Macmillan, coming out of his office and slapping a file into Jean's in-tray. 'Good to see you, Steven,' he said, shaking hands. 'It's been a while.' He turned back to Jean and said, 'If you could get these out by tonight, I'd be obliged.'

'Yes, Sir John.'

Steven reflected on Macmillan's knighthood as he followed him back into his office and closed the door. It had been granted in the New Year's honours list and was, in his view, long overdue. Macmillan had always been his own man and had guarded Sci-Med's autonomy over the years with a zeal that had irritated many in the corridors of power. Suggestions by the powerful that Sci-Med might back off in certain investigations when they came too close to home were always met with refusal and expressions of support for his people. He never excused or ignored any wrong-doing among the rich and powerful of the land and had, as a result, made many enemies along the way. He had once confided in Steven that certain individuals would move heaven and earth to stop him being recognised for Sci-Med's achievements so Steven had been tickled pink to see Macmillan's name come up in the honours list. He hoped that his own success in thwarting a potentially disastrous attack by Al-Qaeda on the UK and US government infrastructures might have helped pave the way for the award because he liked and respected the man enormously and had on several occasions in the past good cause to thank him for his backing when he personally had ruffled the feathers of the establishment.

Steven had been on leave for the past two months, recovering from traumas suffered in his last assignment and regaining fitness at a military camp in North Wales through an arrangement with his old regiment.

'How are you feeling?'

'Fit and well,' replied Steven.

'Jean said you were up in Scotland when she contacted you?'

'I was up seeing Jenny.'

'How is she?'

'I think I've just had a glimpse of the terrible teens to come.'

'Oh dear,' smiled Macmillan. 'Girls are always so much more trouble than boys in my experience.'

'So people keep telling me.'

Macmillan settled back in his chair, looking every inch the Whitehall mandarin, tanned, smooth skin belying his sixty odd years, silver hair swept back, confidence oozing from every pore. He looked at Steven for a moment before saying, 'Nothing too serious I hope?'

'Not in the great scheme of things, I suppose. It was just a bit of a shock to discover that she no longer sees me as her knight in shining armour who appears out of the mist from time to time bearing gifts and telling tales of fighting evil. She now sees me as a flawed human being who chose to abandon her in a far-off land.'

Macmillan smiled and said, 'I'm sure that's not true but it sounds like something all fathers in your position have to go through. The irony is that if you really had abandoned her and she never saw you at all, she'd regard you as a saint and make all sorts of excuses for you.'

'I suppose.'

'Don't let it get you down. You've always had Jenny's best interests at heart. She's always been a much loved little girl. I remember celebrating her birth in this very office.'

Steven nodded, anxious that the conversation should move on.

Macmillan flipped open a file on his desk. 'Dr Scott Haldane, aged thirty-five, general practitioner in a family practice in Edinburgh – at least he was until he took his own life, leaving a wife and two young children behind.'

Steven screwed up his face. 'Thirty-five? No age at all. What's our interest?'

'I'm not sure that we have one but . . . it's possible. His wife is absolutely adamant that he did not commit suicide.'

'Not an uncommon reaction,' said Steven. 'It must be a very hard thing to come to terms with.'

'Well, she apparently has no intention at all of accepting it. She insists that her husband was murdered and has been seizing every opportunity to say so in public. She insists that he was a devoted husband and father, a committed Christian, happy and settled in his work and with everything to live for.'

'What do the police say?'

'The body was found in woodland quite near where he lived – a place known as the Hermitage of Braid. He'd cut his wrists. There was nothing to suggest it wasn't suicide apart from the fact that there was no note and the police failed to establish any reason why Haldane would want to end his life. He seems to have been everything his wife says he was. Perhaps for the same reason, they didn't come up with any reason why someone would want to kill him either.'

Steven thought for a moment before saying, 'This is all very sad but I'm sorry, I don't see where Sci-Med comes in.'

'Haldane's wife is an intelligent woman: she's a nursing sister at the new Royal Infirmary in Edinburgh. She insists that her husband was murdered over something to do with one of his patients.'

'One of his patients killed him?' exclaimed Steven.

'Nothing like that,' said Macmillan. 'The practice was treating a child for a skin complaint. The mother wasn't happy with the way her child's case was being handled by their GP and a transfer was made to Haldane's list. He referred the child to a skin clinic and something called vitiligo was diagnosed.' Macmillan gave Steven an enquiring glance.

'Not really my area but, as I remember, it's a fairly harmless pigment problem leading to patches on the skin – more embarrassing than dangerous.'

'That would fit with what I have here,' said Macmillan. 'Apparently the child, however, was very sensitive about her condition and her mother came home one day to find – in her opinion – that she'd attempted to remove the patch with boiling water.'

'My God,' said Steven.

'According to Haldane's wife, there was some disagreement about this. Haldane was sure the scalding had been an accident.'

'What an awful situation,' said Steven. 'How is the child?'

'She's still in hospital and quite seriously ill.'

'Was she able to throw any light on what happened?'

'She's hardly said a word since the "accident".'

'Poor lass. How old?'

'Thirteen.'

'A very self-conscious age,' said Steven.

'Any thoughts so far?'

'Just from what you've told me, it's not inconceivable that the girl did it deliberately, in which case Haldane may have felt guilt over not having referred her for psychiatric help earlier. Whether that might have tipped him over into taking his own life . . . well, who knows?'

'Haldane's wife is adamant that her husband did not believe for a minute that the child had done it deliberately. He was convinced it had been an accident.'

'I think the popular term could be "in denial",' said Steven.

'Mmm. On the other hand, his wife says that he seemed to be much more upset about some other possibility that he refused to discuss with her.'

'You mean that someone else might have scalded the girl?' asked Steven with wide eyes.

Macmillan flinched at the suggestion. 'I don't think that was what she meant at all. She says that her husband started making lots of telephone calls, demanding to speak to people about the case, but he constantly ran into some problem because the girl was on some monitoring list that she thinks was called "green sticker patients". Apparently it made her notes difficult to obtain.'

'What's this green sticker business all about?' asked Steven.

'That's where you come in,' said Macmillan. 'I'd like you to find out. Have a root around; see what you come up with but most importantly, don't stand on anyone's toes, especially not Lothian and Borders Police. They won't have forgotten the last time you strayed on to their patch. I've asked Jean to find you somewhere discreet to stay while you're up there. She'll give you details on the way out along with the file.'

'On my way.'

Jean Roberts smiled when Steven emerged from Macmillan's office and brought out a folder from the top drawer of her desk which she handed to Steven. 'All we have on the Edinburgh case. Feel good to be operational again?'

'I guess,' smiled Steven. 'Sir John tells me you were arranging accommodation?'

'Yes, he said he wanted it to be somewhere discreet where your presence would hopefully go unnoticed. I've booked you into a B&B in a lovely Victorian building just north of Edinburgh's New Town called Fraoch House – Fraoch means "heather" in Gaelic. My sister and I stayed there last year when we went up for the festival. It has everything you'll need. I've included directions in the file.'

FIVE

It was raining when Steven's flight touched down at Edinburgh airport and the chill wind that caught the side of his face when he stepped out from the aircraft brought back memories of times past in Scotland's capital. He had mixed feelings about the city. He'd had some good times here with Lisa when they'd come through from Glasgow – as they often had – to visit theatres and galleries but he'd also had some bad when past investigations had brought him into conflict with people who could only be described as plain evil. Glasgow, where he and Lisa had lived for a while, wore its heart on its sleeve while Edinburgh hid its face behind net curtains.

A poster on the wall of the terminal building proclaimed Scotland as the 'best small country in the world' while a series of overweight and unsmiling ground staff wearing fluorescent waistcoats herded passengers into snaking queues and shouted at them to keep mobile phones turned off.

'What the hell do they want this time?' grumbled the man in the queue beside Steven. 'Boarding pass? Passport? Shoe size? Inside leg measurement?'

Someone else in the queue whispered, 'Passport.' And the fact that she'd whispered it made Steven realise just how much people had come to fear and dislike authority in airports. Security – or imagined security – had no sense of humour at all and common sense was an alien concept to those charged with implementing it. Anyone displaying dissent would end up in very serious trouble. This in itself was a terrorist victory of sorts.

'Where to?' asked the taxi driver.

'Fraoch House in Pilrig Street,' replied Steven, reading from the note he had in his pocket.

The driver drove without comment, something that suited Steven as he'd had more than enough of taxi drivers' philosophy over the years. Silence was just fine. He could enjoy the sights instead of listening to a treatise on the Iraq war or the virtues of proclaiming Scotland an independent nation, not that the sights today were particularly welcoming but maybe that was the rain. Everywhere looked nice in sunshine. Anywhere could be depressing in the wet.

The driver uttered his first words as they came to a round-about at the head of Leith Street when a woman driving a 4x4 swung out in front of him. 'Bloody loony! No wonder she needs a 4x4 to keep her arse safe!'

Steven didn't comment and silence was resumed until they pulled up outside Fraoch House. 'There you go.'

Steven paid the driver and tipped him well. This brought a smile that looked like an unnatural act.

'Steven Dunbar.'

'Gavin Houston,' said the smiling young man at the desk. 'Welcome. I'll show you to your room.'

Steven had been a bit apprehensive about what a B&B that Jean Roberts and her sister enthused about might turn out to be, but the place was clean, modern and comfortable. It even had wireless broadband available which he used to connect his laptop to Sci-Med to check for any messages. There were none.

Despite having given it some thought, Steven had not yet decided on his first move in the investigation. He wanted to avoid crossing swords with the local police but didn't think that should be a real problem: they had already written Scott Haldane's death off as suicide and closed the book on it. They would have no great inclination to take what his wife was saying seriously. He lay down on the bed and looked up at the ceiling while he thought through his options.

Judging by what he'd learned from the files, Scott Haldane's widow, Linda, might not be the best person to interview first. She was clearly unwilling to even consider the possibility of her husband having committed suicide. Virginia Lyons' daughter, Trish, was currently very ill in hospital so the fate of their GP would not be uppermost in her mind. That just left the medical practice where Haldane had worked. Steven thought he might be able to get a feeling for what had gone on in the disagreement over Trish Lyons' treatment by speaking to someone there and perhaps get someone to throw some light on 'green sticker' patients while he was at it.

A phone-call later and Steven had arranged to meet with Dr James Gault at the practice in Bruntsfield after evening surgery. Bruntsfield was a part of the city that Steven knew well – a nice area about a mile south of the city centre and about three miles from where he was at the moment. Seeing that it had stopped raining, he decided to walk there. It would give him the chance to re-acquaint himself with the city and also afford him some exercise at the end of a travel day with all the enforced inertia that had entailed – especially as it would be uphill all the way.

Steven was a little too early when he reached Bruntsfield Links, the pleasant, green area near to the street where the surgery was located, so he sat down on a park bench and watched the world go by for a few minutes. A child's ball landed at his feet and he picked it up to return it to the child who came to retrieve it but stopped some distance away. 'Hello,' he said.

The child gave him a suspicious look and snatched up the

ball when Steven rolled it to him. His mother called out and it was possible to pick out the anxiety in her voice. He thought it sad that speaking to anyone in the park was a definite no-no for children these days. Steven got up and started to walk towards the surgery, wondering whether the threat to children now was really any greater than it had been in the past or was it perhaps just the perception of it that had changed? He suspected the latter but there was no time to ponder any longer. He'd reached the front door of the surgery.

'What can I do for Sci-Med?' asked James Gault, examining Steven's ID and settling back in his chair.

'I'd appreciate hearing your views on Scott Haldane's suicide. You must have known him well?'

'I did . . . or at least I thought I did. It was as big a shock to me as it seems to have been to everyone else. I would have thought he'd be the last person on earth to take his own life. He had everything to live for.'

'That's what I keep hearing,' said Steven. 'No skeletons in the cupboard?'

'None that I know of. I always found him a perfectly straight-forward chap who cared deeply about his patients – more than me if truth be told,' Gault added with a snort.

Steven gave him an enquiring look and Gault said, 'Call it the cynicism of my years. Forty years of dishing out pills and writing prescriptions can take the shine off youthful zeal.'

Steven nodded. At least the man was honest. 'I understand there was some disagreement over the treatment of a child patient in the practice – a girl with a skin complaint?'

'Not really a disagreement,' said Gault dismissively. 'The child's mother wanted us to pull out all the stops for a condition that I regarded as trivial and harmless. We do not have unlimited resources in the NHS – something I failed singularly to get across to her. In the end she asked for a change of doctor and Scott took her and her daughter on to his list.'

'I understand this child is now seriously ill?' said Steven.

Gault nodded. 'Although not as a result of the original complaint,' he stressed. 'An accident with boiling water, I understand.'

'Her mother doesn't seem to think it was an accident.'

Gault gave him a look that said, *she wouldn't*. 'I wouldn't know anything about that,' he said.

'If the child were to confirm that she did do it deliberately and it was connected with the way she felt about her skin problem, would it alter your view of Dr Haldane's death at all?'

'What are you getting at?' asked Gault suspiciously.

'Dr Haldane's wife is convinced that her husband was murdered and his death was linked in some way to this child's problems. I suppose I on the other hand was considering that he may have taken his own life over feelings of guilt for what had happened to the girl and for not having referred her for psychiatric assessment. Would you consider that a possibility?'

'No way,' said Gault. 'Neither of us saw the need for psychiatric involvement at any stage. The girl had a harmless condition but was being given a hard time over it at school. End of story as far as I'm concerned. She was scalded in an accident, something that played no part in Scott's death.'

'Thank you, Doctor,' said Steven, getting up to go. 'You've been very helpful. Oh, by the way . . . who or what are green sticker patients?'

'No great mystery,' said Gault. 'A number of children from schools all over the country were exposed to tuberculosis at a school camp they were attending in the Lake District – TB is a growing hazard these days with children coming to live in this country from all over the place. Appropriate steps were taken and the children are being monitored as a precaution. They have green stickers on their medical records – hence the name. Any time they appear in the surgery with a problem, a report has to be made and sent off with their records for updating, filing, cross-referencing or whatever the trillions of NHS pen-pushers do these days with the information they keep demanding.'

'I see,' smiled Steven. 'I understand Trish Lyons is a green sticker patient?'

'She is,' agreed Gault.

'Dr Haldane's wife claims that this caused problems in some way for her husband.'

'It might well have done if her records weren't available when he was looking for them – in fact, come to think of it, that might well have happened. The girls in the office would have sent them off the first time she appeared here in the surgery with her skin complaint.'

'So Dr Haldane being annoyed about this would be perfectly understandable in your view?'

'Absolutely, having your patient's medical records lying in some bureaucrat's office when you need access to them had me spitting tacks too.'

Steven thanked Gault again and left. He walked back across the green sward of the links and into the Bruntsfield Hotel where he ordered a gin and tonic and sat down by a window in the lounge to consider what he'd learned. Sci-Med had no interest in whether Scott Haldane had committed suicide or not although his own view was that he possibly had. In his experience, suicide victims often had a deeper, darker side to them than they ever showed to the world and the act often came as a complete surprise to those around them, even to those who knew and loved them most – a bit like serial killers who were nearly always described by neighbours as being quiet and polite, keeping themselves very much to themselves.

Steven had to decide if there was a possibility that Scott Haldane had been murdered and perhaps more importantly from Sci-Med's point of view, for the reason that his wife was suggesting – that it had had something to do with one of his patients. He would have to talk to Haldane's wife to get a feel for what value could be put on her allegations. Was she just a grieving widow who couldn't live with the knowledge that her husband had taken his own life or did she have some good reason for saying the things she was saying?

Using the information contained in the Sci-Med file, Steven rang Linda Haldane as soon as he got back to Fraoch House. The conversation was brief.

'Look, I'm in the middle of bathing the children. Can you call back later?'

Steven called back in an hour and explained who he was. 'I was wondering if we could meet. I'd like to speak to you about your husband and what happened to him.'

'Is there any point?' asked Linda. 'Everyone's made up their minds. He took his own life.'

'I haven't.'

After a sigh and a pause Linda Haldane said, 'All right, come round tomorrow morning when the children will be at school and in the nursery . . . about ten thirty.'

Steven took a note of the address and went out to eat. He chose an Italian restaurant: he felt like having noise and bustle around him. This city held a lot of ghosts for him.

Steven left Fraoch House immediately after breakfast and chose once again to walk across the city on a bright, sunny morning which showed Princes Street and the castle, high on its rock, to best advantage. Linda Haldane lived in what she described as a 'lodge house' in the Grange district of the city – a bit further south than Bruntsfield and one of the most desirable areas of the city with its avenues of mansion houses nestling behind high stone walls and towering trees. He found the Haldane home without difficulty and announced himself at the entryphone at the side of the iron gates, which responded to electronic command and gave a slight shudder as an electric relay released the lock.

Linda Haldane appeared at the side door to the cottage, just inside the gates, and moved a child's tricycle to one side before inviting Steven inside. 'We can talk in the kitchen,' she said.

Steven took a seat at the pine kitchen table and noted the children's breakfast dishes on the draining board. Thomas the Tank Engine was the recurring theme. 'Two boys?' he asked.

Linda followed his gaze to the plastic dishes and smiled. 'Well done . . . but you are some kind of detective. I'm sorry, who are the Sci-Med Inspectorate exactly?'

Steven offered a little more detail.

Linda nodded and said, 'Makes sense. So Scott's death falls within your remit?'

Steven gave a non-committal shrug. 'Possibly.'

'How can I help?'

'We located a newspaper report in which you said that you believed your husband was murdered.'

'I do,' said Linda with more than a trace of defiance. 'There's no way that Scott committed suicide.'

'You also told the police that you thought his death was in some way connected with a patient he was treating, a child named Trish Lyons.'

'And you've come here to tell me to shut up and stop rocking the boat?'

'No, I've come here to establish the truth.'

Linda looked at Steven as if she wasn't sure whether to believe him or not. 'And how will you do that?' she asked.

'What I'm doing right now, talking to people, asking questions.'

'Ask away.'

'I need to know why you think your husband was murdered and why you think it had something to do with a thirteen-year-old girl patient.'

'If you'd known Scott, you wouldn't even consider for a moment that he took his own life,' said Linda with a rueful smile. 'It's ridiculous. He would have been the last person on earth to ever contemplate suicide. He was the most positive person I've ever known.'

Steven's look suggested that this wasn't enough.

'We were happy,' insisted Linda. 'We had everything going for us. Scott had a job he loved, we have two beautiful children, we live in a lovely city. We loved each other dearly ... what more do you need?'

When she saw that Steven was still unconvinced, she added, 'Apart from anything else, Scott was a committed Christian; he spent three years doing voluntary work in Africa before becoming a GP. You really have to be an optimist to do something like that. Talk about lighting a candle being better than cursing the darkness ... Suicide was against everything he stood for.'

'Lives can change in an instant,' said Steven, although not unkindly. 'There's been a suggestion that he might have made a mistake over a young patient which led to her injuring herself. You don't think this could have led to feelings of guilt?'

Linda shook her head. 'No way,' she said. 'I know all about what happened to Trish Lyons. Scott would have been the first to admit to making any kind of mistake if he had made one but he didn't. He didn't believe for a moment that the girl's injuries had been self-inflicted. He was sure it had been an accident and that her mother had come up with the self-harming claim to get her own back on the medical profession who she felt had been less than understanding about her daughter's problems. I'm sure the girl herself will confirm this when she recovers.'

'If she recovers,' said Steven. 'She's very ill.'

'I'm sorry.'

Steven asked the obvious question. 'So, if there was no conceivable reason for your husband to commit suicide, Mrs Haldane . . . what possible reason was there for anyone to murder him?'

'I have no idea,' said Linda through gritted teeth. 'I only know that Scott was found with his wrists cut and he didn't do it – someone else did.'

For a moment Steven saw despair appear in Linda Haldane's eyes along with the grief that was already in residence. 'Look . . .' she began, 'I know how ridiculous this must sound to you and people can be forgiven for thinking I'm just a silly woman who can't cope with her husband's suicide . . . but I am absolutely certain Scott didn't take his own life.'

Steven could see that this was beyond question. 'I'm sorry, I'm afraid I need more than your certainty,' he said. 'I need a motive for his murder. I need to know why you told the police you thought his death was connected in some way to Trish Lyons.' He knew it sounded cold but it was also true.

'Although Scott was convinced that Patricia Lyons' scalding had been an accident, he had some theory about her condition that he couldn't pursue because of obstacles he claimed were being put in his way. He got very angry and upset about it. Scott hardly ever used bad language but I heard him on one occasion calling it "a bloody conspiracy".'

Steven said, 'I understand the girl was one of a group of children being monitored centrally by Public Health people so he might have had difficulty in accessing her medical records?'

'It wasn't just that,' said Linda, 'although he was annoyed about that too. He kept making phone-calls to people who either wouldn't speak to him or wouldn't give him the information he was looking for.'

'What sort of information?'

'Scott wouldn't tell me. He said it was something he would have to be absolutely sure about before he could say anything to anyone.'

'But if it was upsetting him so much, you must have asked him about it on more than one occasion?'

'Of course, but he refused point blank to tell me.'

'Not even you, his wife?'

'Not even me,' agreed Linda with a sad smile, taking the point Steven was making.

'Have you no idea at all who he was trying to phone?'

'I assumed it was the people who were holding the girl's medical records – but that's an assumption on my part.'

'Actually, it's quite hard to see why he would need the girl's medical records,' said Steven. 'I mean, you'd think her medical history wouldn't have had much bearing on the case of a scalding accident.'

Linda shrugged but said, 'You might not think so but I heard him tell whoever it was he was talking to that he needed more information and telling them to stop being so obstructive.'

'And you're absolutely sure your husband never let anything slip about what he was thinking?'

'I think I would have remembered if he had,' said Linda. 'Although there was one occasion when he came off the phone and sat down looking shocked. When I asked him what was wrong he said, "They actually told me to back off if I knew what was good for me."'

'But you don't know who "they" were?'

'Sorry.'

SIX

Steven headed back into town. He decided he would have to access Trish Lyons' medical records for himself in order to see if he could find out what Scott Haldane had been so upset about. The surgery was on the way so he would stop off and ask if the records were there although he suspected they might not be, in view of what had subsequently happened to Trish Lyons.

'I'm sorry,' said James Gault after checking with the practice manager. 'They were returned to us but had to be sent off again to the sick children's hospital to have the scalding incident entered . . . I should think by now the hospital will probably have sent the notes on to the central monitor. Some day they'll come back to us . . .'

'I get the picture,' said Steven. 'Perhaps you could let me have the address of the monitoring body?'

'Of course; I'll have to ask Cathy.'

To Steven's surprise, Gault returned not only with the information he'd asked for but with a woman following along in his wake. She was introduced as Cathy Renton, the practice manager. 'It's not quite as simple as I thought,' confessed Gault.

'Health matters are devolved in Scotland,' said Cathy. 'But monitoring in this instance is part of a UK initiative. The bottom line is that we have to channel the records through the Scottish Executive who then forward them to the UK body and vice versa when they're returned.'

'Why?' said Steven.

'I suppose the Executive needs to know what's going on,' said Cathy with a half apologetic smile. She handed Steven the address and phone number of the Scottish Executive body dealing with the forwarding of medical records.

'Woodburn House,' Steven read out.

'It's not far from here,' said Cathy. 'It's in Canaan Lane, just off Morningside Road.'

It took twelve minutes from the time Steven showed his ID to the girl on the desk until he was shown into the office of someone who 'might be able to help', the intervening time having been taken up with internal phone-calls and subsequent transfers within the building. Miss Collinwood, when he was shown into her office, wasn't too sure either if it was 'within her area'.

'What is it you need exactly?' she asked.

'I'd like to see the medical records for a patient named Patricia Lyons, a thirteen-year-old girl registered with Dr Scott Haldane at the Links Practice in Bruntsfield.'

'Then why come here?'

'Because the Links Practice told me her records were sent here.'

'I'm sorry. Why?'

'Apparently she was a *green sticker* patient – one of a number of children being monitored after having been exposed to tuberculosis at a school camp in the Lake District.'

'The Lake District? That's in England. I don't think we would be monitoring anything as far south . . .'

'No,' interrupted Steven, starting to run out of patience. 'You're not doing the monitoring but apparently medical records from Scottish children on the list have to come to you first before being submitted to the English body.'

'Why?'

'What an awfully good question,' said Steven. 'But they do. Surely somebody here must know where the girl's records are?'

'Give me a moment.' Miss Collinwood picked up the phone.

Steven got up to examine the watercolours on the walls of the office, hoping to find a calming influence in them while the phone-calls mounted up. Lucky number five, he thought when he heard Miss Collinwood say, 'You do, Jan? That's great.'

'Mrs Thomson's been dealing with green stickers.'

'Good show,' said Steven with a smile. 'Where do I find her?'

He was led along the corridor to another almost identical office where Jan Thomson, a short pixie-like woman with bobbed hair and a pointed nose, shook his hand and invited him in. 'How can I help?'

Steven temporarily suppressed his belief that the person asking this question could invariably never be of help and told her what he was looking for.

'I see.' The woman repositioned her computer screen and typed in some details. 'Out of luck, I'm afraid. They've gone south.'

'Don't you keep copies?'

'No, we just forward them and return them to the relevant surgeries when they come back.'

'Like a conduit,' said Steven flatly.

'Well, we like to know what's going on.'

'So what is going on?'

'I'm sorry?'

'If you like to know what's going on, presumably you have some record of what's going on.'

'No, I told you, we just forward the records and then return them.'

'Without noting anything down?'

'Look, Dr Dunbar, I don't make the rules.'

'Of course not, forgive me,' said Steven, back-tracking in a damage limitation exercise. There was nothing to be gained from conflict with authority. 'We're both cogs in the great government machine. Perhaps you can give me the address of the UK body that deals with green sticker patients?'

A few taps on the keyboard and Jan Thomson wrote details on to a Post-it note.

'And maybe some information about the school camp that was the cause of all this?'

More taps and another note.

Steven thanked the woman and left thinking that he had exactly the same feeling inside him the last time he'd been in a government office. He reflected that he was experiencing the same exasperation that had upset Scott Haldane so much. He found a coffee shop in Morningside Road and ordered a double espresso while he brought out the two notes from his pocket. The monitoring body was called 'Lakeland TBMG' – which he guessed stood for TB monitoring group – and was located at an address in Whitehall, London. The school camp was called 'Pinetops' and was sited on the shores of Lake Windermere, not far from Bowness-on-Windermere and not that far from where he himself had been brought up. It conjured up images of *Swallows and Amazons* and children having a good time in glorious scenery.

The TB monitoring group, however, reminded him of stories he'd read in the medical journals recently about tuberculosis making a comeback in the UK after having almost been wiped out in the Sixties. For some years now, it had been thought no longer necessary to test children for the illness or offer them protection against it. This had resulted in a population which was vulnerable to the disease now being brought in by immigrants – a touchy subject in both medical and social terms. On top of this, drug-resistant strains were not uncommon and were proving notoriously difficult to treat.

As he sipped his coffee, Steven wondered if there was any point in his staying longer in Edinburgh. He supposed he could have a word with Trish Lyons' mother but wasn't convinced that that would serve any real purpose apart from upsetting the woman. On the other hand if Trish had said anything about her 'accident' since her admission to hospital it might help a great deal and this was something he should be able to find out discreetly from the hospital itself.

If Trish had scalded herself deliberately when psychiatric help at an earlier stage might have prevented it, then suicide was still a possibility for Scott Haldane despite all that his wife had said. If, however, the girl could confirm that it had been an accident, the puzzle over Haldane's death would remain and the possibility of murder, however unlikely, could not be dismissed entirely although there were no forensics to support this and no apparent motive either, only the belief of a grieving widow.

Steven arrived at the Royal Hospital for Sick Children shortly after 3 p.m. and spoke to the registrar involved in treating Trish Lyons, Dr John Fielding.

'She's still a very ill young lady,' said Fielding.

'The scalding was that bad?'

Fielding appeared to be uncomfortable with the question. He scratched his head in a nervous gesture and said, 'The scalding was bad but . . . it's the healing process that really concerns us . . .'

'In what way?'

Another nervous gesture. 'Well . . . it's not really happening.' The words hung in the air like the calm before a storm. 'It's as if there's some psychological reason for her not improving.'

'I understand she was suffering from vitiligo,' said Steven.

Fielding nodded. 'That's what's making us think there's a psychological factor involved. Apart from the burns, the vitiligo seems to be spreading. She's developed patches on her legs and feet.'

'Poor girl, she's having a nightmare time of it.'

'Actually . . . she's disturbingly calm and detached about it. Worryingly so.'

Steven remembered Trish's mother apparently having said something similar about her daughter's state when she found her on the kitchen floor. 'A long time for shock to persist,' he said.

'Quite,' said Fielding.

'Has she said anything at all yet?'

'Not much.'

Steven put his cards on the table and admitted that his real interest was in establishing whether the scalding had been accidental or not.

'I can help you there,' said Fielding. 'She claims it was an accident.'

'Ah,' said Steven, pleased and somewhat surprised that his question had been answered. 'She did speak about it then?'

'She said she slipped on the kitchen floor and her arm caught the pot handle on the way down.'

'Well, that clears things up,' said Steven but he noticed that Fielding's expression harboured doubts. 'But you don't believe her?' he asked tentatively.

'I don't know for certain but I think there's a possibility she might be saying that to spare her mother's feelings.'

'What makes you think that?'

'When her mother asked her about the agony she must have suffered from the boiling water, Trish maintained that it was nothing, she didn't feel a thing.'

'Oh,' said Steven, feeling a bit deflated. 'I take it she's been seen by a psychiatrist?'

Fielding nodded. 'Who didn't get anywhere with her. She seems locked in a world of her own.'

'Her mother must be going through hell.'

'She is,' agreed Fielding. 'But there's an even bigger hurdle on the horizon. If the healing process doesn't start kicking in soon, Trish is going to lose her arm.'

Steven walked back along the seemingly endless corridors of the Victorian building, noting how out of sync with his feelings the cheerful Disney characters on the walls were. He suspected that generations of anxious parents had felt the same way.

He called Sci-Med to say that he would be returning to London on the following day. He asked Jean Roberts to contact the Whitehall body responsible for 'green sticker' monitoring to request that they send Trish Lyons' notes to Sci-Med.

'Not spending the weekend with Jenny?' asked Jean.

'Maybe next weekend,' replied Steven, suddenly feeling even worse, although when he started contemplating the hell children could put their parents through, he had to admit his own problems faded to nothing when compared to what Trish Lyons' mother was going through.

Jean Roberts had the file waiting for him when he entered her office. He had taken the first BA shuttle down from Edinburgh and had dropped his bag off at his apartment before walking over to the Home Office.

'I hope you appreciate the trouble we had to go through to get these,' said Jean.

'Why so?'

Jean shrugged. 'They really didn't want to part with them. I had to get Sir John to intervene.'

'Can't think why,' said Steven, looking genuinely puzzled. 'But thanks as always.'

'As always, you're welcome,' said Jean, tongue in cheek.

The door to John Macmillan's office opened and he looked out. 'Thought I heard your voice. Got a moment?'

'Wild goose chase?' asked Macmillan when Steven had closed the door.

'Pretty much,' agreed Steven. 'There's no reason to believe Scott Haldane was murdered. On the other hand there was no real reason for him to commit suicide either. The girl patient, however, says her scalding was an accident so there was no reason for Haldane to go off on a guilt trip . . . although that's far from clear too.'

'Sounds like a foggy night,' said Macmillan.

'You could say.'

'Can I ask why you requested the girl's medical notes?'

'Haldane's wife said that her husband had terrible trouble getting his hands on them and finding anyone to talk to about the case. I suppose I wanted to see what the fuss was about. Why do you ask?'

Steven's question was designed to highlight the fact that Macmillan did not usually question his investigators' motives for doing anything.

'Don't misunderstand me; I'm not interfering,' insisted Macmillan with a smile. 'I just thought you should know that I had considerable difficulty in obtaining them after Jean told me she'd hit the wall with a simple request. It may be nothing but if government departments start getting obstructive when we ask them for things, it usually means . . . it's something worth knowing. I just thought I'd tell you.'

'Thanks,' said Steven. 'It's probably tied up with the green sticker business.' He told Macmillan about the children's exposure to TB at the Lake District camp. 'I suspect they're a bit sensitive about giving out information. They wouldn't want the press having a field day over it.'

On impulse, Steven decided to walk back to his apartment and sit by the river for a while to leaf through Trish Lyons' notes. His concentration was interrupted at intervals by the commentary from passing Thames tourist boats as they ploughed their way up and down the river. 'The building on your right is . . .' Not that much concentration was required. It was clear from the notes that Trish had been a healthy baby who had grown into a healthy child. In fact, there was nothing at all out of the ordinary in the notes until she had gone to Pinetops school camp and had been exposed to a child there who had been diagnosed with pulmonary tuberculosis. She'd been given BCG vaccine as a precaution and 'green-stickered' to ensure that her future health and wellbeing was monitored.

Steven was puzzled and disappointed. He couldn't see what all the fuss had been about or why it should have proved difficult to get access to these notes or why Scott Haldane had needed to discuss anything in them. What was there to discuss?

Well, there must have been something, Steven concluded, but he certainly wasn't looking at it. That fact alone was enough to stop him drawing a line under the affair. He hated the idea of missing anything – a good investigator turned over all the stones and there must be one stone missing in this case. They might well be sensitive to outside interest but he would ask the green sticker people a few more questions just to see what happened.

Steven decided to focus on statistics. He would ask how many children were affected by the exposure and just for good measure . . . who they all were. He would also ask for details about the child who had caused the panic in the first place – name, address and current state of health. He called Jean Roberts with his request.

'And if they should baulk at that and ask if this information is really necessary?' she asked.

'The answer's yes.'

It took two days and another intervention by John Macmillan to get the information Steven had requested and even then, details about the child who had contracted tuberculosis were missing. 'Sir John will explain,' said Jean.

'Her Majesty's Government is only too well aware of the potential repercussions of revealing that a non-white immigrant child has exposed a number of British children to the scourge of tuberculosis,' said Macmillan. 'It has been decided that only a select few should have access to the child's identity and where-abouts. A top level decision, I'm told.'

'And we are not among that select few?'

Macmillan paused for a moment before saying, 'I know it's in your nature to dig in your heels and demand to know things. This is not a criticism; you've usually been right when you've smelled a rat but on this occasion I have to ask you formally if it is really necessary for you to know the identity of this child – if it is, I promise I will get it for you but first you have to assure me that it is.'

It was Steven's turn to pause for thought. 'No, it isn't absolutely necessary,' he admitted, although he added quickly, 'at the moment.'

Later, Steven sat down in his favourite chair by the window in his apartment where he could see the river traffic pass by through a gap in the buildings opposite. A Sci-Med salary did not run to a riverside address. He had had to settle for one street back but it had everything he needed and afforded him views of the sky and the river. As he slumped back in the chair looking up at passing clouds, he wondered what Scott Haldane had been so upset about – not being given details of the child with TB? He doubted that. It could have no relevance. No, he concluded, he was still missing something here. Maybe he still hadn't asked the right question.

Yet again, he looked down the list of children who had been green-stickered for follow-up, one hundred and eight from across the UK and all in the twelve- to thirteen-year-old age range. Was it something in the way they had been exposed to the danger that had alarmed Haldane? Maybe a lack of primary checks on immigrant pupils? Possibly something in the way the incident had been handled at Pinetops? Or afterwards? The continuing niggle that he was missing something made Steven decide to drive up to the Lake District in the morning.

SEVEN

After several hours of stop-go travel due to road works and the sheer volume of traffic, Steven finally found some space on the M6 and gunned the Porsche Boxster up to the legal limit. As he'd noticed so many times before, the further north you travelled, the lighter the traffic became. He had bought the Porsche as a replacement for his ageing MGF when it had finally become too expensive to maintain and its British manufacturer looked like joining it in the knackers' yard. He knew that a Porsche might be considered an indulgence when he had so little time to drive it but he had compromised on his original plan to nuke the piggy bank completely and go for the 911 and settled instead for its little brother, the Boxster. Boys' toys? Maybe, but there was no Mrs Dunbar to point this out.

Around two in the afternoon, the soporific boredom of the motorway gave way to the winding roads of the Lake District where the Porsche came into its own, sticking to the road like glue through the curves however hard he pushed it, not that he pushed it too hard, just enough to experience the exhilaration that driving a Porsche could bring.

He had deliberately come a bit further north on the motorway than had strictly been necessary just so that he could drive along the north shore of Ullswater and pass through Glenridding where he'd spent his childhood before heading on down to Windermere. His parents were both dead and he had no siblings so there was no reason for him to stop there but it was nice to flirt with old memories and feel nostalgia for an upbringing that had been idyllic. He coaxed the Porsche up through the Kirkstone Pass and paused at the top to take in the view. It never failed to gladden his heart. Wordsworth could keep his daffodils; for him the mountains were the thing. He had come to know other mountains well in his lifetime – especially those of North Wales, which had featured so much in his military training – but the Lake District peaks would always hold a special place in his heart. Feeling good, he let the Porsche dawdle down the pass into Windermere and started out along the shore road to Pinetops.

The first thing that struck Steven when he drove into the car park at Pinetops was that there seemed to be no children about. He had expected to see lots of them, wearing brightly coloured outdoor gear, chattering, laughing as they wheeled dinghy transporters and carried canoes to and from the water's edge.

'Change-over week,' explained David Williams, the Welsh chief instructor. 'We usually have a five-day gap between groups to allow us to clean and maintain things. You wouldn't believe the havoc children can wreak when they're not even trying.'

Steven could see from the window that several canoes were undergoing patching repairs with fibreglass: he'd noticed the strong smell of solvent in the air when he'd got out of the car. He asked Williams some general questions about the camp to get a feel for the place, establishing along the way the number of instructors employed and the type of activities available for the children.

'It's all about team work and personal responsibility,' enthused Williams. 'When you're out on the hills and something goes wrong, you have to pull together; you share your knowledge, discuss your options and agree on a course of action. You come back safely because you worked as a team; you didn't all run off in different directions doing your own thing.'

Steven knew the philosophy well enough and nodded in the right places. Society needed team players, which was all well and good as long as it didn't lead to the ostracising and exclusion of gifted individuals who preferred to work alone. You didn't often find genius working in a team.

'So, how can I help you exactly?' asked Williams, returning Steven's ID and deciding that the pleasantries were over.

'I understand a group of children were exposed to tuberculosis here a few months ago.'

'So I'm led to believe,' said Williams. 'Nothing to do with the camp, you understand. Some kid brought it in but the relevant medical authorities moved quickly and the children were given protection.'

'BCG vaccine,' said Steven.

'If you say so,' said Williams. 'Not exactly my field.'

'There's one thing I'm not clear about,' said Steven. 'How was the child with TB discovered? Did he or she become ill while they were here?'

'Well, no one reported sick to the camp clinic if that's what you mean,' said Williams, 'or I would have heard about it. We have a full-time nurse on the staff and we can call on a local GP if needed. All incidents are logged.'

'Then how?'

Williams furrowed his brow. 'You know, I don't rightly know. I was informed by telephone of the situation.'

'By whom?'

'A Department of Health official, I think he called himself, snooty bugger as I remember. I guess the kid must have had tests before he or she came here and the results caused the shit to hit the fan.'

'I suppose,' agreed Steven who had noticed that Williams had not given away whether the child was male or female. Was this because he didn't know?

'What happened to the boy?' he asked.

'I've no idea.'

'But it was a boy?'

'I don't know.'

Steven looked surprised in order to provoke further comment.

'I suppose he or she was taken off to hospital but I wasn't asked to make any of the arrangements so I didn't see it happen. I was just asked to organise the other kids for vaccination.'

'Do you know which school the child was attending?'

'I don't think they said,' said Williams. 'Does it matter? What could I have done?'

'You're right,' agreed Steven, backing off. 'The medical authorities seem to have had everything in hand and you had another hundred kids to worry about. Can you remember how long after the initial phone-call the other children were vaccinated?'

'Next day,' said Williams. 'The team was here at ten sharp next morning and we had the kids ready and waiting. I remember we had a late start that day to outdoor activities.'

'Well, no untimely delays there,' said Steven. 'Sounds like a very efficient operation.'

'Maybe you'd like to see round the camp, see the clinic for yourself?' asked Williams, who clearly wasn't at all sure what Steven's interest was in all of this.

Steven said that that wouldn't be necessary, congratulated Williams on having such an enviable job and left. Deciding that he felt hungry – he had missed out on lunch – he drove along the shore to Ambleside and found somewhere advertising all-day-food.

He had to admit that he hadn't come up with anything about

the handling of the situation at Pinetops that could have upset Scott Haldane although he did feel a bit puzzled about the apparent secrecy surrounding the identity and movement of the sick child while at the camp. It was understandable after the event and the reasons given by the authorities to Macmillan and relayed by him had seemed valid enough. Anything to do with race relations issues and possible problems affecting them had to be handled with kid gloves – but the more he thought about it, the odder it seemed that Williams, and presumably his staff, knew nothing about the child. He was chewing his way through a particularly tough gammon steak when another thought struck him. How did the Department of Health know about the child so quickly? Williams had told him that it was someone from DOH who had phoned him. How did the 'snooty bugger' know so quickly?

'Is everything all right for you?' asked the waitress.

Steven nodded. 'Fine.' It wasn't but it was hard to break the habit of a lifetime. Surely, he reasoned, a sick child with lung problems would be seen by his or her GP and referred to a local hospital for X-rays and tests. It was they who would make the diagnosis and arrange for the child to be admitted to hospital. There would have been no need to involve the DOH. Steven paid and left. He walked down to the edge of the lake and threw a couple of pebbles into the water while he continued to follow his line of thought.

TB was a notifiable disease, which meant that the hospital would be obliged to report any incidence of it, but notification would almost certainly be to the local health authorities in the first instance. DOH would be involved in collating national figures but surely not in individual cases and certainly not in the practical aspects of vaccinating contacts.

Maybe he was making a mountain out of a molehill, he

conceded as he started to walk back to the car, but there was something not quite right about how things had been handled at official level and he wanted to know what. It preyed on his mind all the way home. There was a message from Jenny on his answering machine when he got in.

'Daddy, I'm ringing to say I'm sorry about what I said but you're not there. Auntie Sue says I can stay up till nine o'clock if you want to call me back. Love you.'

Steven looked at the time. It was 2 a.m. 'Shit,' he murmured as he poured himself a nightcap. It was impossible not to imagine Jenny's face when 9 o'clock had come and gone. It was an image that reappeared at intervals during a restless night. He was up early to call her before she left for school.

'Hello, nutkin, I'm sorry I was out when you called last night. I was working. I was driving home at the time but it was lovely to hear your voice when I got in.'

'You work very late, Daddy.'

'Sometimes I have to, nutkin.'

'Auntie Sue says that's why you can't look after me and not because you don't love me.'

'Auntie Sue's right, Jenny. I love you very much. We all do.'

'That's what Auntie Sue said.'

'Auntie Sue's very wise.'

'Are you coming up at the weekend, Daddy?'

'You bet.'

'Can we go swimming?'

'Of course we can.'

Steven put the phone down and let out his breath in a long sigh of relief as the tension he had been feeling over Jenny left him. He felt in a good mood as he set out for Great Ormond Street Hospital. He wanted to have a word with an old friend before he went in to the Home Office. Jim Brewer and he had gone through medical school together. Brewer had pursued a more traditional career path and was now a consultant physician, married to Linda, a radiologist who worked at another London hospital. Steven had last seen them both at the christening of Gerald, their third child, some two years ago. He noticed that his friend's reddish fair hair had become thinner in the interim and his waistline thicker as he headed for his forties but he seemed relaxed and at ease with the world. A round peg in a round hole, thought Steven. Can't ask for better than that.

With the pleasantries over, Brewer asked, 'Well, Action Man, what can I do for you?'

'I need some advice,' said Steven. 'I'd like you to imagine that you have a hundred or so children living together at a school camp and one of them is confirmed as having tuberculosis . . . what happens next?'

Brewer rested his elbows on his desk and made a steeple with his fingers. 'Well, let's see. The child would have to be admitted to hospital for assessment and the start of treatment. Assuming that it wasn't a problem strain – resistant to one or more of the front-line drugs – he or she would be started on triple chemotherapy – streptomycin, PAS and isoniazid. They'd be kept on that regime for at least six months but they could be released from hospital once their sputum had gone negative and they weren't infectious any more. Does that answer your question?'

'What about the other children?'

'Close contacts would be screened for the disease, as would family members of course. Depending on the outcome of the tests they would be vaccinated or even put on treatment themselves if they were showing signs of infection.'

'How about non-close contacts, say, children at the camp but from another school group?'

'Skin tests.'

'I take it it's still the Mantoux test we're talking about?' asked Steven.

Brewer nodded. 'Nothing much has changed in the last fifty years.'

'What would you think to the idea of vaccinating the whole camp immediately?'

'With BCG?'

Steven nodded.

'Without skin testing first?'

Another nod.

'Sounds way over the top,' said Brewer. 'Unless of course there was some good reason for doing it.'

'Like what?'

'Like it wasn't a straightforward strain of TB. The World Health Organisation has been reporting multi-resistant strains appearing in Africa and Asia, some of them resistant to all known drugs. If they were to get a grip in this country we could find ourselves back in the nineteenth century with people dropping down with "consumption" all over the place.'

'The affected child was an immigrant.'

Brewer shrugged. 'That could be your answer. The problem cases are coming from the third world. Desperate times, desperate measures and all that.'

'Thanks, Jim, you've been a big help,' said Steven, getting up to go.

'You're welcome. You'll have to come down and see us all soon.'

'I'd like that,' said Steven. 'I'll give you a call.'

It was raining quite heavily when Steven left the hospital but he found a cab that was just turning around to leave and got in, asking to be taken to the Home Office.

'Bit of a mess your place these days,' said the driver.

'Really? I hadn't heard.'

'Yeah, they're going to cut it up into smaller bits. Good idea if you ask me. It's too bloody big the way it is, far too much for one bloke to run.'

'Right,' said Steven. 'Well, another bloke's always welcome . . .'

Steven had coffee and leafed through the current copies of a range of medical and scientific journals while he waited to see John Macmillan. He found a report about what Jim Brewer had mentioned regarding the appearance of drug-resistant strains of TB. It didn't make for happy reading.

'He's off the phone,' said Jean Roberts and Steven nodded that he was ready. She clicked the intercom and told Macmillan he was waiting.

'He isn't going to like this,' murmured Steven as he passed Jean's desk.

Macmillan was standing at the window with his back to Steven. He seemed deep in thought. 'I trust you've brought some sunshine to brighten up a rainy day?'

'Not exactly.'

Macmillan turned round. 'Well, they do say it never rains but it pours. What's the problem?'

'I do need to know more about the child who contracted TB at Pinetops camp – the one they were reluctant to give you information about.'

Macmillan's look suggested that he'd need to hear more than that to comply. He invited Steven to continue.

'There's something they're not telling us. It's not just a case of keeping a low profile for reasons of racial harmony. There's a real chance the kid was suffering from one of the drug-resistant strains that's been reported in the journals of late.'

'Need that concern us?'

'Not directly,' agreed Steven. 'But Scott Haldane was very upset about something that was going on with the green sticker business and I'd like to know what it was.'

'It sounds like you've entirely abandoned the possibility that Haldane committed suicide?'

'The girl herself says her scalding was an accident so there was no reason for him to feel guilty and certainly no other reason for him to take his own life.'

'And the possibility of murder?'

'I haven't been able to rule it out completely and I won't be until I know what upset him about the Trish Lyons case. I need to know more.'

Macmillan sighed and said, 'Well, your instincts are usually spot on. I'll let you know when I get the information. Anything else?'

'Jean got me a list of all the green sticker kids. I'd like to know how many of them have had occasion to visit a doctor since their time at the camp and for what reason.'

'You're not asking for the medical records of over a hundred children, are you?' asked Macmillan, appalled at the thought.

'No, just the ones who've had their records updated since being at the camp – the records submitted to the TB monitoring group.'

'Do you think some of them may have contracted TB?'

'It would be as well to know.'

'All right, you can ask Jean to deal with it on your way out.'

'Thanks,' said Steven, noticing the presence of a red folder on Macmillan's desk. He always used red folders for new Sci-Med cases when they came in. 'Anything I should know about?'

Macmillan looked thoughtful. 'Our computer search picked up on the death of a medical scientist in Cambridge, young chap, hit and run, driver didn't stop.'

The Sci-Med computer was programmed to scan news stories from all over the UK, looking for possible criminal activity related to science and medicine.

'Sounds like a police matter,' said Steven.

'That's my feeling too,' agreed Macmillan. 'But I'm going to keep an eye on how things develop.'

'A university don?'

'No, he worked for a biotech company, St Clair Genomics.'

EIGHT

Steven spent the weekend up in Glenvane. He took Jenny and Sue and Richard's two children swimming on Saturday morning in Dumfries and then for a pizza lunch followed by ice-cream and a telling-off from Sue when they got back for being so indulgent with them. The children enjoyed seeing Steven being scolded, suppressing giggles behind their hands while he did his best to appear contrite, exchanging secret glances with them.

Things between him and Jenny were not as they'd been – the ghost of her outburst on the last occasion still hung in the air – but she seemed more relaxed and even happy again, and that pleased him. There would, however, be no going back. The one sure thing he had to face was the fact that Jenny was growing up.

Steven flew back to London on the Sunday night shuttle from Glasgow rather than wait for the packed flight first thing on Monday morning. He had some paperwork to take care of and some shopping to do. The fridge in his flat was nearly empty as was the freezer and ready meals played a big part in his diet. Cooking did not interest him. He'd had to look after himself at university but student cuisine was no basis for success in the kitchen. Apart from that, his mother had done all the cooking at home and the army had taken care of such matters throughout his time in the military. When he felt like eating 'properly' he would go out to one of a number of restaurants he visited regularly. Tonight, when he'd finished his shopping, it would be Chinese food at the Jade Garden.

'The child's name is Anwar Mubarak,' announced John Macmillan on Monday morning. 'He's thirteen years old and he's currently in the children's hospital in Leicester. He's been diagnosed with pulmonary tuberculosis, affecting both lungs, but the lab reports no problems with the strain. It's sensitive to all front-line antibiotics.'

'Really?' exclaimed Steven. 'That's a surprise.'

'Why?'

Steven told Macmillan about Jim Brewer's assertion that the medical response at the camp had been over the top if there was no reason to believe a 'difficult' strain of TB was involved.

'They wouldn't know at the time if it was difficult or not,' pointed out Macmillan. 'Maybe they were just being ultra-cautious.'

'I suppose,' agreed Steven. 'But it still doesn't explain why Scott Haldane was so pissed off.'

'You don't let go, do you?' smiled Macmillan.

Steven shrugged.

'I need hardly remind you that HMG still wants the identity of the boy to remain a secret.'

'Understood.'

'Jean has the other stuff you asked for. Let me know when you want to lay this to rest.'

Steven smiled as he left Macmillan's office. This was the nearest Macmillan would come to suggesting that he might be chasing rainbows. He collected the file from Jean and went to the unit library to read it, collecting a cup of coffee from the machine in the corridor on the way.

Steven learned that fourteen of the children who'd been present at Pinetops camp when Mubarak had been diagnosed with TB had subsequently sought treatment from their GPs. He read with some alarm that one had actually died. Keith Taylor, a thirteen-year-old boy, had succumbed to the ravages of necrotising fasciitis after having been admitted to hospital in Carlisle. Steven screwed up his face as he read the report, thinking how cruel fate could be and what his parents must have gone through, watching their son die a terrible death.

Patricia Lyons was on the list too, reported as suffering from vitiligo and currently recovering from a scalding accident. Two more children had been treated in hospital for burns. Three had been treated for broken bones – two with arm fractures, one with compound leg fractures after falling off his bike. Four of the children were being treated for impetigo . . .

Impetigo was a skin complaint. Steven had been looking for any early warning signs of TB among the green sticker children but now the four cases of impetigo leapt out at him. Trish Lyons had been suffering from vitiligo, another skin condition. That made five reports of skin complaints out of one hundred and eight children, six if the boy who'd died of necrotising fasciitis was included. Maybe not significant but . . . Steven read on and alarm bells started to ring when he read that three more children had been referred to their GPs suffering from unspecified 'loss of pigment' in their skin. Nine.

What the hell was going on? There was no sign of TB in the children but the incidence of skin complaints must be well above what could be expected in previously healthy twelve- to thirteen-year-old children. Four with impetigo, three with unspecified 'loss of pigment', Patricia Lyons with vitiligo and a boy who'd died of necrotising fasciitis – the flesh-eating disease . . . Surely this couldn't be coincidence but if not, what was he suggesting? That there was some common cause of their ailments? That they had all contracted a skin condition through being at Pinetops camp?

Steven rubbed his forehead nervously as he tried to decide what to do next. The only thing the children had in common, apart from their age, was that fact that they had attended Pinetops camp at the same time and had been given BCG vaccine after a TB scare. BCG vaccine was something that had been used for fifty years so it was hardly likely to be that causing the trouble. According to Jim Brewer, it wasn't the most effective vaccine in the world but it was certainly safe. This left the possibility that something the kids had been exposed to at Pinetops had been the cause of the problem although, he reminded himself, it did not seem to be a single problem. Vitiligo, impetigo, loss of pigment were all vague terms. Even necrotising fasciitis could have a number of causes. Maybe he had been precipitate in lumping them all together as 'skin problems' but he would certainly investigate further and he would start with the one that had caused Keith Taylor's death.

The pathology report wasn't included in the file Jean had given him – the cause of death had simply been put down as necrotising fasciitis. He needed to know more about the bacterium that had caused it. He wanted to know the *exact* cause of death.

Two days later, Steven finally got access to the PM report on Keith Taylor. His physician had made the original diagnosis of necrotising fasciitis after flesh 'instability' had been noted in several areas of Keith's body. The Carlisle hospital pathologist had confirmed the diagnosis at post mortem but no cause had been given. The lab reports had all been negative.

Negative? Steven shook his head in frustration. The boy had an infection that was eating him alive and the lab had come up with nothing? What the hell did they imagine caused it, pixie dust? This was beyond . . . He stopped himself in mid-thought and cautioned himself to calm down. There had to be a rational explanation somewhere. It was just a question of finding it. He phoned the hospital in Carlisle and asked to speak to the consultant microbiologist. He turned out to be an Irishman by the name of O'Connor.

'It was most unusual,' conceded O'Connor. 'We simply failed to grow any bacterium or virus from the boy's tissues.'

'But according to the medical report, his flesh was so infected it was falling off him,' said Steven.

'I know,' said O'Connor. 'But the fact remains, the cultures were all negative and so was the serology.'

'What did you test for?'

'Just about everything we could think of.'

Steven put the phone down, feeling far from happy but not quite sure what to do about it ... or rather, he was sure but was unwilling to contemplate it unless he could convince himself and John Macmillan that it was absolutely necessary. It would involve the exhumation of Keith Taylor's body.

Steven made his request to Macmillan the following morning having agonised about it long and hard and Macmillan had reluctantly agreed after unsuccessfully reminding Steven, unnecessarily, just how much upset and stress this was going to cause to the boy's parents.

'I know,' agreed Steven. 'But there's something very wrong here. I have to find out why Keith Taylor died. I want a Home Office pathologist to carry out a second post mortem and a top lab to analyse the samples.'

Keith Taylor had been buried in a cemetery about half a mile from his home. A new granite headstone recorded his untimely death and the undying love of his parents. Bunches of fresh flowers marked the grave and cards spoke of his youth and all too premature demise. They appeared unreal under the lights from the rig set up by the police to illuminate the scene, an operation which started at midnight behind a canvas awning to avoid prying eyes.

'I hope you've got a damned good reason for this,' said the police superintendent who was overseeing the operation. The disapproval was plain in his voice. 'As if losing their son wasn't enough . . .'

Steven resisted the temptation to snap back: *Of course I've got a good reason. Do you think I do this as a bloody hobby?* Instead he remained silent, eyes fixed on the digging, aware of the patter of rain on the shoulders of his waxed cotton jacket. He saw the coffin hoisted from the ground and loaded into the back of an unlettered black van for transport to the city mortuary where the second post mortem was to be carried out. He left the scene and returned to his hotel to grab a few hours' sleep before joining the Home Office pathologist who was due at nine.

The post mortem was carried out with full bio-precautions being observed. The danger associated with bugs causing necrotising fasciitis was not to be underestimated and the pathologist, Steven and two assistants were fully gowned and masked with full-face visors being employed.

'All right?' asked Mark Porter, the pathologist detailed by the Home Office to carry out the examination. Steven nodded.

'Bloody hell,' were Porter's first words as he began his work. 'I've seen a few cases of Nec Fash in my time but never one as bad as this . . . he's absolutely riddled . . . the flesh is like . . . Jesus, what a mess . . .'

'You're absolutely sure about it being necrotising fasciitis?' asked Steven.

'What else could it be?'

'But the hospital lab couldn't grow anything.'

'Crazy,' said Porter. 'His flesh must be hoaching with bacteria.'

'Can you take lots of samples, please? It's important we find out exactly what caused this. I don't suppose you'd care to hazard a guess about the bug's identity?'

Porter gazed down at the corpse. 'I'd rather not. Like I say, I've never come across anything as bad as this although . . .'

'Yes?'

'It might be a one-off. I mean, the boy might have been ultra-susceptible to the bug. It happens. I've seen AIDS victims succumb to infections that rip through them like a tsunami hitting a beach simply because they have no body defences left when the HIV virus is finished with them. On the other hand of course, it could be the bacterium itself that's ultra-virulent; in which case, we could all be up a certain creek without a paddle.'

Porter turned to the two assistants who were waiting to clean up. 'Be very careful.'

Three days passed without any word from the London lab dealing with the Taylor boy's samples. Steven was collating paperwork he had obtained from various sources over the past couple of weeks when he suddenly saw something that made his blood run cold. It was the entry in Keith Taylor's medical notes that recorded his receipt of a bone marrow transplant and that he was receiving immuno-suppressive treatment. He snatched up his phone and called Jim Brewer at Great Ormond Street.

'Is BCG a live virus vaccine?' he asked.

'It certainly is,' replied Brewer, a reply that made Steven close his eyes. 'It's an attenuated form of TB isolated by two French scientists in the Fifties – Calmette and Guérin, hence the name. BCG. *Bacille Calmette-Guérin.* What's the problem?'

'One of the kids I told you about, the ones who were given BCG vaccine at the school camp, was on immuno-suppressive drugs when he was vaccinated.'

'Jesus,' said Brewer. 'I take it they didn't know?'

'The kid's dead,' said Steven. 'Necrotising fasciitis – it swept through him like a runaway train.'

'Jesus Christ, what a fuck-up.'

'Looks like the medics who gave him the BCG didn't know about the kid's background and the medics who treated him in hospital didn't know he'd been given the vaccine.'

'I take it the lab grew the BCG bug?'

'They didn't grow anything. There are secondary tests being carried out by another lab at the moment.'

'They might not look for TB,' said Brewer. 'It's a lung disease, not exactly the thing you'd expect to cause a rip-roaring flesh infection.'

'The first lab said they'd checked for everything,' said Steven.

'It might be as well to check with them again. TB grows very slowly in the lab compared to other bugs and it needs a special culture medium. It can take six to eight weeks to grow up while something like a streptococcus grows up overnight.'

'I'll do that,' said Steven. 'Thanks again.'

Steven felt sick inside. It looked very much as if a mix-up in paperwork had led to Keith Taylor's death, a mix-up which had also led to his requesting an exhumation and causing the boy's parents a great deal of stress on top of everything else. It had all the elements of a *Bungling Docs* story in the tabloids. He called the lab dealing with the Taylor specimens.

'Nothing yet, I'm afraid.'

'Have you set up cultures for TB?'

'Just a moment . . .'

Steven drummed his fingers on the desk while he waited.

'We wouldn't normally,' came the reply. 'But in this case, because it doesn't seem to be one of the usual suspects, we've set up cultures on every bacterial growth medium we have, including those for TB. If this bug grows in the lab, we'll find it.'

Steven hung up before he was asked about his interest in TB. He wanted to talk things over with John Macmillan first. Knowing now that it would take the lab the best part of six to eight weeks to grow up the BCG bacillus, he decided to check with O'Connor, the microbiologist at the children's hospital in Carlisle. It was he who had told him they'd looked for 'everything we could think of' in the Taylor boy's specimens.

'We got such a surprise when nothing grew up overnight that I told the staff to inoculate his specimens on every other culture medium we use,' said O'Connor.

'Would that include media capable of supporting TB?' asked Steven.

'It would.'

'And?'

'And nothing. No growth on anything.'

'Would you just check again for me please?'

O'Connor put down the phone with a clatter. He returned after two minutes. Steven had followed the second hand sweep of his watch.

'The cultures were discarded as being completely negative after fourteen weeks.'

'Thank you,' said Steven without further comment.

He decided not to talk it over with Macmillan until the following morning. He needed time to get things clear in his head. He had been concentrating so much on Keith Taylor's death that he had lost sight of the connection he was looking for with the other vaccinated children who had developed skin complaints.

He decided to phone the children's hospital in Edinburgh to ask about the condition of Patricia Lyons.

'She's very ill.'

This was not what he wanted to hear.

'She has some kind of an infection in the flesh of her burned arm and it's not responding to treatment.'

'Some kind of an infection?' said Steven. 'What does that mean?'

'It's hard to say. The lab hasn't found anything.'

NINE

The words hit Steven like a body blow. He mumbled a request to be kept informed if and when the lab came up with anything and hung up. He uttered a series of expletives as he thought things through. Surely Trish Lyons' infection could not possibly be the same as Keith Taylor's. If it was, it meant that his logical supposition that the BCG bacillus had somehow rampaged through the boy's body because his immune system had been compromised was wrong. As far as he knew, there was nothing wrong with Trish Lyons' immune system and for two children to have reacted the way they had to a vaccine that had been safely in use for fifty years seemed highly unlikely. Some other factor was involved, possibly something that Scott Haldane had recognised . . . and had been murdered to keep him quiet?

Steven spoke to John Macmillan first thing next morning. 'I'm sorry, there's much more to it than we first thought.' He told Macmillan about Keith Taylor being given BCG vaccine when his immune system had been suppressed, something that brought a frown to his face which was quickly followed by a droop to his shoulders when Steven mentioned that Trish Lyons might also be suffering from the same infection.

'Bad to worse,' complained Macmillan.

'There's more. The lab at the children's hospital in Carlisle should have grown the bacterium if it had been the BCG bacillus to blame but their cultures were all negative even after fourteen weeks. Trish Lyons' cultures are also negative to date. There's a chance that it's a different infection altogether, a vicious, flesh-eating bug that the kids picked up at Pinetops that we can't identify in the lab and can't treat with antibiotics.'

'Just what we need,' sighed Macmillan. 'How exactly are we proposing that the children got this infection – if it should turn out to be the same one?'

'Actually there are several more children on the green sticker list who are complaining about skin problems.'

Macmillan closed his eyes and rubbed his forehead against the palm of his hand in a slow sideways motion. 'Bloody hell,' he murmured.

'The only thing they have in common is the fact that they attended Pinetops school camp together and that they all received BCG vaccine while they were there.'

'And of course, the reason they were given it in the first place,' added Macmillan cryptically.

Steven looked at him questioningly.

'They were all exposed to possible infection from Anwar Mubarak.'

'Which was straightforward TB with no clinical problems according to the lab report . . .' said Steven, his voice fading as he saw what Macmillan was suggesting.

'But against which, as your friend pointed out, the authorities saw fit to vaccinate the whole camp – apparently without reference to medical history or background of any of the children,' said Macmillan.

'Maybe we should call a Code Red on this one?' suggested Steven.

Macmillan nodded somewhat reluctantly but said, 'I agree.'

The change to Code Red signified that a preliminary investigation by a Sci-Med investigator was about to turn into a full-scale investigation with all the powers that entailed. Steven would be able to request help and assistance at any time of the day or night through a specially manned switchboard set up at Sci-Med. He would have access to funds through special credit accounts set up in his name. He would have the authority to request assistance and information from the police authority in any area he was operating in with full backing from the Home Office. He could even request that he be armed should he feel that the situation warranted it. None of this would seem to be necessary in his current assignment but it was reassuring to know that everything was in place should he need it – or would be when Jean Roberts was told.

Macmillan pressed his intercom button and said, 'Code Red on Steven's assignment, please, Jean.'

'What do you plan to do?' Macmillan asked Steven.

Steven thought for a moment before saying, 'I'm going up to Leicester to visit Anwar Mubarak. I want to see the boy; I want to see the cultures they grew and I want to see the drug sensitivity results from the lab. I need to be absolutely certain we've been told the truth.'

'And if we have?'

'Assuming the London lab dealing with the Keith Taylor specimens fail to grow anything, we'll have to accept the possibility that we're dealing with a new infection – probably viral as it seems to be resistant to antibiotics and nothing's coming up on bacteriological culture media.'

'And the first thing to do with a new infection . . .' intoned Macmillan.

'Is to establish the source of it,' completed Steven.

Steven drove up to Leicester, hoping that at least, by the end of the day, one of the variables would be removed from the investigation, giving him a clearer sense of direction. There were just too many possibilities floating around at the moment: he was beginning to feel as if he'd been dropped in the ocean and wasn't sure in which direction to swim. The receptionist at the children's hospital didn't help much.

'We have no one here by that name,' she replied after a brief examination of her screen, apparently not at all concerned that she couldn't help. Steven wondered what it was about the British that so many people who disliked dealing with the public ended up in jobs entailing constant contact with them. He asked her to check again.

'Still nothing,' said the woman, peering over the top of her ornate glasses at the screen.

Realising that Mubarak's name not being on the admissions register might have something to do with the authorities' desire for secrecy over the affair, Steven showed her his ID and asked to speak to the Medical Superintendent.

'Professor Lang is away until tomorrow. He's at a conference in Geneva.'

'Well, his deputy.'

The woman sighed and picked up her phone.

Steven was shown to a bright, modern room on the second floor. The name on the door said Dr N. Simmons. 'Dr Simmons will be with you shortly,' said the junior assistant who had led him up. 'Please take a seat.'

Steven sat down, feeling slightly ill-at-ease staring at an empty chair on the other side of the desk. As the minutes passed, he thought about picking up and flicking through the copy of the *British Medical Journal* that lay there but then thought better of it. It might be construed as an invasion of personal space. As the wait extended to eight minutes, he considered getting up and going over to look out of the window but finding someone wandering about your office could also be intimidating. He sat tight until the door opened behind him and he turned to see an attractive dark-haired woman standing there. She seemed out of breath. 'Hi, I'm Natalie Simmons, Professor Lang's senior registrar. I'm so sorry to keep you waiting. My bleeper went off as I was coming along the corridor and I had to go back to the ward.'

Steven smiled and shook hands with the woman. 'No problem. I'm Steven Dunbar.'

Natalie Simmons plonked herself down behind her desk and pushed her hair away from her face. She took a moment to examine Steven's ID card before saying, 'Well, Dr Dunbar, I'm afraid I've never heard of the Sci-Med Inspectorate but I'm sure you must have every right to be here and this all seems terribly official so what can I do for you?'

Another push of the hair and a big smile revealing even white teeth accompanied this.

Steven decided that he liked her. Natalie Simmons seemed open, friendly but blessed with beautiful green eyes that also somehow suggested an understanding of just how the world worked – a quality that could ultimately lead to cynicism or, as he suspected in her case, to a comfortable acceptance and amused detachment regarding the workings of the human race. He assured her that she wasn't alone in not having heard of Sci-Med and told her briefly what they did.

'I see, and where do we come into that?'

'I need to speak to someone about one of your patients, a boy named Anwar Mubarak.'

'Doesn't ring a bell.'

'He's got TB.'

'Really?' exclaimed Natalie, sounding surprised. 'I wasn't aware we had any TB patients.'

Steven considered, but only for a moment, whether or not he should take Natalie Simmons into his confidence before saying, 'He's a recent immigrant. He attended a school camp up in the Lake District before they found out he had TB. The authorities are keen to keep this under wraps.'

'I can see why – taking our houses, our jobs *and* giving our kids TB. Well, the authorities seem to have done it very well because I know nothing about this child at all.'

Steven felt that familiar sinking feeling come on. 'Is there anyone else who might?'

'I'd be pretty annoyed if there was,' said Natalie. 'I'm acting head of the Infectious Diseases Unit while Ralph is away. I'm supposed to know about these things. Bear with me.'

Natalie made a succession of phone-calls, which all ended in negatives. 'I'm sorry, Dr Dunbar. None of my colleagues knows anything about this either.'

Steven shook his head. 'Bizarre,' he said. 'There seems to have been some sort of misunderstanding but it's my problem, not yours.' He got up to go. As a last resort he asked, 'I don't suppose Professor Lang could be treating the boy somewhere privately because of the circumstances?'

Natalie made a face. 'Frankly, I've never come across circumstances like this before,' she said. 'So your guess is as good as mine. He certainly didn't mention it to me.'

'Maybe I'll call back tomorrow and ask him.'

'Will that involve you making an overnight stop you didn't plan on?'

'I suppose.'

'Look,' said Natalie. 'I have a number for Professor Lang. It's supposed to be for emergencies but I'll ring and ask him.'

Steven said he was grateful. He waited while Natalie called Lang but without success. 'His phone's turned off. Look, leave me your mobile number and I'll try again later. I'll let you know what he says and if it's not too late you can still get off back to London.'

'I'm much obliged,' said Steven.

Steven didn't know Leicester. He drove around for a while, getting a feel for it before finding somewhere to park and going for a walk. He found it easier to think on the move. He decided to save some time and phone John Macmillan before he left the Home Office for the night. He asked him to double-check on the whereabouts of Anwar Mubarak.'

Natalie called him at 5.30 p.m. 'I've just spoken to Ralph; he was in a meeting earlier. He doesn't know anything about this boy. At least, I'm pretty sure he doesn't.'

'I'm sorry?'

'My fault, I'm afraid. I didn't think you'd want me blurting out the question over the telephone in view of its sensitive nature so I got into rather a mess, asking about possible recent immigrant children being admitted with a disease starting with "t" that I didn't know about but he might.'

Steven had to put his hand to his mouth to avoid laughing.

'I think Ralph must have thought I was drunk at first but then I told him that it was an inspector from Sci-Med asking the question and he caught on. The bottom line is that he knows nothing at all about it.'

'Thank you very much,' said Steven. 'I'm very much obliged to you.'

'Not at all. I suppose there must have been some kind of mix-up somewhere?'

'There's not another children's hospital in Leicester, is there?'

'No.'

'Would you care to have dinner with me?' asked Steven, surprising even himself.

'I'm sorry?'

'No, I'm sorry. I asked if you'd have dinner with me without thinking. You've probably got a husband and children waiting for you at home.'

'No . . . I haven't as it happens,' said Natalie.

'Then the offer still stands.'

'I thought you were anxious to get back to London.'

'No, *you* thought I was anxious to get back to London,' said Steven. 'I've contacted Sci-Med about the confusion. There's little point in me going anywhere until I hear back from them and that'll probably be tomorrow – Whitehall goes home at five o'clock.'

'I see, well, in that case I'd be delighted to have dinner with you.'

Steven booked himself into a small hotel, had a shower and changed, using the 'just in case' travel bag he kept in the back of the car. He met Natalie at the restaurant she had suggested, arriving five minutes before she did.

'This is an unexpected surprise,' she said. 'I can't remember the last time I spent an evening alone with a complete stranger.'

'Just means there's so much more to talk about,' said Steven. And there was.

During the course of the next two hours, Steven learned that Natalie – 'Tally' to her friends – had been born and brought up in Bromley, in Kent. She was thirty-five years old and had studied medicine in Sheffield. She'd got married at twenty-seven to Rupert Giles, now an orthopaedic surgeon in London, but they divorced three years later when it was discovered that she couldn't have children. 'That wasn't the only reason,' said Tally. 'But it was quite a big factor. Let's say, it undermined what little foundations we had.'

'I'm sorry,' said Steven.

'Don't be,' said Tally. 'Now I have more children in my life than I can handle. Your turn.'

Steven told her about his army background, his marriage to Lisa and her subsequent death. He told her about his daughter Jenny and her life in Scotland. 'I'm very much a weekend dad – in fact, an every-second-weekend dad if truth be told.'

'It must be difficult being so far apart.'

'It doesn't help,' agreed Steven.

'You couldn't get a transfer?'

'Sci-Med is a very small unit. We don't have northern outposts,' said Steven with a smile.

'Tell me about Sci-Med.'

Steven told Tally about Sci-Med and the sort of investigations it carried out as the waiter replenished their coffee cups for the third time.

'Sounds exciting,' said Tally. 'Very James Bond.'

'Not really,' said Steven. 'Much of the work is just routine investigation work – like clearing up a misunderstanding about the location of a child patient . . .'

Tally smiled. 'I suspect it has its moments.'

'Once in a while perhaps.'

'You didn't tell me why you wanted to see this boy,' said Tally. Then, seeing the indecision on Steven's face, she added, 'Oh, I'm sorry. This is none of my business. I wasn't thinking.'

'No, Sci-Med isn't the secret service,' said Steven. 'Although we do like to operate discreetly. Anwar Mubarak having TB was the reason given by sources in the Department of Health for giving BCG vaccine to over a hundred children at a school camp. One of these children is now dead and another is seriously ill because of an infection which the labs are having great trouble in identifying. Several other children in that group have reported ill. I need to be sure that it is TB the boy Mubarak is suffering from and not something else.'

Tally's eyes opened wide. 'Like what?' she said.

114

'I don't know.'

'But surely if a government source says it's TB . . .'

Steven smiled. 'It must be TB?'

'Well, yes. I mean, they wouldn't lie about something like that . . . would they?'

'Not without considering they had good reason to,' said Steven.

'What does that mean?'

'There is a long tradition in government of not telling the public what they don't want them to know. They imagine they're doing it to avoid causing fear and alarm among the population or out of security concerns – another favourite of theirs – but it's not true. They do it because it's second nature to them. Their automatic response to any unusual problem arising is to pretend there isn't a problem at all: *No cause for fear or alarm.*'

'But you work for them.'

'Sci-Med's attached to the Home Office but we have a mandate to operate independently of any government department.'

'Doesn't that lead to conflict?'

'From time to time.'

'What's to stop the government getting rid of you if you start biting the hand that feeds you?' asked Tally.

'Her Majesty's Opposition would start asking awkward questions if they did.'

'Well, well,' smiled Tally. 'Who would have thought . . .'

'Sorry, I'm boring you.'

'Far from it!' exclaimed Tally. 'It's been fascinating. The trouble with working in a hospital is that all your friends tend to do the same. You become isolated in an enclosed community without even realising it so it's good to meet people outside the circle – even if you happen to be a doctor yourself.'

'It's been a while,' said Steven.

'But you were a doctor in the army?'

'Field medicine.'

'Medicine under fire? Gosh, you have led an exciting life.'

'That was yesterday,' said Steven. 'Now I ask questions for a living.'

'I'd like to hear the answer to these questions – about the boy, I mean,' said Tally. 'Or is that not possible?'

'I'd like to see you again so let's make it possible,' said Steven. 'How about lunch tomorrow. I should have heard back from London by then.'

Tally laughed at the suggestion. 'You've obviously not worked in the NHS for a long time,' she said. 'Lunch is a sandwich grabbed at my desk if I get the chance.'

'Well, maybe I'll call you anyway?'

'That would be nice . . . and thank you for a lovely evening.'

Steven paid and left a big tip for the staff in deference to the fact that they were the last two to leave the restaurant, something he'd only just noticed. He'd only had eyes for Tally.

There was a taxi rank across the road with two cabs waiting. 'Obviously isn't London,' said Steven as he beckoned one.

'Obviously isn't raining either,' said Tally.

Steven saw her to the door of her apartment building where she thanked him again for a nice evening. Steven kissed her on the cheek and took the cab back to his hotel.

TEN

Macmillan rang while Steven was having breakfast. 'Can you talk?'

'One moment.' Steven left the small hotel breakfast room via French doors leading out into the back garden and followed the winding path down through an arch of forsythia to the fake wishing well at the end, where a garden gnome fished off its edge. Steven sat down beside it. 'Go ahead.'

'I'm now told there was a last-minute change of plan and the Mubarak boy was not admitted to the children's hospital in Leicester after all. My contact at DOH apologises for the confusion. They took the view that that might be too public and arranged for the boy to be treated at a private clinic instead.'

Steven took out the notebook he always carried in his pocket and pulled the pen from its spine with his teeth. 'Do you have the address?'

'Actually . . . it's in Sweden.'

'Sweden,' repeated Steven as if challenging what he'd just heard.

'I'm just as perplexed as you,' said Macmillan.

'They took a kid with TB to Sweden just to avoid publicity?' exclaimed Steven.

'A bizarre decision, I agree,' said Macmillan.

'Do we have the address of this Swedish clinic?'

'They said they'd get back to me today with the details. I take it you're planning to follow it up and go there?'

'You bet. All this nonsense for a straightforward case of TB with no treatment difficulties? I don't think so. I'll stay up here and catch a flight from Birmingham.'

Steven returned to the breakfast room, smiling his apologies to the couple who'd come in to breakfast in his absence and chosen to sit in front of the French doors. He asked the Polish waitress for more toast and coffee while he digested this latest revelation.

He returned to his room and used his laptop to check out options for Swedish flights leaving from Birmingham: he made a note of their departure times. It was now going to depend on when John Macmillan got back to him. In the meantime, he called Tally with the information that the boy never had been admitted to the children's hospital in the first place: there had been a 'misunderstanding'.

'Good,' she replied. 'Then I can stop looking through cupboards for secret patients. Where is he?'

'Er . . .'

'Oh, I understand. If you told me, you'd have to kill me. Right?'

'He's in Sweden.'

'Why?'

'God knows but that's the reason I'll be leaving for Sweden as soon as I get the address of the clinic there.'

'Well, I wonder what wonderful medical facilities the Swedes have got that we haven't,' said Tally. She'd said it tongue in cheek but it triggered off something in Steven's memory – something that alarmed him. 'They are world leaders in bio-hazard containment,' he said distantly.

'What?'

'The Swedes are often called in as consultants whenever there is a threatened epidemic of a killer disease. Find an outbreak

118

of Ebola or Marburg virus and you'll find people wearing Swedish-designed bio-hazard suits working in Swedish-designed mobile labs.'

'Surely you're not suggesting that the boy has anything like that?' said Tally.

'I'm not suggesting anything right now,' said Steven. 'I'm stumbling around in the dark. I take it lunch is still not possible?'

''Fraid not,' said Tally. 'But thanks anyway. Let me know how you get on in Sweden.'

John Macmillan called just after noon. Steven could tell by the tone of his voice that something was wrong. He tried pre-empting him. 'You're going to tell me that you don't have the address of the Swedish clinic?' he said.

'Steven, I have been approached by people at the highest level . . .'

Steven could hardly believe his ears. John Macmillan was going to ask him to back off, the John Macmillan who had gone to war with 'people at the highest level' so many times in the past to maintain the integrity of Sci-Med and establish the truth.

'They have asked me to take their word for it that Anwar Mubarak is not suffering from any unusual or exotic disease and is in no personal danger. When I told them about our concern for the green sticker children, they also assured me that Mubarak's condition had absolutely nothing to do with the death of Keith Taylor or Patricia Lyons' illness. They have given me their absolute word on that.'

'I see,' said Steven in a tone that prompted more comment.

'I think, in the circumstances, I have to accept what they say. The alternative would be to accuse people in the top echelons of government of lying without having any foundation for the charge.'

'So you're asking me to drop the investigation?'

'You know better. It's always been my practice to let my people make their own decisions in the field. I'm just asking you to bear in mind what I've just told you. The decision is still yours but I have to know. Are you still going to insist on travelling to Sweden to see the boy?'

'I suppose not,' said Steven although the words almost stuck in his craw. He was frustrated and angry that Macmillan had put him in such a position and felt hamstrung about saying so because he owed so much to the man. His thinking, however, was tempered by conceding that Macmillan himself had been placed in an almost impossible position. 'Shit,' he murmured as he put down the phone. 'Shit, shit shit.'

A knock came to the door. It was one of the hotel receptionists. 'Will you be checking out soon, sir?' she asked.

Steven glanced at his watch and took her point. He apologised because it was nearly twelve thirty. 'Actually, no,' he said. 'I'd like to stay one more night if that's possible?'

'I'll check downstairs for you.'

Steven stood by the window, watching the traffic pass. He felt uncomfortable at having no clear objective. Perhaps it was because he had spent so long in the military but he hated the feeling of being at a loose end. Macmillan's call had effectively put a halt to his investigation when he felt that it was far from over. There had been no explanation of why the boy had been taken to Sweden and there had been no resolution of the cause of death in the case of Keith Taylor or any clue as to what was behind Trish Lyons' condition.

The phone rang. 'Your room will be available for another night, sir.'

Steven's spur-of-the-moment decision not to go back to London had been taken largely to give him the opportunity to calm down. He needed time to free himself of anger and frustration. If he returned to the capital in his current state of mind he would be liable to come out with something he might regret. He decided – as he had so often in the past – to use physical exertion to help him battle stress. He fetched track suit and trainers from the car, changed and set off on a run with no particular route or destination in mind.

The hotel was well away from the city centre so crowds were not a problem and he was able to pound the pavements of suburbia until he was sweating freely and the endorphins released by physical effort did much to create an inner sense of calm. Apart from that, it felt good to stretch his muscles and feel assured that his physical condition gave no cause for concern. Common sense told him that there was no way that he could be as fit as he'd been some ten to fifteen years before when serving as an operational soldier with 'the best' as 'the Regiment' liked to see itself but it still *felt* as if he was and that was a major feel-good factor. Running and swimming kept him lean and occasional sorties into the mountains of North Wales by arrangement with his old regiment let him test himself to the limit. It just took longer to recover these days.

He stood in the shower for a good ten minutes when he got back to his hotel room, letting the warm water soothe away the aches and pains of the run. He towelled himself dry, dressed in jeans and a plain white T-shirt and called Tally.

'I thought you'd be on your way to Sweden by now. Where are you?'

'Change of plan, I'm still in town. How about dinner this evening?'

Tally hesitated for a moment before saying, 'Ye . . es, if we could make it a bit later. I have a class.'

'Of course. What are you doing?'

'Conversational French. I'm planning on going touring there in the late summer with friends.'

'Good for you. 'Tell me where the class is and I'll pick you up.'

Steven asked at the reception desk whether there were any French restaurants in Leicester.

'Indian, no problem,' said the girl with what Steven thought might be an edge to her voice. 'But French . . . I'll have to ask Carol.'

The girl returned from the back office with the name and phone number of a restaurant written down on a 'with compliments' slip. Steven called the number and made a reservation at Le Gavroche for nine.

It was raining when Tally emerged from the school her class was being held in. She held her briefcase over her head as she looked right and then left for Steven outside the gates and before he got out the car and waved to her.

'Gosh, I've never been in one of these before,' said Tally as she made a meal of getting into the Porsche while Steven held the door. 'Not exactly conducive to decorum . . . are they,' she exclaimed as her knees came up almost to her chin. 'I feel as if I'm sitting in the road.'

Steven ran round and got in. 'You're a good . . . two inches off it,' he grinned as he started the car.

'Where are we going?'

'It's a surprise.'

Ten minutes later, Tally leaned forward in her seat to read the name above the restaurant they were stopping near. 'Oh, how sweet,' she exclaimed on seeing the French name. 'And how thoughtful, thank you.'

'Have you been here before?'

'I didn't know it existed,' confessed Tally.

'So neither of us know what the food's like,' said Steven with a smile. 'Fingers crossed.'

On entering the restaurant, first impressions were good. The place was warm and welcoming and they were shown to their table by a waiter who seemed either French or very good at affecting the accent in the cause of ambience. They sipped Kir Royale while looking at the menu.

'So, why no Swedish trip?' asked Tally.

'I've been warned off,' said Steven, still smarting at what had happened.

Tally read the signals well and decided not to probe too much. 'That must have been disappointing.'

'People "at the highest level" have assured my boss that the kid is okay and doesn't have some awful disease. That being the case, there is no need for me to visit him at the clinic . . . is there?'

'You obviously think otherwise?' Tally asked calmly.

They paused while the waiter took their order.

'I still don't know why he was taken to Sweden or what's going on with the other kids from the school camp,' said Steven.

'Does this mean you'll have to drop the investigation altogether or can you work round the problem?'

'I've only agreed not to go to Sweden but that was the next logical thing for me to do so I'm not sure where I go from here.'

'You could talk to the boy's family,' suggested Tally.

'I don't have an address,' said Steven. 'It was hard enough work getting his name. If I now ask to get his address . . .'

'They'll know what you're up to and it might be seen as a breach of your . . . gentlemen's agreement.'

'Something like that.'

'Well, there's more than one way to skin a cat,' said Tally brightly. 'You could get it from the boy's school.'

Steven looked at her.

'You said there were around a hundred pupils at the camp?'

'A hundred and eight.'

That suggests maybe ten school parties at most, probably fewer. You should be able to find out which schools were there at the time and then establish which one the boy was at. It shouldn't be too difficult to get his address from the school records. All you need is a plausible excuse.'

'Brilliant,' said Steven. 'Remind me never to underestimate you.'

'I hope you weren't even considering it . . .' smiled Tally.

Their first course of deep fried Camembert with redcurrant jelly arrived and Steven said, 'Let's talk about sunnier things. Tell me all about your trip to France.'

At the end of a pleasant evening filled with laughter at reminiscences of times past, Tally invited Steven in for a nightcap. 'I really enjoyed this evening,' she said, returning from the kitchen with two small cups of coffee and two balloon glasses of Calvados. 'I thought we'd maintain the French flavour to the evening.'

'I had a good time too,' said Steven, raising his glass to her.

'Here's to ships that pass in the night,' said Tally, raising hers.

Steven smiled at the point she was making.

'Back to London tomorrow?' asked Tally.

'Not until I find out what school the boy was attending. If the original intention was to admit him to your hospital then it seems probable that he attended one of the schools here in the city.'

'Good thinking.'

'Can I call you tomorrow?'

'Yes, I'd like to know how you get on.'

'That wouldn't be my reason for calling you . . .' said Steven, making deliberate eye contact.

Tally smiled and said, 'Steven . . . I know we're attracted to each other but logic says that this isn't going anywhere . . . My life is here and you're just passing through.'

'It's not that far from London.'

'It would never work.'

'We could make it work.'

Steven put down his glass and took Tally's hands in his. Tally looked as if she was having difficulty with an inner struggle. Her head was telling her one thing but her body quite another. Steven took her in his arms and kissed her. Tally was tentative at first but then seemed to relax but only until her head won the battle. She put both hands on Steven's chest and pushed him away gently. 'No,' she said. 'I only met you a couple of days ago and you'll probably be gone tomorrow . . . It's been nice but let's just leave it at that.'

'If you say so,' said Steven sadly. He smiled and kissed her gently on the forehead. *'Bonne nuit, madame.'*

First thing next morning Steven called Pinetops school camp and asked for the names of the schools which had pupils staying there at the time of the TB alert. There were nine in all and one of them was in Leicester. Seeing this as being the favourite, he obtained the number from Directory Enquiries and called the school office, saying that he was a Department of Health official, checking on the pupils who'd been given BCG vaccine when staying at Pinetops. Steven ticked the names off his list of green sticker children as the woman read them out. She stopped after twelve and Steven prompted, 'And of course, Anwar Mubarak?'

'He's not one of ours,' said the woman.

'You're absolutely sure?' said Steven.

'I've never heard of him.'

'Really? He's the boy who was taken ill at the camp; I thought he was one of your pupils?'

'Definitely not. Sorry.'

Steven tried the school nearest to Leicester and got the same result. He grew more puzzled and frustrated as the schools dwindled to leave just one, the school Trish Lyons went to in Edinburgh. As there were only twelve names left on his green sticker list he asked the administrator to confirm the names as he read them out. He ticked off twelve before adding, 'And Anwar Mubarak.'

'No, he's not one of ours.'

Steven closed his eyes and said, 'He was the boy who caused the scare, the one who fell ill.'

'That may well be but he wasn't from our school.'

Steven threw his pen down and let out a long sigh. What the hell was going on? Mubarak hadn't been a pupil at any of the nine schools who'd sent pupils to Pinetops. He'd made a point of telling each of the schools that Mubarak had been the boy who caused the panic just in case there had been a 'misunderstanding' about the name like there had about the hospital he'd been admitted to. He'd expected to be corrected by the relevant school but this hadn't happened. All nine were under the impression that the boy had been a pupil at another school.

Steven phoned Tally. 'I'm going back to London. I have to speak with John Macmillan. The boy, Mubarak, wasn't a pupil at any of the schools staying at Pinetops.'

'What? How can that be? Maybe they changed his name?'

'I thought of that. They didn't. All the schools are under the impression that the sick boy was a pupil elsewhere. Thinking

126

back, the staff at Pinetops weren't told which school he belonged to either.'

'How odd. It doesn't make any sense.'

'It does if he didn't exist,' said Steven.

ELEVEN

'What?' exclaimed John Macmillan when Steven told him. 'How dare they send us off on a wild goose chase? They gave me their absolute word and I promised cooperation on that basis.'

Steven thought about this while Macmillan stalked around the office, giving vent to his anger. 'I suppose in the strictest sense of the word, they didn't lie,' he said, secretly knowing that he was just adding fuel to the fire. The Whitehall Mafia were not his sort of people and he enjoyed seeing them found out. 'Mubarak can't be in any danger if he doesn't actually exist . . . and by the same token, he couldn't have been responsible for what happened to Keith Taylor or Trish Lyons, I suppose . . .'

'Don't play semantics with me,' fumed Macmillan. 'Clinics in Sweden . . . requests from the highest level . . . double-dealing bastards.'

'It could be to our advantage that they don't know that we know they were lying,' said Steven.

Macmillan stopped stalking round the office. 'Go on.'

'If you go back to DOH with all guns blazing before we even have an inkling about what they've been up to, they'll find some way to bluster their way out of trouble. They'll muddy the water with the usual nonsense about failures of communication and unfortunate misunderstandings. The end result will be that they'll batten down all the hatches and tough it out. We may never find out what went on at Pinetops.'

'What do you suggest?'

'We say nothing, let them think we're playing ball while we try to find out what's really been going on.'

'Makes some sort of sense, I suppose,' said Macmillan, calming down a little.

'Let's take stock,' said Steven. 'We have a situation where one hundred and eight children were given BCG vaccine without any apparent cause . . . if indeed, that's what they were given.'

Macmillan rolled his eyes.

'Several of these children have presented with skin complaints. One has died of necrotising fasciitis although the diagnosis remains incomplete because the lab can't confirm it and another girl looks like she's developing a similar problem. First, I think we have to establish exactly what the kids were given and why, and see if that provides clues as to what's been happening to them. I'll leave the "whys" up to you.'

'Where will you start?'

'Pinetops has its own small clinic and at least one fully qualified nurse on the staff. I'm hoping that they were involved in the administration of the vaccine – it's my guess they were if only because it might have aroused suspicion if they hadn't been. I'll go up there and talk to them, ask them if they noticed anything out of the ordinary at the time. Then I'll pay another visit to Edinburgh and see how things are with Trish Lyons. I'll also have another talk to Scott Haldane's widow. Something still tells me that her husband figured out something that I should know.'

'Maybe the something that got him killed?' said Macmillan.

'Quite so.'

In contrast to his first visit, Steven found the activities at Pinetops in full swing when he arrived. The camp had its full complement of children enjoying the outdoor life and a series of character-building experiences under the eyes of ever-vigilant instructors. Steven paused to watch a number of them practise rolling and righting their canoes near the edge of the lake. He'd never been fond of that manoeuvre himself – water always got up his nose – although he recognised it as being an essential skill to have. He empathised with one boy who was coughing and spluttering after his roll to the amusement of the others. Their accents said they came from London.

'You just can't stay away from here, can you?' said David Williams when Steven put his head round the door.

'Makes me wish I was a kid again,' said Steven, looking back at the water. 'The lake looks wonderful this morning.'

The instructor joined him. 'Takes some beating, doesn't it? God's own backdrop. What can I do for you this time?'

Steven asked if he could talk to the clinic staff.

'No problem. I know that Joan, our registered nurse, is dealing with a cut knee at the moment. I'll take you across.'

Steven and the chief instructor walked across the camp compound passing as they did a posse of children about to depart for a walk in the hills, all clutching maps and compasses.

The smell of disinfectant assaulted their noses as they entered the clinic where the camp nurse had just finished bandaging a young boy's knee. She was telling him to come back in the morning for a change of dressing. 'And don't get it wet, young man.'

'Joan, this is Dr Dunbar from the Sci-Med Inspectorate; he'd like to ask you a few questions,' said Williams.

'Hope we're not in any trouble,' said the nurse with a smile.

'Nothing like that,' said Steven, nodding his thanks to the instructor, who took his leave. 'It's about the BCG vaccinations that were administered to a number of children here a few months ago. Were you involved in that?'

'Yes, I helped administer them.'

'Excellent,' said Steven. 'I was hoping you'd say that. Tell me about the team. How many people were involved?'

'Let me see, the doctor and four assistants. Six including myself and Carol my assistant.'

'Did you know this doctor?'

'I'd never seen him before.'

'So he wasn't local?'

'No, I think someone said they all came up from London.'

'You didn't happen to catch his name, did you?'

'Leyton, I think. Yes, he introduced himself as Dr John Leyton. Is there something wrong? Why are you asking?'

'No real problem,' said Steven, anxious to dispel the seeds of suspicion the nurse was showing. 'But a few of the kids have fallen ill since getting the vaccine so we have to be sure that correct procedure was followed; you know how it is these days?'

'Tell me about it, forms for everything and an entire nation waiting for the chance of compensation.'

'Exactly,' said Steven. 'I take it you noticed nothing out of the ordinary about Dr Leyton and his team?'

'Nothing at all, they seemed very nice.'

'Did they bring the vaccine with them or was it ordered in for them?'

'They brought it.'

'Can you remember anything at all about it . . . what it said on the labels for instance?'

'It said BCG,' said the nurse as if she were talking to an idiot.

'Well, that's a good start,' said Steven with a smile. 'Anything else? Dates? Manufacturer's name?'

The nurse looked askance at him. 'Surely no one is suggesting they were given the wrong vaccine?' she exclaimed.

'No,' sighed Steven. 'But these days you and I both know that we have to dot all the I's and cross all the T's.'

'I checked the expiry date out of habit. I can't remember what it said but it was fine.'

'Manufacturer?'

'Sorry, wait, no, there was a name . . . Nichol, I think. I can't be a hundred per cent certain but I'm pretty sure it was something like Nichol or Nichols. I didn't pay that much attention.'

Steven thanked the nurse and told her she'd been an enormous help. He struck up a conversation with her about her background in nursing and the types of injury she came across at Pinetops just to reinforce the friendly, routine nature of his inquiry but in reality hoping that she wouldn't bother to mention his visit in any formal record she had to submit.

Before driving off, Steven phoned in a request to Sci-Med, asking them to check up on any pharmaceutical company having a name like Nichol or Nichols who was involved in the manufacture of BCG vaccine. At the same time he checked to see if the London lab had managed to grow anything from the post mortem samples taken from Keith Taylor. 'No, nothing,' came the reply.

It was about nine in the evening when Steven arrived in the outskirts of Edinburgh and decided to use the place where he had stayed last time, Fraoch House. He phoned ahead about a room and was told he was 'in luck'. Keeping a low profile was still a good idea, he reckoned. The fewer who knew where he was and what he was doing, the better.

He hesitated before he phoned Scott Haldane's widow, wondering if it might be too late to call, but then did it anyway, apologising for the lateness of the hour but asking if he might meet with her in the morning.

'Is there really any point?' snapped Linda Haldane. 'Everyone still believes my husband committed suicide. In fact, I think I'm even beginning to believe it myself.'

'But not really?' said Steven.

'No,' she sighed.

'If it's any comfort, I'm not entirely convinced myself,' said Steven. 'That's really why I'd like to talk to you.'

Linda gave another long sigh. 'I don't think so,' she said. 'The house was burgled three nights ago and I'm still in the process of clearing up. I really don't have the heart for any more dealings with officialdom. I'm sick of policemen and endless questions.'

'God, I'm sorry,' said Steven. 'That was the last thing you needed but I'm not really a policeman and frankly, I think I'm on your side. Maybe just half an hour?'

'All right,' conceded Linda, as if against her better judgement. 'Come round at ten. You remember where?'

Steven said that he did.

'Why don't we sit outside in the garden while we have the chance,' said Linda, glancing up at the watery sunshine when Steven arrived promptly at ten. 'Apart from that, I still haven't finished clearing up the mess inside.'

'Did the police have any ideas about the break-in?' asked Steven.

'No, not really, just that it was probably drug addicts who knew that Scott was a doctor and imagined he kept cupboards full of heroin all over the house. They certainly gave the place a thorough examination,' she added bitterly.

'I'm sorry,' said Steven. 'Many people don't realise what an awful experience it is to have your home invaded by strangers.'

'I can still feel them in the house,' said Linda with an involuntary shudder. She left Steven alone to enjoy the morning sunshine and blackbird song while she went back inside to make coffee.

'Nice garden,' he said when she rejoined him.

'Mmm,' agreed Linda. 'Unfortunately we're not going to be able to stay here much longer. We'll have to learn to live within our means as my old gran used to say.'

'I'm sorry, I thought . . .' began Steven, feeling embarrassed.

'Suicide tends to negate life insurance policies,' said Linda with undisguised venom. 'So, unless you know differently . . .' She fixed Steven with a steely gaze.

'I've no evidence,' confessed Steven. 'Only a feeling that there's more to the green sticker children than I've been told. I suspect it was what your husband was concerned about rather than Trish Lyons' accident.'

'So you do now believe it was an accident and not the reason for some guilt trip that drove Scott to his death?'

Steven nodded and conceded the point. 'Like your husband, I do believe it was an accident.'

'Well, that's something, I suppose. How can I help you?'

'You told me that Scott was very upset after making various phone-calls connected with the Trish Lyons case but wouldn't say why. I just wondered if you'd remembered anything else since the last time we spoke, no matter how small or seemingly insignificant. I desperately need something to point me in the right direction. I've got the same uneasy feelings your husband had but he obviously figured out more than I have.'

'God knows I would love to be able to say yes to that question,' said Linda. 'But I haven't. Scott wouldn't tell me anything. He kept saying he had to be sure before he said anything.'

'Didn't you pick up the odd clue from his phone-calls? A name? An organisation? Anything at all?'

'I think I already told you about him complaining that people were being downright obstructive.'

'Nothing else?'

Linda looked doubtful. 'I suppose I may have picked up the odd word here and there when he raised his voice on the phone . . . I think I once heard him ask, "Who made the bloody stuff?" but I've no idea what he was talking about.'

Steven repeated the quote. 'That's interesting,' he said, thinking about the vaccine. 'I think I may even know what he was asking about.'

'Really?'

'Trish Lyons isn't the only child to have fallen ill after attending the camp in the Lake District. Apart from their attendance there, the one common factor among them was that they were all vaccinated with BCG vaccine.'

'And you think Scott was suspicious about it?'

'It's possible. Not only that, I think he may even have worked out what was wrong with the kids. If you do happen to think of anything else please call me, any time, day or night.' Steven handed her his card.

'I will. I promise.'

Steven couldn't have arrived at the children's hospital at a worse time. Patricia Lyons' mother, Virginia, was clearly upset and arguing with doctors having just been told they would have to amputate Trish's arm to stop the infection spreading throughout her body. Raised voices meant that he could hear much of what Virginia Lyons was saying as he waited outside the room.

'What infection?' she demanded. 'You haven't come up with anything yet. You're just guessing. How can something you can't even grow be spreading throughout her body?'

Steven could only just pick up the muted murmur of reasoned response before Virginia Lyons broke down in tears and was led out from the office by one of the doctors to be handed over to a nursing sister who wrapped her arms round her and led her away for tea and sympathy.

Steven recognised one of the doctors as John Fielding, the man he'd spoken to last time. 'I came to see how Trish was. I think I may already have my answer,' he said.

Fielding shook his head in a gesture of hopelessness and said, 'The lab still can't grow anything and she continues to deteriorate no matter what antibiotics we give her. We're fighting a losing battle here. Even if her mother gives us the go-ahead for amputating her arm, she's still not out of the woods. The patches on other parts of her body are beginning to look as if they might go the same way.'

'You mean the infection is not a result of her burns becoming infected?' asked Steven, feeling some trepidation.'

'That's what we all thought at first of course,' replied Fielding. 'Burns are notorious for becoming infected but none of the usual suspects grew up in culture so we're beginning to have our doubts. If only the lab could find the bug responsible, life could become a whole lot easier for everyone.'

Steven nodded, thinking he'd heard all this before from the doctors who treated Keith Taylor. It could not be a coincidence. 'How about necrotising fasciitis,' he said.

'Without a cause?'

'But not without a precedent,' said Steven under his breath.

'Would you like to see her?' asked the doctor.

Steven nodded and was led to a small ante-room to don mask and gown before entering the room where Trish lay, heavily sedated.

'The nurses removed the dressings so we could show her mother the extent of the problem and they haven't been re-applied yet so you can see it for yourself,' said Fielding. He removed the light gauze covering from Trish's arm and Steven saw the damage and grimaced at the sight.

'The flesh is just sloughing off,' said the doctor. 'There's no chance of recovery and every chance of gangrene setting in if we don't act quickly.'

Steven nodded and the doctor replaced the gauze before moving down to Trish's feet and saying, 'These are the areas we fear might go the same way.'

Steven saw the discoloured patches on Trish's legs. 'Do you mind if I take a closer look?' he asked.

'Please do,' said the doctor, holding out a box of disposable gloves for Steven to help himself.

As he bent down, Steven became aware of a woman standing at the viewing window next door – it was Trish's mother. Her wan expression spoke volumes about the stress she was under. Steven went ahead and examined the patches, running his fingers over the surface in all directions and pinching at intervals before saying, 'The flesh seems firm enough. What makes you think they might be becoming infected too?'

The doctor opened a sterile stylet pack and said, 'Watch.'

Steven saw Trish move in her sleep when the doctor pricked an area of normal looking skin but fail to react when he did the same in the centre of one of the patches.

'She's losing sensation in these areas. Not a good sign.'

'And not a recorded symptom of vitiligo either if I remember rightly,' added Steven.

'Good point,' agreed Fielding.

'Thank you,' said Steven, stripping off his gloves and dumping them in a pedal bin. Both men left the room and joined Virginia Lyons and the nursing sister next door. Steven was introduced simply as Dr Dunbar without any further details being given.

'Mrs Lyons has come to a decision,' said the nurse.

'I want you to go ahead with amputation,' said Virginia as

if every word had to be forced from her lips. 'If it's the only way to save her . . .'

'I'm afraid it's the only chance she's got.'

Virginia made to move away but stopped and turned when she reached the door. 'What were you doing with the needle to Trish's legs?' she asked.

'Reaction testing,' said the doctor.

'Dr Haldane did that too,' said Virginia vaguely.

'It's a fairly routine test, Mrs Lyons.'

Virginia Lyons looked as if a nightmare had just been born in her head. 'My God, you're not thinking of cutting her legs off too?' she gasped.

'Good heavens, no, nothing like that,' said Fielding, clearly flustered as the nurse quickly put her arm round Virginia's shoulders and led her away. She would have found the look that passed between Steven and the doctor far from reassuring.

TWELVE

Macmillan and Steven sat in silence for what seemed to be a very long time before Macmillan finally said, 'You are seriously suggesting that someone in government presided over the injection of a noxious substance into over a hundred schoolchildren under the pretence of protecting them from TB with a vaccine?'

'That's what it's beginning to look like,' agreed Steven. 'I don't believe the kids were given BCG vaccine – there was no reason to give it to them. The kid who was supposed to have TB was a myth.'

'So what did they give them and why, for God's sake?' mused Macmillan.

'I think in the circumstances you may have to ask the DOH that after all,' said Steven. 'Jean has just told me that there is no pharmaceutical company with a name like Nichol or anything close to it. That being the case, my investigation has just hit the wall.'

Uneasy at the prospect of going to war with the upper echelons of government, Macmillan got up and walked over to the window. 'God, will it ever stop raining,' he complained as he looked out at the slow-moving snake of traffic outside.

'Yes, if you believe the climate experts who predict imminent drought from climate change,' said Steven. 'No, if you believe the ones who predict widespread flooding and water-skiing in Whitehall.'

'So cynical and you're not even forty yet,' sighed Macmillan.

'All I ever ask for is proof,' replied Steven, 'and all I ever get is plausible-sounding bullshit.'

'You do have a point,' murmured Macmillan. 'Plausibility is the new currency in science. I suppose it's easier to come up with than fact.'

Steven had stopped listening. He was leaning forward in his chair, inclining his head to read the label stuck on a red folder lying in Macmillan's 'pending' tray on his desk. 'Nichol!' he exclaimed.

'What?' asked Macmillan, turning away from the window.

Steven lifted the folder from the tray and said, 'That was the name on the vaccine vials.'

'It was the name of the young scientist who was killed in the hit and run accident I told you about a couple of weeks ago. Nichol, Alan Nichol. Could just be coincidence, I suppose ...'

'But there again, I remember you said he worked for a biotech company,' said Steven. 'D'you mind?' He held up the folder and Macmillan nodded his assent.

Steven read through the report. 'St Clair Genomics ... I wonder.'

'It was just sitting there waiting for the final police report,' said Macmillan.

'I'd like to check this out,' said Steven.

'If it gets me out of a head-to-head confrontation with DOH,' said Macmillan, 'by all means go ahead.'

'Do we have anything more than this?' asked Steven, holding up the slim report.

'I did ask Jean to see if she could get more details just in case the police came up with anything that should concern us,' said Macmillan, pressing the intercom button.

'I have a file,' came Jean Roberts' reply.

* * *

Steven decided to read it before he left the building just in case there was anything else he needed to ask or request. As it turned out, there wasn't. He had the names of the managing director of St Clair Genomics and a little about his background and also the name and address of the dead man, Nichol, along with some background information and his home address. There was also an accident report from the local police now some three weeks old.

Nichol had been walking his dog along an unclassified country road outside the village of Trenton where he lived in a rented cottage with his wife, Emma, when he had been hit by a car travelling at speed. The car had failed to stop and had not as yet been traced despite a villager claiming to have seen a red 4x4 moving at speed through the village around the time of Nichol's death. No description of the driver had been forthcoming and Steven had the distinct impression that the police were treating the incident as a drunken hit and run.

Alan Nichol, he read, had been twenty-eight years old, a graduate of Glasgow University in Molecular Biology with first-class honours, who had gone on to do a PhD at Edinburgh University on genes affecting viral pathogenicity, followed by a three-year post-doctoral research position at the University of Cambridge. This was where he had been approached by Phillip St Clair, who ran his own small biotechnology company and who maintained good relations with the biological sciences departments at the university. He did this out of self-interest – he was always on the look-out for good ideas or promising researchers to recruit – although he liked to insist that the relationship was symbiotic and that he was always keen to share information.

St Clair's charm and gift of the gab had helped enormously with this and, although everyone knew that his real interests were commercial rather than academic, he was generally accepted around the university. Although he had graduated in biological sciences himself, he had always planned to set up in business as soon as he could to exploit what he saw as the huge potential of molecular biology in medicine. His father had made a one-off investment in his son's future some ten years ago by funding the set-up of St Clair Genomics, insisting that Phillip then stand or fall on his own merits.

It had been touch and go in the early years but the company had come up with a few minor diagnostic aids over the past three years and had attracted some venture capital investment. As yet, it had failed to bring anything major to the market-place. Steven decided that he would call on St Clair Genomics unannounced.

Unlike Cambridge University, which nurtured and guarded its history in the ancient stone of its colleges and quadrangles, St Clair Genomics was a building of its time – functional and with a very temporary feel about it. An attempt to grow Virginia creeper along the front had not been entirely successful and could not disguise its construction from prefabricated concrete panels. It was, however, light and airy inside thanks to a number of glass roof panels which allowed natural light to fall on the plants in a small atrium. Steven read that they had been supplied on a rental basis from 'Woodland Office' as he sat down beside one while the receptionist investigated whether or not Phillip St Clair would be 'available'.

'You'll have to forgive me, Dr Dunbar, I don't think I've come across Sci-Med before,' said Phillip St Clair with what Steven thought was a nervous smile as he returned his ID card.

'No reason why you should,' replied Steven, stating briefly what he and the organisation did.

'Sounds like a good idea,' said St Clair. 'There's obviously a need . . .'

'Really? Why do you say that?' said Steven. He knew perfectly well that St Clair had said it out of politeness but thought he'd see if he could rattle the man – maybe find out why he seemed so nervous.

St Clair shrugged and opened his palms. 'Technology moves forward at such a rate these days. The police can't possibly hope to keep up with every development . . .'

Steven smiled and nodded.

'I have to confess however,' continued St Clair, 'that I don't quite understand what you could possibly want with us?'

'One of your people died recently,' said Steven. 'In unfortunate circumstances, I understand.'

'Alan Nichol,' said St Clair. 'Hit and run.' He rubbed the side of his forehead with the tips of his fingers. 'I hope the bastard who did it rots in hell. Drunken yob! Alan was one of the nicest guys you could ever hope to meet and one of brightest of his generation. He had so much to offer and such a brilliant future ahead of him. What a waste. And poor Emma . . . they'd only been married a year. This has absolutely destroyed her. I suppose it's a blessing they didn't have any children.'

Steven nodded, thinking that St Clair had just about covered all the bases in his impromptu eulogy but wondering why his hands were shaking – something he attempted to hide by interlacing his fingers on his lap.

'What was Alan Nichol working on?' Steven asked.

'He was one of our best researchers, a first-rate virologist and a wizard at the bench when it came to molecular biology. The two don't always go together, you know. I've known brilliant people who didn't have the practical ability to post a letter . . .'

'I'm sure, but what was Alan Nichol working on?'

St Clair looked uncomfortable. 'I'm afraid I can't tell you that.'

'I do have the right to ask,' said Steven, nodding to his ID which he'd left lying on the desk. He could see perspiration break out on St Clair's face.

'I'm sorry, I can't tell you.'

Steven disliked playing the heavy but saw no other way forward. 'I'm afraid I must insist,' he said. 'We can do this at the local police station but I was hoping that that wouldn't be necessary? Believe me; I have no interest in compromising any commercial considerations you might be worried about.'

'It's not that,' said St Clair.

'Then what?'

'Dr Dunbar, have you signed the Official Secrets Act?'

Steven said that he had.

'So have I. Alan's work was classified.'

Steven looked at St Clair, barely able to disguise his surprise. 'Are you telling me that Alan Nichol was working for the government?'

'No, he worked for St Clair Genomics but what he was doing was covered by the act. It still is.'

Steven took a moment to digest what he'd heard. It prompted St Clair to add, 'You people don't seem to talk to each other much, do you?'

'Indeed we don't,' agreed Steven. 'Thank you very much, Mr St Clair, you've been very helpful.'

'I haven't told you anything at all.'

'More than you think,' said Steven with a smile that was not designed to put St Clair at his ease. 'By the way, does the name Scott Haldane mean anything to you?'

St Clair looked momentarily blank. 'Haldane ... ? I don't think so. Should it?'

'You tell, me, Mr St Clair. Thank you again for your time.'

Steven sat in the car for a few minutes before driving off. For once, he couldn't complain about his luck. The chance sighting of a document lying in Macmillan's in-tray had led to this . . . and this was certainly no coincidence. There was no doubt at all in his mind that the name the nurse at Pinetops had seen on the vials of supposed BCG vaccine referred to Alan Nichol of St Clair Genomics. Something designed by Alan Nichol had been injected into over a hundred children with the collusion of Her Majesty's Government.

'Bloody hell,' whispered Steven. St Clair's nervousness now made sense but the man wasn't just nervous; he was afraid.

Steven considered talking to Emma Nichol but decided against it. There was a good chance that St Clair had phoned ahead to remind her of her duty to say nothing. Apart from that, there was a good chance that she hadn't known what her husband had been working on anyway if he'd signed the Official Secrets Act. For the moment, he would leave her to grieve in peace.

Steven turned to the file beside him on the passenger seat and checked out the name and address of the witness who claimed to have seen a red 4x4 in the vicinity at the time of the accident. Maurice Stepney, 1 Apple Cottage Row, Trenton. A brief reference to the road atlas he kept tucked into the pocket on the back of the passenger seat and he was on his way to Trenton.

At three in the afternoon, the village appeared to be asleep. There was no one about, no sounds, not even a dog barking as Steven crawled through, looking for Apple Cottage Row. The Porsche was unhappy at low revs, obliging him to blip the throttle intermittently to stop the spark plugs fouling and bringing on feelings of guilt at interrupting the rural calm. As he turned into Apple Cottage Row, he saw his first person, a man working in the garden of the end cottage. The man paused to lean on his hoe and look at Steven and, as he drew nearer, Steven saw that he was standing in the garden of number one.

'Maurice Stepney?' he asked as he got out the car.

'Who wants to know?' replied the man.

Ye gods, thought Steven. Why did everyone behave as if they were a hit man on the run these days? He showed the man his ID and said who he was. 'It's about the car accident a few weeks ago.'

'Have you got him then?'

'Afraid not. I wanted to ask you if there was anything else you'd remembered about the car?'

'What's all this then?' asked a small, plump woman, emerging from the house, wiping her hands on her apron. She didn't introduce herself but Steven assumed she was Mrs Stepney.

'This fellow's asking about the hit and run. Wants to know if I've remembered anything else.'

'You remember anything?' exclaimed the woman. 'Most of the time you can't remember what day of the week it is.'

'Be that as it may,' said Stepney, looking down at his shoes to hide his annoyance, 'I can't tell you any more than I already told the police. It was a red 4x4, travelling fast, not from around here. I'd never seen it before.'

'And I keep telling you it was probably the same red car I'd seen sitting up by the post office the week before,' said Stepney's wife, a comment that got Steven's full attention.

'Nonsense,' said Stepney.

'It was sitting in the lane the last two Thursdays when I went round to Ellen's.' She looked at Steven. 'Ellen's my friend. She lives by the post office. I always go round on a Thursday for a cuppa and a chinwag. Her Bill goes out to his club, you see.'

'Stupid woman,' said Stepney. 'You wouldn't know a 4x4 if it ran over you.'

'I just said it was a red car.'

'That should narrow it down to twenty million,' scoffed her husband.

'Did you tell the police this, Mrs Stepney?' asked Steven.

'He said not to bother,' said the woman, inclining her head towards Stepney.

'Where exactly is the post office?' asked Steven.

Both gave him directions at once but he managed to deduce where he should be heading. 'Many thanks, you've been a great help.' He got back into the car, leaving the Stepneys arguing in the garden.

Steven stopped the car just past the lane near the post office and reversed back into it. He saw that he now had a clear view of Elm Street without being too noticeable himself. Elm Street rang a bell. It was where . . . He checked the file beside him again. It was where the Nichols lived . . . Another check of the file for the date of Nichol's death and a quick calculation in his head told him that Nichol had been killed on a Thursday.

Steven breathed an expletive as he put things together. The person or persons sitting in the red car when Mrs Stepney had come round to visit her friend on a Thursday evening could have been establishing Alan Nichol's routine. They would have discovered what time he took the dog for a walk and what route he took and used that information to intercept him somewhere along the way. Alan Nichol might well have been murdered.

THIRTEEN

Not for the first time in his career with Sci-Med, Steven found himself reluctant to accept the evidence he was uncovering. It was an uncomfortable feeling, one that seemed to undermine everything he stood for. He had long ago stopped believing that the UK government couldn't possibly get involved in anything underhand or downright illegal. Common sense demanded that they be as ruthless as any potential enemy when it came to matters affecting state security. But it was important to him to believe that he still worked for the 'good guys'. The distinction however seemed to have been becoming more and more blurred.

Some kind of experiment carried out on unwitting school children with government approval and involving the murder of a scientist connected with the affair was pushing things to the very limit. Had Nichol got cold feet about what he was doing and decided to blow the whistle? Had he been 'silenced' because of it? Had Scott Haldane in Edinburgh been murdered because he'd suspected that something unethical or even illegal was going on? Steven drew the line at believing in state-sanctioned murder but on the other hand, Dr David Kelly's suicide had never struck him as being entirely convincing. He would check first thing in the morning on the state of health of all the green sticker children. If any more had developed conditions like Keith Taylor or Trish Lyons, the time for discreet inquiries would be over. Like it or not, Macmillan would have to tackle the Department of Health head-on and demand an explanation. As to what that explanation could possibly be . . . Steven shivered as he considered that someone might see it as being more expedient to do away with Sci-Med than come up with one. He called Tally's number.

'Hello, how are you? Where are you?'

Steven was pleased that Tally sounded happy to hear from him. 'I'm just outside Cambridge; I wanted to hear your voice.'

'That's nice,' said Tally. 'I'm glad you phoned. Any particular reason?' She couldn't hide the mischief in the question.

'The foundations of my life are being swept away and I thought you might be able to help . . .'

'How?'

'Strong drink and a shoulder to cry on would be a good start.'

'But you're in Cambridge.'

'I've got a Porsche.'

Tally laughed and said. 'All right, come up but if you're not here by ten, forget it and don't bother ringing the bell. I've got a very busy day tomorrow.'

'On my way.'

Steven pushed the entry-phone button outside Tally's apartment block at a little after nine thirty and was rewarded by an invitation to enter. He sprinted up the stairs and found her standing at her front door, leaning on the jamb with an amused smile on her face. She gave a slight shake of the head and said, 'For a man who's had the foundations of his life swept away, you're moving rather well . . .'

'The Dunbars have always been resilient,' smiled Steven,

taking her in his arms and giving her a big hug. 'Nice to see you.'

'You too.'

Tally poured Steven a large gin and tonic and topped up her own wine glass. 'Well,' she said, sitting down beside him on the couch. 'Tell Aunt Tally all about it . . .'

Steven smiled wryly and said, 'I'm trying to make light of it but it's deadly serious and I wasn't joking about the way I'm feeling. I think I'm losing the place here . . .'

Tally could see that Steven was genuinely undergoing some kind of a crisis. 'Go on,' she said.

He told her what he had uncovered and deduced, admitting, 'I can't see any other way of looking at it.'

'But this is outrageous,' exclaimed Tally. 'Experimenting on children? It beggars belief.'

'It won't be as cold-hearted as that when the truth comes out, I'm sure,' said Steven. 'It'll be a case of someone meaning well but screwing up big time – it usually is where HMG is concerned – but two murders to keep it quiet? That's taking things to a whole new level.'

'You can't be sure these people were murdered,' said Tally.

'No, but it's looking odds on.'

'Any idea what they gave the children?'

Steven shook his head. 'Something they thought would do them good,' he intoned.

'Like a vaccine?'

'Like a vaccine,' agreed Steven. 'Only it's hard to see how a vaccine could cause what I've been seeing. Have you ever seen necrotising fasciitis?'

'No, thank God, I never have.'

'You don't want to. Believe me.'

'But if it was the "vaccine" that caused it, doesn't this mean that all the children are at risk?'

'That's my real fear,' said Steven. 'I'm going to run a check in the morning on all the kids involved, just to see what the current situation is.'

'And if there are any more who've fallen ill?'

'Then it's a national disaster in the making and one which might well bring down the government . . . if they let it.'

Tally looked at him. 'You mean if they've murdered two people to keep this quiet, they may murder more?'

'That's what I'm having trouble getting my head round. I thought I worked for the white hats . . .'

'I can see the problem,' said Tally thoughtfully, her eyes breaking contact.

'No one knows I'm here,' said Steven. 'No one in my world knows you exist. You're quite safe.'

Tally gave a slightly embarrassed smile. 'You read my mind,' she said.

'Can you read mine?' asked Steven softly, taking both her hands in his.

'Steven . . . I thought we agreed this isn't a good idea . . .'

'I think it's a very good idea.'

'I see. I just see you in times of national crisis?'

'If we both want it, we can make it work . . .'

'Steven . . .'

Steven brought her closer and a first hesitant kiss led to passion that rose inside both of them. 'Oh bugger . . .' murmured Tally as she wrapped her arms around Steven. 'I'm going to regret this in the morning . . .'

'Good morning,' said Steven as he delivered coffee to a sleepy Tally who was still in bed.

'Oh my God,' she exclaimed in alarm. 'What time is it?'

'Just after six.'

Tally relaxed. 'God, I thought for a moment you were going to say nine.'

Steven kissed her lightly on the forehead. 'Full of regrets?' he asked.

Tally smiled and reached up to touch his face. '*Je ne regrette rien.*'

'Good.'

'Why so early?'

'I have to go.'

'And so, farewell?' said Tally.

'You know it's not like that,' said Steven. 'I'll call you later?'

'Make it evening. I've got a busy day ahead. You're off to London?'

Steven nodded. 'You're not the only one with a busy day ahead,' he said ruefully.

Steven set off, hoping to miss the worst of the rush hour traffic before he joined the M1 motorway. The street outside Tally's apartment block seemed quiet enough so he took this as a good sign although, as he looked both ways before crossing, he took in that a dark grey Jaguar saloon was sitting about a hundred yards away with two men in the front. He smiled to himself at his observation and remembered that his wife, Lisa, had always maintained that he was never really off duty. Two men in the front of a parked car were always worth noting and usually keeping tabs on someone. As to whether they were policemen in an unmarked vehicle or privateers noting who was sleeping with whom, it didn't matter. It couldn't possibly be him they were interested in. No one knew he was here.

Steven felt a chill when he saw that the Jaguar had taken off from the kerb a few seconds after he pulled away and was keeping station about a hundred metres behind the Porsche. He was sure he hadn't been followed here. He didn't even know himself he was coming up to Leicester until he'd phoned Tally from the village where the Nichols had lived and he would have noticed if there had been a car behind him on the quiet country roads leading over to the motorway. It had to be coincidence. At any moment the Jaguar would turn off and he would think of what Lisa would have said to him about seeing baddies round every corner . . . but it didn't. It joined the M1, heading south behind him.

Again, Steven tried convincing himself that there was nothing sinister in the situation. The men had probably just come out of a building up the street at the same time as he left Tally's apartment this morning and were heading down to London just like him. He accelerated to 70mph and held the Porsche on cruise control. He was tempted to go faster but the car was a magnet for police road patrols and he'd rather not get another ticket. The Jaguar remained behind him as the Mondeos and Vectras of the nation's sales force swept past in the outside lane.

Steven's argument with himself progressed to considering that the Jaguar was probably just obeying the law as he was and after all, what would be the point of following him all the way from Leicester to London after having followed him all the way up to Leicester? He reinforced this by again concluding that there was no way that anyone could have known where he was staying last night.

A glance in the mirror to check that there was no other vehicle in the gap between him and the Jaguar and Steven took his foot off the accelerator. The Jaguar closed quickly and Steven read its registration plate. He picked up speed again and called it in to Sci-Med. Two miles passed by before he was told, 'It's a dark grey Jaguar belonging to a Mr Geoffrey Slessor of Greenhill Avenue, Dover.'

'Thanks,' said Steven. He considered reporting that the car was following him but deferred this because he still wasn't sure that it was. One final test, he thought. He waited until he saw a long gap appear in the road ahead and dropped a gear before sinking his foot to the floor, making the Porsche take off like a scalded cat. His heart sank as he saw the Jag accelerate too. He took his foot off the accelerator, letting his speed drop back to two figures and expecting the Jag to do the same, but instead it maintained speed and came up fast in the outside lane as his own speed dropped to eighty. Steven glanced to the side as it came alongside and saw the Jag's passenger window opening. His initial fear that a gun was about to appear in it was dispelled as the Jag continued to pass and pull in in front of him. He prepared himself for a sudden braking manoeuvre but, instead and before he had the chance to react, the air was suddenly full of metallic objects flung from the Jag, sunlight reflecting off their sharp points. The fat tyres of the Porsche hit them before Steven could do anything, causing them to burst and shred, sending the car slewing across the hard shoulder and up the banking where it took off in a graceful arc before touching down and somersaulting end over end, finally coming to a halt on its roof in a field.

Steven felt disorientated but was still conscious and the smell of fuel was telling him that he had to get out fast. His immediate problem was to escape the suffocating attention of the airbags in order to release his safety belt. There was a nightmare moment when he thought his left leg might be trapped by the deformed metal of the footwell but he managed to free it by twisting, turning and pulling in a variety of directions although his shoe remained behind. He thanked God for the fact he was wearing loafers with no laces.

There was no possibility of climbing out through the driver's side because it had taken the brunt of the heavy landing after the last somersault but there was a gap on the passenger side through which he could see green grass. The smell of petrol grew ever stronger, adding panic to his efforts as he fought to manoeuvre his large frame into a position where he could squeeze into the gap and pull himself out head first. He found the body-hugging seats that were so good in high-speed cornering an absolute nightmare to get out of in his current situation. Sweat was pouring down his face and mingling with the blood from superficial cuts by the time he managed to turn himself round and get his head into the gap to take a big breath of fresh air. Another bad moment was to come when he thought his shoulders weren't going to go through the gap but a superhuman effort, which ripped the shoulder padding off his jacket, won the day and he finally dragged his legs out to corkscrew round and lie face down on the ground.

Fear of an imminent explosion made him roll away from the car and scramble over a small rise to lie there, looking back. The seconds passed and Steven saw that two men were running over the field from the motorway. He assumed at first that they were people who had seen the accident occur and were coming to help but he also had to consider that these might be the two from the Jag. He stayed where he was, pushing himself even closer to the ground behind the small rise, finding a clump of grass to hide behind as he watched.

One of the men was carrying a plastic container. Both seemed unwilling to get too close. Steven wasn't near enough to hear what they were saying to each other. He watched as one dropped to his knees, trying to establish if he was still inside the car. The man shrugged at his accomplice as if to signify that he couldn't be sure and followed up by making a large balloon shape with his hands. The deployed air balloon was obscuring his vision through the gap.

The man got to his feet and joined his companion. The two looked around at the countryside as Steven pressed his face to the earth, bringing back memories of how many other times he'd had to do this in his life.

When he thought it was safe again, Steven raised his head for another look and saw the man with the container open it and return to the car to splash the contents into the small gap. He was clearly nervous and moved as if he were standing on hot coals. He retreated quickly as soon as the container was empty and joined his accomplice in crouching down about twenty metres back from the car, forearms held up against their faces in anticipation of the explosion to come.

The seconds ticked by in silence with nothing but contracting metal noises coming from the Porsche as a slight pall of blue smoke drifted up from the wreckage. The faint sound of sirens in the distance was making the men even more edgy as it became clear to them that one of them might have to go back and ignite the car.

Steven, feeling a moderate breeze against his cheek, appreciated their dilemma. The wind was dispersing the highly explosive air/petrol mix before it could reach critical levels. He watched as the two men approached the car together, preparing to set fire to the petrol-soaked wreckage themselves, under the impression that they were about to immolate Steven Dunbar. They were only about three metres from the wreckage when Steven felt the wind drop to a flat calm, making his eyes open wide in anticipation. The men obviously didn't realise the significance of the wind in the equation. Steven just had time to start considering the poetic justice of what was about to happen when the Porsche exploded, sending a sheet of yellow flame high into the air and enveloping his two would-be murderers in burning fuel as they were blown off their feet to land about fifteen metres from where he lay. Neither man moved as the flames consumed them, making Steven think that the blast alone had probably killed them. The air was filled with the smell of roasting flesh, which only added to the heavy cocktail of fuel and smouldering grass.

FOURTEEN

Steven could see activity on the banking where he'd come off
the motorway and figured that the emergency services had
arrived. It only took a second to decide that he did not want
to be part of any police investigation at that particular moment.
What he needed was time and space to work out what was
going on, not get bogged down in police routine. He rolled
back down the rise he had been hiding behind and into a ditch
that ran along the length of the field. He maintained a crouching,
scrambling run until he reckoned he was far enough away from
the scene of the accident to stand up and take his bearings.
There was a farm house about a quarter of a mile away and,
between him and it, what looked like a minor road. He made
for the road and a track he could see leading up to the farm,
hoping that there might be some sign there. There was. It said,
'Moorfields Farm'. Steven looked about him, taking in that the
land round here was hilly but there was a relatively flat field about
half a mile south of the farm house. He brought out his mobile
phone and called Sci-Med. This was going to test Condition
Red to the limit.

'I need a helicopter to pick me up as fast as possible. I'll be
in a field about half a mile south of Moorfields Farm house to
the east of the M1, travelling south from Leicester.'

'Taking you to where?' asked the calm voice of the duty
officer.

'London.'

'Anything else?'

'A car to meet me at the other end to bring me to the Home Office. I also need you to alert Sir John, please.'

'Will do. I'll call you back with an ETA for the 'copter.'

Steven closed his phone. Not for the first occasion in his time with Sci-Med he had cause to give thanks for the way Macmillan had set up the organisation. When it came to support for investigators in the field, everything ran like clockwork. Sci-Med's administrative brief was to provide support for front-line people, not, as in the case of so many other government organisations, treat them as a source and supply of information for them to make reports and fill in forms of their own making.

Macmillan recruited the best for his investigators. He trusted their judgement implicitly and what they asked for they got. In the case of 'Condition Red' people, the rider 'without question' was applied. Recriminations, should there be any, would come later, not in the middle of an investigation.

Steven left the road and hid himself in a copse of trees at the southernmost edge of the field to wait. He used the time to reflect on what had happened and inspect his body for cuts and bruises. He had been remarkably lucky, he concluded – not even a sprained ankle from an incident he felt sure he would revisit in bad dreams throughout his life to come. He managed a wry smile when he thought it would have to take its turn among all the rest but the smile turned to feelings of bitterness when he started wondering who exactly his enemies were on this occasion. He'd been in similar circumstances before, waiting for pick-up from either a jungle or a desert rendezvous, when he'd known exactly who the enemy were but he'd never found himself doing it in the heart of the English countryside.

His phone rang and he flipped it open.

'Air sea rescue helicopter flying in from Hunstanton; estimated ETA, thirty-five minutes.'

'Roger that,' said Steven.

'Sir John will await your arrival.'

Steven whiled away the time, lying on his back watching the clouds pass over. He thought of Tally and Jenny, separately and together . . . together and separately . . . pleasant daydreams of family life, outings, picnics, Christmas time, holidays in the sun . . . Christ! thought Steven, suddenly fully alert and rolling over on to his stomach, Tally could be in danger. He steeled himself to think logically. The two hit men in the Jag had known he was staying in Leicester last night and where . . . but they were now both dead. The chances were that they had been following him and had no interest at all in Tally but a nagging doubt persisted. If the opposition, whoever they were, suspected that he had told Tally anything that might concern them . . . she could be at risk. He would have to arrange protection for her until he'd worked out what was going on. The sound of rotor blades broke his train of thought and he ran out into the open to signal as he saw the helicopter appear.

'I'm grateful to you,' said Steven as he was pulled on board.

'Our pleasure, Doctor,' said the winchman, closing the door. 'Makes a pleasant change from waiting for some clown to set to sea in a plastic dinghy.' The man looked at the state of Steven and opened his medical kit. 'Maybe we can do something about cleaning you up,' he said.

With his cuts and bruises cleaned and dressed where necessary and with a rescue service anorak taking the place of his torn jacket, Steven jumped down from the helicopter, crouching from the downdraught, and running somewhat unsteadily in service boots a size too large for him, which the winchman had also come up with, to the waiting car. He turned and waved an acknowledgement to the helicopter crew who waved back before lifting off and leaning heavily over to port as they climbed away.

Macmillan's first words when Steven appeared in his office were, 'This had better be good.'

'Good is not a word that's going to come into this,' said Steven. 'Before we go any further I need a police guard put on Dr Natalie Simmons in Leicester – a discreet guard. I don't want her to know. At this stage, it's just a precaution.'

'Address?' asked Macmillan, picking up the phone.

Steven gave him details of Tally's work and home addresses. With that done, Macmillan looked to Steven. 'Now?'

Steven told Macmillan everything leading up to the attempt on his life, watching him become more and more disturbed.

'Over a hundred children injected with something that looks like it could kill them all?' he exclaimed as if unwilling or unable to believe it.

'Something that St Clair Genomics designed and two people have already been murdered to keep it quiet. It was going to be three until I got lucky . . . They do say it's an ill wind that blows nobody any good, only in my case it was the calm that did the trick.'

'I think we can do without gallows humour. How could they have known where you were last night? We didn't.'

Steven shook his head. 'I can't work it out. I didn't know myself until . . .' Steven paused in mid-sentence. 'It was the car,' he exclaimed. 'They knew where the car was, not me.'

Macmillan looked blank.

'The Porsche was fitted with a tracker device in case it got stolen. 'May I?' Steven used Macmillan's phone to dial the emergency number of the tracker service. He said who he was and gave details of his car when asked.

'Everything all right now?' came the reply.

'In what way?' asked Steven cautiously.

'You reported your car as being stolen and then when we told you where it was you said everything was okay: it was a misunderstanding.'

'Yes . . . thank you, fine . . . I just thought I'd call and apologise for the trouble I caused.'

'No problem, sir. All in a day's work.'

'It was the car,' said Steven to Macmillan. 'They, whoever they are, reported it stolen. The tracker service told them where it was.'

Macmillan nodded. 'If I remember rightly, that kind of device saved your life once when the police used it to track you down.'

Steven smiled. 'Well, at least we know the how . . . all we need now is the who and the why.'

'I'm going to call a meeting at the highest level,' said Macmillan. 'No more pussy-footing around. Someone has some explaining to do. In the meantime we'll have to square things with the police up in Leicester and see if we can get some ID on your attackers.'

'And if they should turn out to be MI5 doing HMG's bidding?' asked Steven.

'That doesn't bear thinking about,' said Macmillan.

'Personally, I can think of little else.'

'You should be armed. Ask Jean to fix it. Keep a low profile for the time being. I'll let you know when the meeting is set up.'

Steven got up to go.

'About the police guard on Dr Simmons?'

'Maybe keep it on until we know a bit more about what happened and why?'

'Very well. By the way, Jean mentioned something about having something for you,' said Macmillan as Steven opened the door.

In the outer office Jean Roberts said, 'This came in for you this morning. It's the update on the green sticker children you requested.'

Steven thanked her and said that he needed to make a weapons requisition.

Jean brought out the relevant form from her desk and asked Steven to sign. 'I'll phone ahead so the armourer will expect you,' she said. 'Be careful.'

Steven smiled and nodded in recognition of the concern that had been in her voice. He disliked carrying a gun for all the usual reasons that surfaced when the suggestion that the UK police be armed was made but when his life was under threat – as it clearly was after this morning's incident – he felt more comfortable with the odds redressed a little.

He picked up a Glock 23 automatic pistol from the armourer, who also fitted him with a shoulder holster. 'Neat weapon,' said the man. 'No one will notice it. Not much good for invading Iraq but fine for just-in-case duties.'

'Good,' said Steven flatly.

The mere presence of the weapon underlined the fact that he was now involved in the type of investigation which distanced him from normal life. He'd have to make excuses to Jenny about not being able to come up to Scotland and to Tally because he didn't want to put her life in danger. It was a depressing thought. How could any relationship flourish in such circumstances? How could he put it to Tally that there had been an attempt on his life this morning? What did he expect her to say? *Gosh, that's exciting, you'd better take care?* On the other hand, how could he not tell her if he didn't want the relationship to be built on lies from the outset?

He could hardly dismiss what had happened as a bit of a hard day at the office. He couldn't even tread a middle path and tell her that this was an unprecedented occurrence and unlikely to ever happen again when the weapon currently nestling under his left armpit had been there before and probably would be again . . . unless he left Sci-Med and got himself another job, an ordinary 9 'til 5 – catch the 8.15 every morning, three weeks holiday a year – job. This was the bottom line he always baulked at despite knowing that he wasn't getting any younger and there would come a time when he would have to leave front-line investigation to someone younger while he . . . did what?

As always, Steven put an end to this line of thought but remembered the maxim, *Life is what happens to you while you're planning for the future. Embrace today, not tomorrow.*

Before he went home, Steven decided to sort out his transport problem. He would need a car to use while Sci-Med dealt with the paperwork surrounding the demise of his Porsche. Insurance for Sci-Med people, be it home, personal injury, car or life, was covered by the organisation. He had already decided against using a pool car because details would be too readily available. It might be paranoia but he would make his own arrangements for the time being.

Steven caught a cab and got out about a quarter of a mile from where he actually wanted to go and used a succession of side streets to get to Stan Silver's garage in Dorset Mews. Silver had also served in the Regiment although not at the same time as Steven but it was enough to cement a bond of respect and friendship between the two men.

'So where's the Boxster?' asked Silver when they'd shaken hands and given each other a hug. It had been Silver who had sold Steven the car. He wiped his hands on an oily rag as he took an exaggerated look along the lane in both directions.

'It is no more,' replied Steven.

'You haven't trashed another motor?' laughed Silver.

'I wasn't entirely to blame.'

'Bloody hell. That was a real nice car. So, does this mean you're looking for a replacement?'

'As soon as the paperwork's sorted out,' said Steven. 'I'll give you a ring but in the meantime . . .'

'You need wheels.' Silver led the way to his yard at the back of the mews garage where half a dozen cars were parked. 'A bit of a come down but you can have one of these for the time being although I may have to call it in if I find an interested party.'

'Fair enough,' said Steven.

Silver looked around and pointed to a small, black Honda. 'How about that one? It's a Civic Type R. Looks nothing special but hides its light under a bushel you might say.'

'Sounds good,' said Steven.

'I'll get the keys.'

Steven followed Silver into the garage preparing to formalise the loan of the car and pay up-front. Silver handed him the keys. 'We'll sort that out later when you've got less on your mind.'

Steven gave him a quizzical look.

'You're carrying. I felt it when I hugged you. You're into some-thing heavy. We'll leave the paperwork for another time.'

'Thanks, Stan.'

'Just don't go trashing my motor.'

Steven drove the Honda round to his apartment block and parked it in the basement garage, deliberately not using his own space but that of a neighbour he knew to be away in Australia visiting relatives.

Once inside his apartment, Steven took a cold beer from the fridge and settled down by the window. He knew he would have to phone both Jenny and Tally before the day was done

– something he wasn't looking forward to – but first he wanted to read through the update on the green sticker children.

His brow furrowed as he discovered that twenty-eight children had now had occasion to consult their family doctors: three had been admitted to hospital, fourteen had been referred to specialist clinics for further investigation and the remainder had been diagnosed and started on treatment. To the uninitiated, it would have looked as if they were suffering from a wide range of problems but Steven saw the common thread. The kids had skin problems. The three in hospital had been admitted for other reasons but skin complaints still featured somewhere in their notes. One girl had suffered severe lacerations to her left arm after an accident on an artificial ski slope and the failure of her skin to heal properly was giving concern. Steven heard echoes of Trish Lyons in every word he read. Another child, a boy, had crushed his foot in an accident involving farm machinery and post-surgical healing was not progressing as well as had been hoped. Doctors had expressed concern that an infection might be taking hold.

Steven put down the file and rubbed his eyes as he considered this latest instalment of the nightmare. He wondered if it would be worthwhile visiting any of these children and speaking to their doctors but concluded not, feeling that all that would yield would be a succession of medics puzzling over infections with persistently negative lab reports. It might be better to wait until Macmillan had set up the high-level meeting with health officials and hear an explanation of what was going on.

Steven was thinking about phoning Jenny when his own phone rang. It was John Macmillan.

'We put a priority on identifying the two men who tried to kill you on the motorway and they've come up trumps.'

'Tell me.'

'Both were ex-security service men.'

Steven closed his eyes as his worst fears were realised. His own side was trying to kill him.

'Ex-Russian security service men.'

Steven imagined his mind was playing tricks on him. 'Say again.'

'Oleg Malkov and Yuri Valchev, both ex-KGB operatives. MI6 had them on file but were unaware of them being in the country. Neither is known to be employed by the current regime but that is as much as they know.'

'It just gets better . . .' sighed Steven, not sure whether to feel relieved that his own side were not hunting him down or alarmed because the KGB – or whatever they were called these days – apparently were.

'Bizarre, I grant you,' said Macmillan. 'I take it you haven't done anything to offend our friends from the east?'

'Not that I'm aware of. What about the car owner?'

'The car was cloned. They copied the registration number of another Jaguar and stuck it on an identical model they'd stolen. The original is still in Dover with its owner currently wondering why his house was surrounded by armed police this afternoon. He's a chartered accountant with the county council.'

'At last . . . some excitement in his life,' said Steven.

'The security services will be in touch if they come up with anything more about the two Russians.'

'Good. Any word about the meeting?'

'3 p.m. Home Office, day after tomorrow. Come in earlier; we'll have lunch.'

FIFTEEN

Steven sat wondering for fully ten minutes how two Russian hit men could fit into the picture. There was no obvious way but the fact that it was the car they had traced and followed rather than him made him wonder if it could have been a case of mistaken identity. The car had not been new when he'd bought it from Stan Silver; it had been eight months old. He phoned Stan and asked about the previous owner.

'A little old lady who only used it to go to church on Sundays,' said Silver with a chuckle. 'Like all my cars.'

'I'm serious, Stan. Someone tried to take me out the game today. They got to me through the car.'

'Hang on a mo . . .'

A rustle of paper announced Silver's return to the phone. 'Lieutenant Cyril Ormsby-Frew, with a hyphen, Grenadier Guards officer, needed some readies to pay off some gambling debts as I remember.'

'Mmm, I suppose he might just fit the bill if he didn't actually use the money to pay off his debts,' mused Steven, thinking to himself that Russian Mafia were not exactly thin on the ground in the capital at present. 'Thanks, Stan.'

Steven felt better. Mistaken identity was by far the most attractive explanation. Even if it came to be known that there was no body in the wreckage of the Porsche, the good lieutenant would be the target of whatever vendetta was going on and not him. Embracing this explanation meant that he would no longer have to tell Tally about an attempt on his life . . . it would only be a white lie if he told about the car accident without giving too much detail . . . but first he would phone Jenny.

Susan answered the phone.

'How are things?' asked Steven.

'Better after your last visit but we're still having our moments.'

'I'm so sorry.'

'Don't worry, Steven, it's only a stage she's going through. We'll all ride out the storm, I'm sure. Can I take it you'll be up at the weekend?'

'Actually . . . that's a bit doubtful. I'm in the middle of an investigation and I'm not quite sure how things are going to turn out in the next few days.'

'I see,' said Susan, making it sound like, 'Oh dear'. 'That's a pity. I think Jenny wanted to show you off to her school friends. I said she could ask a few round for tea on Saturday afternoon.'

Steven closed his eyes. 'Sorry . . . look, I'll see what I can do but . . .'

'It's okay, Steven, I understand, I really do. We've known each other long enough to know that we don't bullshit each other. If you can't come up, I know you've got a damned good reason and there's nothing you can do about it with a job like yours. Unfortunately, it's Jenny you have to convince.'

'You'd better put her on,' said Steven. He heard Sue call out her name above background hubbub. 'Jenny . . . it's your daddy.'

'Hello, nutkin, how are you?' he asked as the phone was picked up.

'I'm good, Daddy. I'm playing a computer game with Robin and Mary. Robin's winning but only because he's been practising round at his friend Colin's house after school. Boys always have to win.'

'I suppose,' said Steven.

'My friends Louise and Carol are coming round for tea on Saturday so you can meet them. I've told them you're some sort of policeman in London. They asked if you had a gun but I told them that was just silly.'

'Absolutely,' said Steven, eyeing the Glock pistol hanging over the back of a chair in its holster. 'Look, Jenny . . . I'm afraid I'm awfully busy just now. We're on the trail of some really bad people and Daddy may not be able to get away to come up at the weekend . . .'

There was a long silence, which Steven found deafening. 'Jenny?'

'Yes, all right. Well, I'll have to get back to the game now. Bye.'

Steven let out his breath in a long sigh before Sue picked up the phone again. 'I take it that didn't go down too well,' she said *sotto voce*.

'Like a lead balloon,' said Steven. 'I'm sorry if you're going to get the fall-out from this . . .'

'Like I said, don't worry about it. She's been quite happy being one of our family for long enough. She's just experimenting with the people around her, seeing if they'll dance to her tune. It's all part of growing up.'

'Thanks, Sue. You really are a special person, Richard too. I don't know what I would have done without you guys . . .'

'Let's not go into all that again,' said Sue. 'You know we love Jenny as our own and that's an end to it. Get on with your job and don't let this worry you. It'll sort itself out.'

Steven poured himself a drink and gave himself a few minutes before calling Tally. The feel-good factor he'd got earlier from concluding that the attempt on his life had been down to mistaken identity had all but evaporated in the space of Jenny's long silence on the phone.

He was just about to hang up when Tally answered. 'Sorry, I was in the bath. I usually take a phone in with me but I'm so tired I forgot. I was going to let it ring but then I thought it might be you.'

Steven smiled at the wealth of information. 'And now you're dripping all over the floor?'

'I'll just take you back into the bathroom . . . and put you down while I climb back into the bath . . . There, that's better. God, I'm bushed. What a day.'

'As bad as you feared, huh?'

'And then some. Sometimes I hate my job.'

'Really?'

'Well, maybe it's not my job I hate; it's the NHS. I'm sick to the back teeth of being manipulated by bureaucrats so that they can meet targets and tick boxes for a bunch of stupid politicians who don't know up from down when it comes to health care.'

'Let it all hang out, girl.'

'Setting targets hasn't improved patient care at all; it's just created thousands of jobs for people who can manipulate figures to make it appear as if targets are being met. It's a nonsense.'

'It's not the first time I've heard that,' said Steven.

'I'm sorry . . . it's been a long day and here I am, taking it out on you. Sorry, how was your day?'

'Well, I came off the motorway at 80mph, did a couple of somersaults, landed in a field and then the Porsche blew up . . . apart from that, nothing special.'

'You are joking. Right?'

'Afraid not but I'm absolutely fine apart from a couple of scratches here and there.'

'Oh, Steven, how awful. What happened?'

'Front tyre blow-out. Nothing much you can do when that happens.'

'It must have been absolutely terrifying.'

'I've had better experiences. Still, no real harm done and I live to fight another day.'

'I take it Sci-Med knows what happened?'

'Yes, I've been in touch. There's a top level meeting scheduled for Friday about the Pinetops affair.'

'My God, I'd certainly like to be a fly on the wall at that,' said Tally.

'I'll let you know what happens.'

'If you can.'

'The Official Secrets Act is not there for the convenience of politicians although you might be forgiven for thinking so sometimes. They're not going to get away with using it this time without coming up with an explanation which I can't begin to imagine.'

'I've got a weekend off,' said Tally.

Steven hesitated as guilt welled up inside him over his earlier exchange with Jenny. 'I can't see me getting one,' he said. 'The chances of everyone shaking hands after this meeting and agreeing it was all a mistake must be less than zero. People are going to be fighting for their political lives and others are going to be baying for blood and then there's the question of the children and what happens to them . . .'

'And I'm complaining about targets . . .' said Tally.

'I don't suppose you can get off tomorrow?' asked Steven. 'I've got a free day tomorrow.'

'No way, I'm afraid. If anything it's going to be worse than today.'

'Call you tomorrow night?'

'Please do.'

Steven rested his head on the back of the chair and thought through what he'd told Tally. Nothing had been a lie; everything he'd said had been true and yet he didn't feel as comfortable doing this as he'd hoped. How the front tyres on the Porsche had burst had been quite a big thing to leave out. Maybe another gin would help him feel better.

Steven used his free day to drive down to the south coast: he felt the need to go beach walking. He wanted to taste salt on the breeze and generally escape from the pressures of life by watching the sky fall into the sea on a horizon that would seem suitably far away. The outward trip was a bit of a struggle against a stiff breeze that whipped sand up into his face, causing him to shrug down into the collar of his jacket, but the return leg enabled him to enjoy the sight of the beach becoming almost liquid as its surface moved in deference to the will of the wind. He felt so much better when he got back and sought out beer and a sandwich in a harbour pub before driving home, his skin still tingling and his calf muscles reminding him of the exercise.

Lunch with Macmillan at his club on Friday proved a sombre affair. Macmillan was very much aware that in a few hours' time he would have to make Sci-Med's position clear to the government and the consequences of doing this could be catastrophic for many if, as was his intention, he refused to be any part of a cover-up. With this in mind, he told Steven that he had lodged a report of his findings along with all relevant files with a well-respected firm of solicitors in the City together with instructions as to whom the information should be sent to in the event of any concerted efforts to discredit Sci-Med or its people.

'Or any accident befalling us,' added Steven.

The two men paused in order to let a waiter refill their coffee cups.

'I don't think anyone can afford to be that silly,' said Macmillan.

'Good,' said Steven, not sounding entirely convinced.

Macmillan noticed this and said, 'After your little off-road experience – and before we knew of any Russian involvement – I made a point of telling all our investigators what's been going on. I let this fact be known to the powers that be. But of course, this was before your assailants were identified and there was still a possibility that our security services were involved. Maybe we've both been guilty of paranoia.'

'I'd like to think so,' agreed Steven, feeling uncomfortable with the general tenor of the conversation. The lights went on in the club as the sky darkened outside and rain started to fall.

'Are we all done?' asked Macmillan.

'I think so. Thanks for lunch.'

Macmillan smiled and said, 'Let's hope that eating a hearty meal doesn't imply anything about the afternoon.'

Although they went into the meeting on time, Steven saw that he and Macmillan were the last to arrive. He wondered if this was some psychological ploy on the part of the twenty or so sombre people seated there – many of them instantly recognisable as senior government figures, others not so well known.

The Home Secretary formally acknowledged them but made as little eye contact as possible with either of them. Sci-Med did fall within the auspices of the Home Office although Macmillan was not personally answerable to the Home Secretary – a grey area perhaps but this was not the time to explore it.

The Home Secretary, appearing gaunt and serious, said, 'I see no point in beating about the bush, ladies and gentlemen. Sci-Med has uncovered a situation relating to a number of school children attending a school camp in Cumbria which they are extremely concerned about. They have requested an explanation, as is their right. We for our part have been some-what reticent in complying with their requests for information and I can only apologise. If ever there was a case of the road to hell being paved with good intentions, this is it. Gerald, would you be so good as to put our Sci-Med colleagues in the picture?'

Sir Gerald Coates, looking equally grave, got to his feet and said, 'Gentlemen, it's important that you understand the background situation that Her Majesty's Government finds itself in.' He gave Macmillan and Steven a rundown on the impasse that had surfaced between themselves and the pharmaceutical industry. 'It's something we simply have to find ways around.'

Steven and Macmillan remained impassive.

'All the intelligence that we have been getting recently has suggested that a terrorist biological weapon attack is imminent,' continued Coates.

'Forty-five minutes to an anthrax attack,' said Steven, attracting hostile stares.

Coates ignored him. 'If we are to have any chance at all of countering such an act, we desperately need new vaccines so we've been encouraging the best biological brains to design them.'

'I don't think I understand,' said Macmillan. 'You've just told us that the pharmaceutical companies wouldn't cooperate.'

'We went to the smaller ones, the biotech companies that were set up at the height of the new technology boom. We offered them incentives in terms of prizes, accelerated-tracking through the licensing process, long-term contracts with the NHS for success.'

'What exactly does "accelerated-tracking through the licensing process" mean?' asked Macmillan, dissecting the real information from what Coates was saying.

'The decision-making process would be speeded up, delays cut to a minimum, fewer referral bodies, that sort of thing.

175

There just isn't time to put new vaccines through what has become the normal schedule of trials and safety evaluation,' said Coates. 'There's a chance we could all be dead before anyone was vaccinated.'

'So you tried out a vaccine on a hundred and eight children without their knowledge or consent or that of their parents?' said Macmillan.

Many in the room thought it an opportune moment to look down at the table surface and say nothing.

'I hope I can assure you that wasn't the case,' said Coates solemnly. He paused for a moment to make eye contact with both Steven and Macmillan. 'Knowing that HMG were keen on cutting bureaucracy to a minimum where new vaccines were concerned, a number of junior people in the Department of Health hatched a plan they imagined might, in the long run, endear them to their superiors. They colluded with the bio-technology company St Clair Genomics in setting up field trials for the company's new vaccine against tuberculosis, the Nichol vaccine. The people at St Clair convinced them that obtaining the necessary paperwork for the trial would be little more than a time-consuming formality: all preliminary tests had been carried out and passed with flying colours so many months could be saved by simply going ahead. The children at Pinetops comprised a perfect cohort. After vaccination, the plan was to monitor them so that their antibody levels could be checked.'

'The green sticker children,' said Macmillan.

'Yes. The anticipated good levels would be used as the basis for bringing the vaccine into regular use.'

'And protesting after the event would be useless,' murmured Macmillan with a shake of the head.

'I can't stress how much we need a new vaccine against TB. BCG is well past its sell-by date and the disease is making a big comeback. If we don't do something soon about protecting our young people, we could be facing a return to the dark days of the early twentieth century where death through "consumption" was a regular visitor to homes across the land.'

'But instead, the company came up with something that's put the lives of over a hundred children at risk?' said Steven.

'I think that's going too far,' said Coates. 'Although we are, of course, aware that there is a problem. . .'

'You're aware there is a problem?' exclaimed Macmillan as if he couldn't believe his ears.

'Let me explain,' said Coates, appealing for calm with the palms of his hands. 'There is actually nothing wrong with the vaccine *per se*.'

Macmillan looked as if he was preparing for another outburst but Coates used his hands again to calm him. 'The Nichol vaccine passed all its lab tests and was tried out very successfully on animals. I assure you, no short cuts were taken at any stage. By any criterion, it is an extremely good vaccine and much superior to BCG in giving protection against the tubercle bacillus.'

'But?' asked Steven.

Coates nodded. 'And I admit it is a very big but, something went dreadfully wrong when the vaccine was handed over to the company who were contracted to prepare the injection vials.'

'What kind of something?'

'Somewhere along the line in the production process the vials were contaminated with a toxic agent, a poison that attacks human tissue cells. It's that that's been causing the trouble in a few cases. We believe that there were only traces of it present but obviously enough to cause illness in some of the children.'

'So the children were poisoned, not infected?' said Steven.

'Yes.'

'Where did this toxin come from?' asked Macmillan.

'We understand that Redmond Medical, the company tasked with preparing the vials, had been contracted to bottle several new compounds for another company who were looking for new anti-cancer agents. It seems likely that traces of one of these compounds found its way into the vials used for the Nichol vaccine which was the next job on their production schedule. The company still aren't sure how it happened. They thought their cleaning and sterilisation procedures were foolproof. Needless to say, work at the plant has been suspended and vaccine production has been transferred to another company.'

'One of the children who was given the vaccine was immuno-compromised,' said Steven. 'He had a bone marrow transplant a year ago.'

At this, another man stood up and introduced himself as Dr John Leyton, the doctor who had administered the vaccine supplied by St Clair. 'I'm aware of that,' he confessed. 'But as the Nichol vaccine is a non-live vaccine, there was no danger to the child. He may not have produced antibodies in response to the vaccine but there was no chance of him being infected by it.'

'But he's dead,' said Steven.

'Not because of the vaccine.'

'It's something we all regret, I'm sure,' said the Home Secretary, a view echoed solemnly by the others.

'But why should this child have been more susceptible to a poison than the others?' asked Steven.

Leyton shrugged and said, 'I'm afraid you have me there. Maybe just normal human variation. We all have different levels of susceptibility to a lot of things. It could be the same for toxins.'

'Was it a case of corners being cut in the manufacturing process?' asked Macmillan point blank. 'Sloppy procedures?'

'Absolutely not,' countered Coates. 'We've been over the firm's practices with a fine-tooth comb. They couldn't be faulted.'

'But a poison still ended up in the vials,' said Steven. 'A poison that's killed one child and looks like killing another soon.'

'I'm afraid so,' said Leyton. 'And we all deeply regret that.'

'I take it you're still investigating what exactly happened?' asked Macmillan.

'We're currently examining all the equipment used in the vial manufacturing process.'

'So where does this leave us?' said the Home Secretary. 'Sci-Med has caught us – and by "us" I mean Her Majesty's Government – *in flagrante delicto*, for this is something for which we must take collective responsibility. Although it was the fault of a few over-zealous individuals and a misunderstanding perhaps over how *flexible* the rules might be in the current climate, we are responsible for administering a new vaccine to one hundred and eight of our school children and, it has to be said, unwittingly putting their lives at risk. You don't have to be a tabloid editor to see where this is going to end up should it become public knowledge.

'Just in case there is any doubt,' the Home Secretary continued, 'the government will fall, the children's parents will launch criminal and civil actions, the vaccines programme will grind to a halt and we will be left defenceless against anything the terrorists care to throw at us. They will be free to launch plague after plague until we succumb totally and our green and pleasant land becomes a barren desert.

'Health and Safety officers, however, will be able to dance on our mass graves – once suitable safety barriers have been erected – from Land's End to John o'Groats, comfortable in the knowledge that they stopped vaccine safety regulations being breached.

'Food for thought, eh, John?' said the Home Secretary to break the silence that ensued.

'And if we do nothing?' asked a sombre Macmillan, causing Steven's heart to miss a beat.

'I'll be perfectly frank with you; nothing much will change. We must go on pressing for new vaccines and streamlining the testing process. We have to. Time is not on our side and letting Health and Safety decide whether we live or die is not an option. There may well be occasional victims but this is the way it has to be if our way of life is to survive.'

'At least you're honest,' said Macmillan.

'Can I ask what happens now to the Nichol vaccine?' said Steven.

'We see it as a perfectly good vaccine. It will go into production with a different manufacturing company.'

'Before you've established the exact cause of the problem last time?'

'We know what the problem was. Establishing at which point in the production process the contamination occurred is purely academic. The company won't be used any more.'

Macmillan sensed that Steven was squaring up to argue so he interrupted. 'What about the affected children?' he asked.

'We will award generous financial compensation to their parents under the guise of medical insurance covering the children while they were at camp.'

It was Steven's turn to look down at the table.

SIXTEEN

'What a mess,' growled Macmillan when he and Steven got back to his office. He poured sherry into two glasses and handed one to Steven before settling in behind his desk.

'Do we really believe it was down to a few ambitious civil servants and a *misunderstanding* over the rules?' asked Steven.

Macmillan looked at him thoughtfully. 'I think we have to, don't you? The alternative that a British government presided over such a completely unlawful experiment is just too much to contemplate.'

'It's not without precedent for people in high places to let it be known that they are unhappy about certain situations and for more junior people to *take the hint*,' said Steven.

'So if it goes wrong, the powers that be can deny all knowledge of it,' added Macmillan.

'They do all the wrong and we end up with all the angst,' said Steven.

'It was certainly the time to play the collective responsibility card, I'll grant you,' said Macmillan ruefully. 'One out, all out and it will all be Sci-Med's fault, the fall of the government, a monumental scandal . . . the incoming government faced with an impossible situation . . . the country hopelessly vulnerable to biological attack. Ye gods, you couldn't make it up.'

After a few moments of deep thought, Macmillan asked, 'What are your feelings?'

'The need for new vaccines has certainly put them between the proverbial rock and a hard place but occasionally, that can be more comfortable than it sounds. It can be used as an excuse for all sorts of suspect decisions and actions. The pendulum may have swung too far in the direction of health and safety legislation where vaccines are concerned – and it has – but actually there's still something that worries me about the Nichol vaccine.'

'What's that?'

'They've decided that there's nothing wrong with it before establishing exactly how the problem arose last time. They're using a presumption as a basis for conclusion – never a good move.'

'They would argue that time is not on their side.'

'Another comfortable excuse.'

'So what do we do?' asked Macmillan, giving birth to yet another long silence that neither found easy. The weight of responsibility on their shoulders was almost unbearable but the seemingly impatient patter of rain on the windows served as a reminder that a decision had to be made.

'It's incredible,' said Steven. 'We went into that meeting holding all the aces and we came out with a pair of twos and it's our turn to bet or fold . . .'

'I don't think we have any option,' said Macmillan. 'We have to keep this quiet. The alternative just doesn't bear thinking about.'

'You're right, of course,' agreed Steven. 'But it doesn't half leave a nasty taste in the mouth . . .' He was thinking of the parents of the dead boy, Keith Taylor, and of Trish Lyons facing life without her arm if indeed she had a life to look forward to at all. Guinea pigs used in a good cause? Just one of these things? You can't make an omelette without breaking eggs? Sacrifices for the common good? Tough choices, difficult decisions? They died so that others . . . Bollocks to the lot of it. The big picture just did not translate to personal circumstances.

'Then we're agreed?' asked Macmillan before Steven talked himself out of going along with it. 'We say nothing?'

Steven nodded. 'Yes.'

'Can I take it that Sci-Med's interest in the Pinetops affair is now officially at an end?'

'No,' said Steven. 'Not yet, I need a bit of time to mull things over. There are some things that still bother me.'

'Like what?'

'Scott Haldane's death . . . why the poison raced through Keith Taylor's body the way it did . . . why the kids are reacting to it in different ways at different times . . . how the poison managed to survive the cleaning process and get into the vials . . . things like that.'

Macmillan nodded. 'Does that mean you want me to tell the Home Secretary about your continuing interest despite the fact we won't be taking things any further?'

'No,' said Steven. 'I'll just pick away at it on my own for a bit.'

'I know this is not the sort of ending we might have hoped for but you did well taking things as far as you did,' said Macmillan.

'Thanks,' said Steven but his heart wasn't in it.

Steven decided that he needed fresh air and walked by the Embankment for a bit, low in spirit and with a sense of anti-climax that seemed to be accentuated by the very normality of everything around him. Did these people pushing prams and carrying briefcases appreciate what was being done on their behalf in the name of security? Of course they didn't, but they expected it. In fact, they demanded it. They expected government to respond to every threat to their person, even the merest suggestion of a threat or woe betide them come election time.

The sun broke through the clouds and Steven took the opportunity to sit down for a few minutes and enjoy its warmth on his face. How good was the intelligence that suggested biological attack was imminent? How imminent was imminent? Was the information more reliable than the intelligence that sent the army to war in Iraq? Or less? Had it been filtered, manipulated, sexed-up, made to fit an alternative agenda? Or might even the suggestion of that lead to personal disaster as it had for Dr David Kelly in the weapons of mass destruction furore?

For his own peace of mind, he felt that the deaths of both Scott Haldane and Alan Nichol had to be fitted into the picture before he could fully accept the explanation given by Coates for the Pinetops disaster and, for the moment, he could not see how that was going to come about.

He thought about each in turn as he continued to enjoy the sunlight on his eyelids. If Scott Haldane's unease over Trish Lyons had centred on a suspicion that she had been poisoned, why hadn't he said anything about it at the time? There was no reason to keep such a theory to himself, particularly when her doctors at the time were failing to find any cause of infection. There was certainly no reason to keep quiet 'until he was sure' – the explanation given to his wife for his silence. It didn't make sense.

Apart from that, harbouring such a suspicion would certainly be no reason to commit suicide but on the other hand, could voicing it to the wrong person have provided grounds for murdering him? It was certainly true that the government had no desire to see what had happened at Pinetops being made public – in fact, they had everything to lose – but Haldane had displayed no desire to tell anyone: he didn't even want to tell his wife. Introducing state-sanctioned murder into the equation seemed to be going a little far.

As for Alan Nichol, the designer of a new TB vaccine, something that was still being regarded as a big success despite the contamination problems, why should anyone want to kill him? Nichol would have been among the first to see from the green sticker survey that all was not well with the kids on the trial. He or one of his colleagues would have raised the alarm and started an immediate investigation. They would have left no stone unturned before establishing the presence of a toxin as the cause of the trouble. Nichol probably had less reason than anyone to make this public, so killing him to keep it quiet seemed a non-starter. As the designer of the vaccine, he would automatically get the blame from the public whatever the truth of the matter.

It occurred to Steven that it might be worth checking with Phillip St Clair the series of events leading up to the discovery of the contamination problem. He also reminded himself that his search for a murder motive was personal. Officially, Alan Nichol's death had been an accident.

Steven phoned St Clair Genomics and was relieved to get an answer considering that it was nearly seven o'clock on a Friday evening. It was Phillip St Clair himself who answered the phone because – as he pointed out – he was the only one there.

'What can I do for you, Dr Dunbar?'

'I wondered if we might have another chat,' said Steven. 'Now that we're both aware of what's been going on?'

'Yes, I heard there had been some sort of meeting,' said St Clair. 'When would you like to come?'

'I don't suppose you work on Saturdays?'

'I work every day that God sends,' said St Clair. 'This is a small business, remember. The buck stops with me.'

'Then tomorrow?'

'I'll be here from about ten: I allow myself a long lie-in at the weekends,' said St Clair with what Steven felt was a somewhat strained attempt at humour.

'See you then.'

There was only one other car in the car park when Steven arrived, a black Porsche Cayenne, which he assumed would belong to Phillip St Clair. The Honda looked like a toy beside it. The door to the building was locked so he rang the bell and waited for a voice from the grille beside it. Instead, St Clair came and opened the door personally. 'Come on in. I'm just about to have some coffee. Will you join me?'

Steven thanked him. 'Black, no sugar. Nice car,' he said, looking back at the Cayenne.

'Thanks, a 4x4 with the performance of a 911, what more could you ask? You're a Porsche man too, aren't you? In the garage?'

'Bit of an accident,' said Steven.

'Sorry to hear that, not your fault, I hope. Insurance is a bit of a killer on these things.'

'Not exactly,' said Steven as St Clair went next door for the coffee.

'Thank God you didn't ask for a skinny, decaf latte or some such thing,' laughed St Clair when he returned with two mugs bearing the company logo. 'Coffee seems to have become an A level subject these days.'

'Know what you mean.'

'So, how can I help you?'

'The Nichol vaccine,' said Steven. 'Tell me about it.'

'What's to say? It's a brilliant piece of work from a brilliant scientist who tragically won't see his work receive the acclaim it richly deserves. I understand they still haven't got the bastard who ran him down.'

'Was anyone else involved in the design?'

St Clair shook his head. 'Not really. Alan had technical help but it was really all his baby. He snipped away at the genome of the TB bug until it was no longer infectious but still stimulated good levels of antibodies against TB – exactly what the doctor ordered, you might say.'

'Absolutely, but I'm afraid I'm still not quite clear about the funding for the work,' said Steven. 'Vaccine design and production isn't something you associate with small companies, no disrespect.'

'None taken and you're quite right but times have changed. Government needs all the help it can get these days and cash incentives were on offer to those who could come up with the goods, small or otherwise.'

'Incentives?' asked Steven.

'If you were willing to take the risk and could find financial backers to support your confidence in your researchers and they came up trumps, the rewards for success were substantial – an initial seven-figure prize plus reimbursement of development costs, a further lump sum on completion of field trials and finally a government contract to supply the vaccine for general use.'

'I see,' said Steven. 'But then you fell at the last hurdle and one hundred and eight children were injected with something that's already caused one death with the possibility that it may still cause more?'

St Clair stopped smiling as if conceding that he had been insensitive in over-emphasising the positives. 'You're right,' he said. 'An unfortunate accident did occur, there's no denying this but it was something beyond our control, a chance in a million, a problem in the manufacturing plant leading to contamination of the vials, something we worked day and night to help uncover, I have to say.'

'How many were involved in that?' asked Steven. 'Alan Nichol and who else?'

'Not Alan,' said St Clair. 'Alan died shortly before we discovered the source of the problem.'

'I didn't realise that,' said Steven.

'I had every other member of the scientific and technical staff drop whatever they were doing to work on it. The manufacturing company, Redmond Medical, had a team working round the clock and a government lab was also involved.'

'Which one of you discovered the toxin?'

'We did,' said St Clair. 'Traces of a cytotoxic agent were found in the injection vials. We discovered this by taking samples from the vials and injecting them into human cell cultures. When the cells started to die, the alarm bells started ringing. Naturally we informed both the DOH and Redmond Medical immediately and the plant was closed down.'

'Does anyone know how the toxin got into the vials?'

'Only that Redmond had been producing ampoules of these cytotoxic chemicals for a pharmaceutical company investigating combinations of these agents for anti-cancer properties. It's pretty obvious there must have been cross-contamination at some stage but, as yet, we don't know at which one.'

'A worry,' said Steven.

'Tell me about it. Redmond is still at a standstill. The government has withdrawn their accreditation and we've had to use another company to start production again.'

'Was Alan Nichol alive when kids started to fall ill?'

St Clair nodded. 'Yes, it was Alan who drew our attention to it in the first place. He raised the alarm. He'd been keeping a close eye on the children's health records.'

'The green sticker monitor?'

'Exactly. It wasn't obvious to the rest of us at first but Alan saw a pattern emerge and hit the panic button.'

'I think I may have asked you this before, but does the name Scott Haldane mean anything to you?'

St Clair appeared to give the question some thought before saying, 'I do remember you asking but it meant nothing to me then and nothing now. Should it?'

'He was a GP in Scotland who also suspected there was something wrong with the vaccine. I just wondered if he'd made contact with you or Alan Nichol at any point.'

'Sorry, doesn't ring a bell.'

'No matter,' said Steven pleasantly, getting up to go. 'Many thanks for your help.'

'Not at all,' said St Clair. 'I'm glad I was able to talk openly to you this time. Living with secrets is not as easy as people might imagine.'

'No,' agreed Steven, thinking of Tally.

Steven drove into Cambridge proper and found a place to eat: he had skipped breakfast after a restless night. He parked the car and looked around, finally settling for coffee and croissants in a small café boasting Tudor beams and a frontage leading down to the river. A couple of punts moored at the water's edge and nestling under a weeping willow set the scene for calm reflection on what he'd learned.

It was Alan Nichol himself who had raised the alarm over what was happening to the green sticker children but he was dead by the time three separate groups had set out to establish the source of the problem. It was the scientists at St Clair Genomics who had uncovered traces of the toxin in the vaccine vials and the problem had been ascribed to Redmond Medical, the company contracted to prepare injection vials of the Nichol vaccine. Redmond had been bottling toxic compounds for another company immediately before starting the vial run for St Clair so everything seemed to fit . . . except for Alan Nichol's murder.

Steven ordered more coffee from a waitress who looked and sounded as if she belonged in a Jane Austen novel. She was doing a Saturday job, he concluded. She'd be back studying English Lit on Monday morning. He wondered if he could have been wrong about Nichol being murdered. If his death *had* been an accident, he wouldn't be currently left trying to fit a square piece into a round hole.

Try as he might, Steven could not bring himself to believe that Nichol's death had been accidental. He remained convinced that he had been murdered. The strange red car, parked at the head of Nichol's street, had been just too much of a coincidence. This still left him looking for a motive. Nichol had died after raising the alarm about the health of the green sticker children but before the vial contamination had been discovered. The answer had to lie somewhere in that time frame. Nichol couldn't have been killed to stop him talking about the possibility of contamination because it was common knowledge among the others in the lab. In fact, just about everyone at St Clair Genomics had been detailed to work on it. His death didn't make sense unless . . . someone was lying about something. But what?

Steven paid the bill and left, choosing to walk by the river for a bit and feeling nostalgic for the days of his youth when he came across groups of students enjoying a sunny Saturday, free of lectures and all care it seemed as they laughed and chatted their way along the banks of the Cam. It made him wonder if he had already reached the age where he had become invisible to the young. The argument that he was only . . . twice their age – my God, was it really that much? – failed to provide reassurance.

Was he looking for a big lie or a little one? Start with the big. Could what he and Macmillan had been told by people at ministerial level be a complete load of nonsense, designed to elicit their sympathy and gain their collusion in keeping it quiet? Maybe the children had not been given a new anti-TB vaccine at all? Perhaps they had been given something else entirely and for some other reason?

Steven shook his head in an involuntary gesture of dismissal, noting that he'd just got a nervous sideways glance from a man out walking his dog. This was going too far, he reckoned, and would demand the involvement of too many people. It made him think of the old adage, *Two can keep a secret if one of them is dead.*

He felt inclined to accept that the Nichol vaccine was exactly what the authorities maintained it was – a new and much needed vaccine against TB. So, what did that leave to lie about? The problem with the toxin, that's what, he concluded, the contamination of the vials with an unidentified poisonous substance. There was something wrong with that story.

Phillip St Clair had told him that it had been one of a number of compounds being checked out by a pharmaceutical company looking for new anti-cancer drugs so, being experimental, it wouldn't be listed in any lab handbook but, even if it wasn't a listed substance, shouldn't one of the labs investigating the samples taken from Keith Taylor or Trish Lyons have noted the presence of a toxin, even an unknown one?

Steven wasn't sure. It may have been present in such small quantities that it hadn't been picked up. Maybe the automated analytical equipment had simply not recognised it and therefore failed to report it. It was also possible that the vials had been contaminated to varying degrees so that some children got a bigger dose of toxin than others but that seemed less likely. If this had been the explanation for the toxin rampaging through Keith Taylor's body like a full-blown infection, the lab would almost certainly have uncovered evidence of its presence and they hadn't.

SEVENTEEN

Steven called the duty officer at Sci-Med and asked him to ring round the labs involved in analysing material taken from either Trish Lyons or Keith Taylor to ask about the presence of toxic compounds – identified or unidentified. He had his answer within an hour. The hospital labs in Carlisle and Edinburgh both reported that they had carried out routine biochemical analysis on a number of samples: all were negative for toxins. The London lab which had analysed the samples taken from Keith Taylor at the second post mortem and which was furnished with the best equipment money could buy had also drawn a blank.

Steven sighed but had to admit that the lab results were pretty much what he'd expected. After all, if any of them had noted the presence of a toxin, they would have reported it before now, but the negatives did raise an obvious question. If St Clair Genomics had detected the presence of a toxin in the vaccine vials, why hadn't the relevant labs found it in the patients? He supposed it might have had something to do with breakdown of the toxin in the body – some poisons did this and could therefore remain undetected – but this was outside his area of expertise. He would have to seek expert advice but first he needed to gather more information about the contaminating toxin. Phillip St Clair didn't have any chemical details; a talk to Redmond Medical was called for. He phoned Sci-Med and asked that they make contact with a senior person at Redmond Medical. He also asked for business background information on both St Clair and Redmond.

'It's Saturday afternoon,' said the duty man. 'It'll probably mean getting someone at home.'

'Fine.'

'And the background info, when do you need that?'

'Now.'

'Watch this space, as they say.'

Steven smiled at the good-humoured response. He liked laid-back people.

The duty man called back forty-five minutes later. 'Sorry, all the senior people at Redmond seem to be away for the weekend but I've managed to contact a Mr Giles Dutton; he's the line maintenance manager at the company. He lives in Moulden at 34, Lipton Rise. He's expecting your call.'

Steven noted down the number. 'Okay, thanks.'

'Jean Roberts has some stuff on Redmond. She says she'll email it to you. She's working from home.'

'Thanks again.'

Steven had doubts about whether a line maintenance manager would be able to give him the information he was after, namely the identity of the toxic agent. He suspected not but, as he had nothing else to do meantime and nuggets of information often came from unlikely sources, he called Dutton and asked if he could come and speak to him.

'Please yourself,' replied Dutton.

It wasn't quite the response Steven had expected but he took it as a yes and said that he'd be in Moulden in a couple of hours.

'Right.'

Steven set off, feeling less than optimistic about getting

anything at all out of Dutton who had sounded less than interested and hadn't even bothered to ask what it was about but at least he was doing something. He was pleasantly surprised when a friendly looking woman opened the door to him at the pretty white bungalow in Lipton Rise. She invited him in. 'Giles is in the conservatory,' she said. 'It's through here . . .'

Steven followed her through a living room smelling strongly of furniture polish and out through French doors into a conservatory where the temperature was several degrees higher because of the sun on the glass. A man with thinning red hair and a matching pale complexion sat there in a cane armchair, glasses on his nose, feet up on a small footstool as he read his newspaper.

'It's the gentleman you're expecting, dear.'

'Steven Dunbar,' said Steven.

Dutton grunted and pushed his glasses up his nose but didn't get up.

'Perhaps you'd like some tea or coffee, Dr Dunbar?' asked the smiling woman. Steven got the impression she might be well used to being excessively polite and helpful in order to make up for her husband's shortcomings.

'Coffee would be lovely, thank you.'

Steven showed Dutton his ID card but he waved it away. 'Makes no odds, just state your business.'

Steven sat down on the other cane armchair and said, 'I'd like to ask you a few questions about the chemical that contaminated the St Clair company vaccine.'

'Like what?' said Dutton, making a point of looking out of the window at a high conifer hedge in the garden rather than at Steven.

'Ideally, I'd like to know what it was, where it came from and how it got into the vaccine vials.'

'Me too,' said Dutton.

'I'm sorry?'

Dutton turned to face Steven. 'I'd like to know that too,' he said.

Steven sensed there was more to this comment than he was taking on board. Dutton wasn't just being rude; he was very bitter about something. 'You've no idea?' he asked.

'None whatsoever.'

'But if the company don't know what happened, you have no way of stopping it happening again,' said Steven.

'Very true,' said Dutton with what appeared to Steven to be a wry smile.

'If you'll pardon my saying so, Mr Dutton, you don't seem to be very concerned about something so serious,' said Steven. 'Surely, as production line maintenance manager, it's your responsibility if contamination occurs?'

'It would be if that's what happened,' said Dutton, adding to Steven's mounting frustration.

'Mr Dutton, you do accept that a toxic substance was found in the vaccine vials prepared by your company?'

'So they tell me.'

'But you're not concerned?'

Dutton looked at Steven and shook his head. 'Nope.'

'My God, man, if your maintenance schedules allowed a toxic chemical to get into a vaccine . . .'

'I should be on my knees asking the Almighty for forgiveness,' said Dutton. He leaned towards Steven. 'But it never happened.'

At that moment Dutton's wife came into the conservatory with a silver tea tray and laid it down between them. 'There you are. I hope you two are having a nice chat. The scones are freshly baked – just out the oven . . .'

Steven did his best to fake up a smile and said, 'Thank you, Mrs Dutton, that's very kind.'

'Just shout if you want more . . .'

Mrs Dutton backed out through the French doors and closed them with a last beaming smile.

'What d'you mean, it never happened?' demanded Steven as the electric atmosphere returned. 'The scientists at St Clair Genomics found toxin in the vials, the same one that you had been bottling the day before.'

'So they did.' Dutton resumed his watch on the conifers in the garden.

'Are you saying that it didn't come from the production line?' asked Steven.

'Well, you got there in the end,' said Dutton.

Steven's senses were reeling. 'But how else would it get in?'

'I've no idea,' said Dutton. 'It's true that we'd bottled a number of toxic compounds for a pharmaceutical company in Kent the day before we did the vaccine vials for St Clair and everyone thought they'd jump on the obvious bandwagon. But what the smart arses didn't know was that the main production line broke down that day and I had to move the job to our back-up facility in C building. The technicians fixed the problem with the main line overnight and we were able to use that for the St Clair job. The contaminating chemical was never near the main line. It wasn't even in the same building.'

Steven swallowed as he felt his throat dry. 'But you must have told someone this?'

'Of course,' said Dutton. 'They didn't want to know. I was told not to worry. It was a technicality. Everything would sort itself out.'

'So how did the vials become contaminated?'

'Your guess is as good as mine.'

'But unless that is established . . .'

'Redmond Medical can't reopen for business?'

'Exactly.'

'Redmond Medical isn't going to open again for business,' said Dutton. 'Our owners have decided to close it down. The staff have been told they'll be paid to the end of the month and that's it. Finito.'

'Bloody hell, that's a bit over the top,' said Steven. 'Have you any thought about what you'll do?'

Dutton gave Steven a look that suggested he'd been thinking about little else. 'Word gets around in the pharmaceutical business, Mr Dunbar. Who's going to employ a production line manager held responsible for the fuck-up that closed down Redmond Medical?'

'But from what you say, you weren't.'

'Yeah, I could tell them that,' said Dutton sourly.

'But there must be others who know what happened?'

Dutton gave a contemptuous snort. 'Staff are in line for a bonus if they sign up to a confidentiality clause. They're being paid extra to say nothing about anything they did at Redmond. It almost doubles their redundancy money.'

'Surely that kind of clause wouldn't extend to something like saying which production line was working and which wasn't on any particular day?' said Steven.

'It covers everything.'

'You're making it sound as if Redmond are quite content for people to think the contamination happened on their production line?'

Dutton shrugged and said, 'They don't seem to care too much about how or where it happened. They've accepted it was their fault and rolled over. Any further inquiries would just be an academic exercise as far as they're concerned.'

Steven heard echoes in that of what the Home Secretary had said at the Home Office meeting. 'It's not exactly what you'd expect a company like Redmond to do in a situation like that,' he said. 'Denial and counter claim is usually the order of the day until someone proves what happened.'

'Well, not in this case,' said Dutton. 'When a toxic chemical being processed by us on one day is found in vials in the production run on the following day, you don't have to be a rocket scientist to figure out what the conclusion's going to be. All I'm saying is that it didn't happen on my production line.'

'Thanks for telling me all this, I appreciate it,' said Steven, preparing to leave and feeling absurdly guilty about not having sampled Mrs Dutton's scones.

'If you find out what did happen, will you let me know?' asked Dutton.

Steven assured him that he would.

He shook his head as he got into the car and sat for a few moments thinking about what he'd just learned. It was a totally unexpected twist and not at all what he had been looking for in an investigation in which the ground continually seemed to move beneath him. A boy with TB in a Leicester hospital? – no such boy – a boy with TB in a Swedish clinic? – no such boy – the boy disappears completely. All lies, smoke and mirrors designed to obscure the truth about a secret trial of a new vaccine. Children receiving the new vaccine fall ill and a rogue toxin getting into the production process is blamed. But now . . . there was no rogue toxin in the production process of the vaccine according to Dutton, so where did it come from?

Steven called Tally. There was no reply from her home phone so he left a message saying he'd called. He set out to return to London but had barely gone a mile when she rang.

'Hi, I've just got in. I found your message. Where are you?'

'Near Milton Keynes. I thought I might come up but maybe if you're just in . . .'

'No, that would be great. I look forward to seeing you.'

Steven suddenly felt a whole lot better. The thought of seeing Tally was just so good – the prospect of light, warmth, company and intelligent conversation – not to mention sex – instead of going home to sit in silence and brood about the latest puzzle in the green sticker saga was the perfect antidote to feeling depressed about his progress. He joined the motorway and gunned the Honda up to seventy, reckoning that he should be there in about an hour.

Traffic was light and, as the miles passed by, he allowed himself to wonder if it could ever be this way on a more permanent basis. Driving home to Tally was a nice thought; it had a comfortable ring to it . . . or maybe it was just a daydream? Yes it was, but there was no harm in that, he reckoned. He started to wonder how Jenny would take to Tally and vice versa if they should ever meet. The two ladies in his life, would they get on? Could they get on? It was seductive to imagine that they would and a short step from that to thinking about picnics, days out, whispered confidences, Christmas at home . . .

The reality would probably be different, he conceded. Tally's career was every bit as demanding as his own and equally important to her. His cosy notion of domestic bliss – if it really existed – probably required a completely different cast or enough commitment to change things to make it possible . . . Old doubts returned. Were the problems really insurmountable or was he looking for an excuse to treat his association with Tally as a finite thing, a beautiful love affair but doomed from the start because of fate – his preferred reason – or maybe the fact that he was a selfish bastard – a strong contender.

Steven turned the car into Tally's street and drew heavily upon his favourite mantra: *Life is what happens to you while you're planning for the future . . .*

Tally was waiting for him at the door to her apartment when he emerged from the lift. She was dressed casually in a sweater and jeans, barefoot and her hair still damp from the shower and smelling of shampoo. Steven kissed her and wrapped his arms around her, unwilling to detach himself from the perfumed heaven he found himself in.

'What have you been up to?' he asked.

'Working,' replied Tally ruefully. 'I should have known. As soon as I arranged to meet up with my sisters for a boozy lunch and a long gossip, something turned up at the hospital and I had to work on my weekend off.'

'Bad luck,' said Steven. 'I didn't know you had sisters.'

Tally laughed and said, 'I've got two. There's a lot you don't know about me. We hardly know each other. And if you say it seems like we've known each other for ever, I'll knee you where it hurts.'

'I suppose you're right,' said Steven with a smile.

'Anyway, what have you been up to? That's got to be much more interesting. What happened at the meeting?'

'The government are hell-bent on developing new vaccines because of fears of a biological attack.'

'And?' asked Tally when she saw Steven hesitate.

'It seems a number of over-ambitious civil servants thought they'd please their masters and accelerate their own careers by setting up an unofficial trial of a new vaccine against TB using the kids at Pinetops. The company involved, a biotechnology outfit called St Clair Genomics, convinced them that getting the necessary paperwork was just going to be a time-consuming formality. There was some talk of a misunderstanding over how far the officials could bend the rules but, in any event, it all went terribly wrong when the vials got contaminated with a toxic agent on the production line.'

Tally was speechless for a few moments during which she spread her hands and looked up at the ceiling. 'A *misunderstanding*?' she exclaimed. 'How could you have a *misunderstanding* over something like that? And then they managed to poison them? How on earth could something like that happen? That's absolutely outrageous. They should all be hung, drawn and quartered . . .'

Tally suddenly realised what Steven's long silence implied. 'Oh God, you're not going to tell me they're going to get away with it, are you?'

'I'm afraid that's the bottom line,' said Steven. 'I'm as sick about it as you but the alternatives are just too awful to contemplate.'

'I don't understand,' said Tally, her eyes full of accusation.

EIGHTEEN

Steven talked Tally through what would happen if the Pinetops affair was made public and saw the same frustration grow inside her that he had felt – the battle against an inescapable logic which concluded that saying nothing was the right thing to do – however unpalatable.

'The bastards,' said Tally. 'There's a reason for all these safe-guards.'

'My heart agrees but my head understands why everyone wants to speed things up if we really are at risk of a biological attack.'

'What's the evidence for that?' asked Tally.

'I haven't seen it but the government believes an attack is inevitable. They insist that the intelligence is overwhelming. There's no chance of getting the vaccines we require developed and tested through the normal channels so they're smoothing the way wherever possible.'

'And giving rise to *misunderstandings* . . .'

'So it would appear,' agreed Steven.

'Do you believe them?' asked Tally, watching Steven closely for the slightest flicker of his eyes or any change in body language that might belie his response.

Steven was aware of her scrutiny. 'There are still some things that disturb me,' he said. 'Yet I have no option but to accept what they say. On the other hand . . . I don't think I've been told the whole truth about the Pinetops disaster ... There's something not quite right with their version of what went wrong with the vaccine and how.'

Tally saw this as a scaling down of the main argument and it showed on her face but she reined in her temper, recognising that continuing to express outrage wasn't going to get them anywhere. She poured them both a drink and sat down. 'How so?'

Steven told her about his discussion with Dutton.

Tally looked doubtful. 'If that's what they were bottling before the vaccine run, surely it has to be the number one suspect?' she said. 'Even if they didn't actually use the same production line, they might still have transferred parts from it, a filter, a dispensing head, a piece of tubing. How else could it get in, or are you suggesting that someone actually injected it into the vials deliberately?'

Steven made a face and shook his head. 'No, you're probably right but Dutton is an experienced man ... He wouldn't have made an elementary mistake like transferring a contaminated filler head from one line to another ...'

'It didn't have to be him,' said Tally. 'I still think it's odds on the fault was in the production process.'

'Maybe that's what we were meant to think ...'

Tally looked at him questioningly. 'Very cryptic,' she said. 'You could write tag lines for *EastEnders* ... Doof, doof ...' She hummed the theme tune.

'I just don't feel comfortable about it. And now they are closing down the company. Something doesn't ring true.'

'You're right,' said Tally. 'A company admitting liability and doing the decent thing doesn't ring true at all these days.'

'But don't you see, there was no pressure on them,' said Steven. 'The affair's not going to be made public so there will be no tabloid editors demanding blood, no TV reporters standing outside the building, demanding to know what happened. It's a small company so there are no shareholders to worry about. Why shut up shop before any detailed investigation has taken place?'

'I hate to say it but isn't this a minor consideration, Steven?' asked Tally. 'Does the precise mechanism of how the toxin got into the vials really matter in the great scheme of things when the damage has already been done and these children have been harmed? Isn't it academic?'

'No, it isn't,' insisted Steven. 'People keep saying this but it's like the piece of a jigsaw puzzle left over at the end when you thought the picture was complete. You can either hide it and pretend everything's okay or admit there's a problem and take a closer look only to discover that some of the pieces don't really fit at all: it's all just an illusion.'

Tally looked at him with an indulgent smile. 'If you say so,' she said. 'I don't know about you but I think I've had enough of cold reality for one week. I think we should make good our escape from it by drinking far more than the BMA would recommend and end up behaving in an absolutely outrageous and wanton manner, finishing up in a scenario featuring my bed with my backside bouncing off it . . . like there was no tomorrow.'

Steven broke into a huge smile. 'Talk about good ideas . . .' he said, slipping his hand slowly under Tally's sweater. 'But let's not rush things . . .' He pushed Tally's bra up and sought out her right nipple with his tongue.

'If you . . . say so,' murmured Tally appreciatively.

'Oh, I do,' said Steven. 'I have a feeling this is going to take . . . ages.' He moved his attentions to Tally's left breast while continuing to circle her right nipple with the side of his thumb.

'Oh, that is gorgeous . . .'

Steven saw that Tally had her eyes closed but the smile on her lips spoke volumes. He continued his adoration of her breasts while he loosened her jeans and eased them off: Tally assisted by raising her bottom, letting Steven's right hand roam freely over her buttocks and between her thighs, taking direction from the sighs and groans he was provoking.

'You're all wet . . .' he whispered as he slipped his hand into her panties while moving his mouth down over her stomach and tracing a line with his tongue. 'Deliciously wet . . .'

'And you are all hard,' groaned Tally, reaching down to free what was pressing for release from Steven's trousers.

'Time to see if your mattress will take it . . . ?'

'Absolutely,' gasped Tally.

'The sun's shining,' whispered Steven in Tally's ear. She responded by turning away and pulling the covers up.

'It's a beautiful day.'

'It's Sunday,' complained Tally. 'Have you no heart?'

'No . . . I think I've lost it to a beautiful lady,' whispered Steven as he kissed Tally's neck gently.

'Mmm . . . You're a heartless monster . . .' she murmured but a smile had settled on her lips. 'How is a girl to get her beauty sleep . . . ?'

'She doesn't need it. She's already gorgeous.'

'Too much,' giggled Tally. 'What is it you're after, Dunbar? As if I didn't know . . .'

Steven smiled broadly. 'Well, that too,' he agreed. 'But I thought we might have the perfect Sunday. We'll have a walk in the sunshine, find some place that'll serve us Bloody Marys while we read the papers and then have a long, self-indulgent lunch . . . before we come back and watch the football on TV.'

Tally's eyes shot open. 'What?' she exclaimed.

'Just joking,' smiled Steven. 'But I got your attention.'

'Monster, monster, monster,' complained Tally as she rained mock blows on Steven's chest. 'What am I going to do with you?'

'Well, first . . .' murmured Steven. 'I thought you might . . .'

Tally had a fit of the giggles. 'You are impossible,' she said but she gave in.

Tally, dressed in jeans and a soft leather blouson over a white T-shirt, slipped her keys into her handbag and gave the flat door a final check before saying to Steven, 'You know, I don't think I've ever had a Bloody Mary before.'

'It'll give you an appetite,' said Steven, slipping his arm round her shoulders. 'But I'm depending on you to suggest a nice place?'

'My sister keeps talking about a place called the Riverside Tavern, out by Marley Wood. We could try that?'

'Excellent.'

They stepped outside into the sunshine and paused for a moment to enjoy its warmth on their faces. 'Mmm,' said Tally. 'This is how weekends should be.' She looked up at Steven who smiled and hugged her closer.

'No argument there.'

'Let's go in my car,' said Tally. 'Then I won't have to shout directions at you.'

Steven rested his arm on the roof of Tally's Renault Clio while she got her keys out. He was about to say something about women and handbags when he felt a sudden pain in the back of his left thigh as if he'd been stung by a wasp. He clutched at it and turned to see a male figure who had been walking towards them turn on his heel and run off.

'What the . . .' he gasped as his senses started to reel and he felt his knees become weak.

'Steven!' Tally cried out in alarm as she ran round to the passenger side to find him slumping to the ground. 'What's happened?'

Steven was fighting a losing battle but he pulled out the thing that was sticking in the back of his leg. It was a small dart – the kind that could be fired from an air pistol. He matched this up with his observation of the man who had taken to his heels. Something about his suit said that he wasn't English . . . he was east European, maybe Russian. 'Sweet Jesus,' he murmured as he realised that he had been wrong about the two Russians who had driven him off the road. It hadn't been a case of mistaken identity at all. It had been him they'd been after all along.

Steven looked at the dart through blurred vision as consciousness threatened to leave him. 'Ricin . . .' he murmured. 'Ricin . . . There's no antidote. I'm so sorry.'

Tally, her eyes wide with horror, saw the dart fall from Steven's hand and did her best to cushion his head as he slumped unconscious to the pavement. She put him in the recovery position and snatched her mobile phone from her bag to dial three nines. With her fingers resting lightly on the carotid pulse in Steven's neck and feeling a mixture of shock and anguish, she brought out a pair of tweezers from her bag and picked up the dart from the pavement.

'Welcome back,' said the voice as Steven blinked at the whiteness of the ceiling and started to take in his surroundings. He tried to focus on the figure in white who had spoken but everything was just too bright.

'Before you ask, you're in hospital: it's ten thirty on Tuesday morning and you are a very lucky man.'

'Tuesday?' murmured Steven, suddenly realising that he had lost a couple of days of his life. 'Tally . . . must see Tally.'

'I take it you mean Dr Simmons? She asked to be kept informed when you woke up. I'll give her a call in a moment,' said the nurse. 'Mind you, she'll have to fight her way through the heavies on the door. I thought it had to be Brad Pitt or George Clooney lying helpless in here when I came on duty last night.'

'Sorry,' said Steven with an attempt at a smile.

'Oh, I don't know . . .' said the nurse with a grin as she left the room.

Steven had barely a moment to rest his head on the pillow and think back to Sunday before a middle-aged man in a suit came into the room and introduced himself as George Lamont, the doctor in charge of his case. 'How are you feeling?'

'I thought there was no antidote to ricin,' said Steven.

'There isn't,' said Lamont. 'But it wasn't ricin.'

Steven looked at Lamont, feeling confused and wondering if his recollection of events might be flawed. 'But the dart . . .'

'Was poisoned, but not with ricin,' interrupted Lamont. 'And you have Dr Simmons to thank for saving your life. She picked up on the slight smell of almonds coming from the dart when she picked it up to examine it and you can be eternally grateful that she made the right call. The dart delivered cyanide not ricin. She and the paramedics managed to counteract the poison with amyl nitrite when your heart stopped and then we took over.'

'My God . . . I assumed . . .'

'Everyone remembers the Georgi Markov story,' said Lamont. 'Poisoned-tip umbrellas and all that.'

Tally arrived and entered the room, wearing a white coat and with a stethoscope slung round her neck. Lamont smiled and made to leave, saying that he would give them a few minutes together before having to give Steven a thorough examination.

'I hear I owe you my life,' said Steven.

'The very least I could do . . . after Saturday night,' smiled Tally. 'How are you feeling?'

'Like I've got the worst hangover in the world,' replied Steven. 'I'm so sorry for exposing you to danger like that. Christ, it could have been you.'

'You weren't to know that somebody was going to make an attempt on your life,' said Tally, sitting on the edge of the bed and smoothing his hair back. 'But I am curious to know why . . .'

'I got it wrong,' said Steven. 'I should have known better at the time but I made the wrong call. I believed what I wanted to believe.'

Tally looked puzzled and vaguely uneasy as if she suspected that she was about to hear something she really didn't want to know. 'I don't understand.

Steven told her about the attack on the motorway and the two Russians who had perished in the flames. 'I thought it was a case of mistaken identity . . . that they were after the previous owner of the car but that's what I wanted to believe when it was me they were after all along.'

Tally had gone pale. 'Steven, you're scaring me. I know you're an investigator but I thought . . . you were sort of like a tax inspector . . . You might have to ask awkward questions from time to time . . . But Russians forcing you off the motorway and cyanide darts . . . This is all getting a bit much for me.'

'I think that's what I was afraid of hearing when I went for the mistaken identity conclusion rather than even consider it had been me they'd been after,' said Steven.

'What else haven't you been telling me?'

'You know everything else,' said Steven.

Tally looked less than convinced. 'So where exactly do Russians and poison darts fit into an investigation into British children being given unlicensed vaccines?'

'I don't know,' he confessed.

Tally looked as if she didn't know whether to believe him or not.

'I really don't.'

'Oh God,' sighed Tally, putting her hand to her forehead. 'I knew this was a bad idea . . .'

'No,' said Steven, stretching out to take her hand. 'It's a good idea,' he insisted. 'When this is over, I promise I will do whatever it takes to make you see that it is, even if it means giving up my job and selling double glazing in Leicester . . . Just don't give up on me?'

Tally's expression softened. 'You know very well how I feel about you,' she said. 'But this . . .' Words failed her and she looked everywhere but directly at Steven. 'I need a bit of time. Dr Lamont wants to examine you and there are a lot of people out there waiting to speak to you. I'll come back later when I've finished my shift.' She kissed Steven gently on the forehead but left him feeling uneasy in his mind.

NINETEEN

As soon as Lamont had finished examining Steven and given him a clean bill of health, Steven requested that he be allowed to make some telephone calls.

'Calling Sci-Med?' asked Lamont.

Steven nodded.

'I've already informed Sir John Macmillan that you're back in the land of the living. He left instructions when you were admitted that he be kept informed of your progress at all times. I gather he's the one responsible for the guards on the door. He'll be expecting your call.'

Steven called Macmillan but spoke first to Jean Roberts who said how worried they had all been. 'I'm so glad you're all right. When we heard it was cyanide . . . well, you know . . .'

Steven was touched by the note of genuine concern in Jean's voice. He had to swallow before saying, 'Thanks, Jean. I was very lucky. I wonder if you'd mind phoning my sister-in-law in Scotland and telling her why I've not been in touch. Don't tell her the whole story, maybe just that I've been away on operations and I'll call as soon as I can? Give her my love and ask her to tell Jenny that Daddy loves her very much. He'll be in touch as soon as we've caught the bad guys.'

'Will do. John's had a bit of a job squaring things with the local police and trying to keep the story out of the papers.'

'But he managed?' asked Steven anxiously.

'Yes, after enlisting some pretty heavy assistance from the Home Office.'

'Good.'

Steven spoke to Macmillan for more than ten minutes, both trying to come up with some explanation for the attacks on his life but in the end failing.

'It has to have something to do with what I've been working on' insisted Steven. 'But I can't see any conceivable Russian connection with the green sticker kids. Can you?'

Macmillan said not. 'Someone obviously thinks you know more than you do about something,' he said.

'Which puts me in a very uncomfortable position.'

'Especially as they'll probably try again,' said Macmillan.

'I need you to step up protection for Tally,' said Steven. 'They might well try to get to me through her.'

'I did that as soon as I heard what had happened,' said Macmillan. 'I think the history of your car and its previous owner lulled us both into thinking it was someone else they were after.'

Steven nodded.

'How is Dr Simmons taking things?'

'Pretty much as you'd expect,' said Steven, the tone of his voice suggesting not well.

'Well, it's a bit much for anyone to take on board. Give her time.'

'I'm hoping that's what she might give me,' said Steven ruefully.

'The sooner this investigation's concluded the happier we'll all be,' said Macmillan.

Steven took the phone from his ear and looked at it in disbelief. He'd just been told to get on with things in ever such a civilised way. He fought the urge to point out to Macmillan that he'd been knocking on death's door for the past couple of days. Instead, he said, 'I should be out of here in the morning but one thing . . .'

'Yes?'

'I returned my gun to the armoury when I thought I wouldn't be needing it. I'd better have it back.'

'Glock 23, wasn't it?'

'Yes.'

'I'll have it delivered to the hospital. It'll be there before you leave in the morning.'

It was a little after six in the evening when Tally came back. She was dressed in her outdoor clothes with a bag slung over her shoulder. 'How are you feeling?'

'How are *you* feeling which is more to the point?' countered Steven. 'All this must have come as a hell of a shock to you.'

'Life's rich pattern, I suppose,' said Tally with a sigh. 'But I must say I didn't plan on being a Bond girl: I'm really not the type. I'm quite happy as a paediatrician.'

'My life isn't usually like this,' said Steven. 'I'm not a spy or any kind of secret agent. You know what I do: I told you. I wasn't lying.'

'And the Russians?'

'I've no idea why they want me dead. I can only think I must have stumbled across something and upset the wrong people. The trouble is I've no idea what it is or who they are.'

'Which makes things even more dangerous,' said Tally.

'It does,' agreed Steven, deciding not to even try putting a gloss on things.

'I hear I am to have people looking after me?'

'Special Branch. John Macmillan thought it would be a wise precaution. He arranged it while I was in the land of nod. They'll be discreet.'

214

'And the men outside your door?'

'Special Branch too. They'll be gone in the morning when I check out.'

'You're expected to look after yourself?'

'Yes.'

'I suppose that means you're an expert in unarmed combat and carry a gun under your arm?' asked Tally. There was no mistaking the accusation in her voice.

'Yes,' said Steven flatly.

There was an uncomfortable pause before Tally shook her head slightly and her eyes filled with renewed doubt.

Steven took her hand and said, 'I served with Special Forces. I was a doctor but I acquired certain other skills along the way – but they're a legacy of the past – nothing to do with my current job, and I only carry a gun when there's cause to believe my life's in danger. I don't have a double 0 licence . . . although I have a TV one . . . and a driving one with three points for speeding on it.'

Tally couldn't resist a smile. She sat down on the edge of the bed and looked Steven straight in the eye. 'I hope I don't live to regret this but I'm going to believe you,' she said.

Steven closed his eyes and gave silent thanks.

'What are your plans when you leave here?'

'Back to London. I'm going to pick up the pieces of the investigation.'

'Please be careful.'

'I will, I promise. I've got too much to live for.'

'You could always stay at my place until you decide what you're going to do . . . Special Branch could look after both of us?'

Steven kissed Tally and thanked her for the offer. 'I have to talk things over with John Macmillan face-to-face. We've not been told the whole story about the vaccine. I'm convinced of it.'

'Keep in touch,' said Tally. It sounded so poignant that Steven took her in his arms and held her close. 'As soon as this thing's over we'll start making plans about us, right? We come first.'

Tally gave a slightly distant smile and nodded. 'Take care, Steven.'

Steven was officially discharged next morning after final tests on his reflexes and cardiac and respiratory functions were completed to George Lamont's satisfaction. 'You'll never be that lucky again,' said Lamont. 'There can't be too many people in the world who've been injected with cyanide and lived to tell the tale.'

'I believe you.'

Steven dressed and thanked the unit nurses for looking after him before having a word with Jenkins and Ritchie, the two Special Branch men on the door. 'Thank you, gentlemen, I'm grateful to you but happily I won't be requiring your services any longer.'

'Oh, just when we were beginning to enjoy ourselves,' said Jenkins, a thickset, bald man who would not have looked out of place in the front row of a rugby scrum. 'Nothing we like better than baby-sitting Sci-Med agents. Delicate flowers they are, George,' he said, turning to his colleague. 'Did you know that?'

Ritchie, his more thoughtful-looking colleague, gave an embarrassed smile.

'They're all graduates,' continued Jenkins. 'Brains the size of planets, some of them, they reckon. Isn't that right, Doctor?'

'Well, all things are relative,' said Steven, making sure he was looking directly at Jenkins when he said it.

'But when push comes to shove . . . it's Special Branch they call on when noses need blowing and arses wiping . . .'

'And an excellent job you do,' said Steven.

Jenkins bristled at being patronised. 'Now are you sure you wouldn't like us to see you across the road, Doctor?' he asked Steven. 'Check to see if there are any bad people out there? I mean, are you quite sure you're fighting fit again . . . ?'

Before Jenkins knew what had hit him, Steven had his arm twisted painfully up his back, his legs splayed apart and the side of his face rammed hard up against the wall in the corridor so that he looked like a gargoyle on a cathedral wall. 'Yes,' said Steven thoughtfully. 'Everything seems to be working well . . . but thanks for asking. It's always just as well to check . . .'

As the two Special Branch men walked away, Steven heard Ritchie say to Jenkins, 'You arse, didn't you know he was ex-Regiment?'

Steven found an official government courier waiting patiently for him in Reception. The man smiled politely and examined Steven's ID carefully before handing over the package Steven knew would contain the pistol and ammunition he'd requested. He signed three forms and wished the man a safe return to London before following the signs for the ground floor visitors' toilets where he used a cubicle for privacy while he loaded the weapon and secured it in its shoulder holster which he put on with some difficulty in the confined space. Finally, he adjusted the straps for comfort before putting his jacket back on and coming out to check in the mirror that there was no telltale bulge showing.

He used the exit nearest to where taxis dropped off their passengers and timed it so that he was exposed for the minimum of time before jumping into one that was just about to drive away after dropping off an elderly couple.

'You're supposed to wait at the stand,' growled the driver.

'Twenty quid says you'll overlook it this once.'

'Where to?'

Steven deliberately had the driver follow a circuitous route to the police compound where his car had been taken at Macmillan's request. He first asked to be taken to the hotel he'd stayed at on his first visit to Leicester, changing his mind half way to ask instead for the French restaurant that he had taken Tally to before finally directing the driver to the police compound when he felt sure that they weren't being followed.

'Are you having a laugh?' the driver growled.

'Call it the gypsy in my soul,' replied Steven.

He picked up the Honda and drove back to London without incident but spent the entire journey wondering why anyone should want to kill him, trying his best to work through things logically but without much success. Both attacks had originated in Leicester not London. He was certain that the first had been because of the tracking device on his Porsche – the fact that someone had reported his car stolen in order to get the information on its whereabouts seemed to confirm that. But that couldn't have been the method employed to trace him for the second attack. The Honda wasn't fitted with a tracker – at least he didn't think it was ... He called Stan Silver.

'No, it isn't. Don't tell me you've lost the bloody thing,' said Silver.

'Nothing like that,' Steven assured him. 'I was just wondering how somebody knew exactly where I was the other day.'

'If you think you've been followed and the car's to blame, maybe someone stuck one on?'

'It's a possibility,' agreed Steven.

'Bring it round.'

Steven glanced at his watch. 'I'm driving down from Leicester. I'll be there in about half an hour.'

'Inside's clean,' said Silver, finishing his inspection and edging out backwards. 'I'll put her up on the ramp.'

Silver drove the Honda on to the hydraulic ramp and pressed the button to raise it. He lit a cigarette while they waited for the vehicle to clear head-height. 'So, are you winning?' he asked Steven above the noise.

Steven shook his head. 'Somebody wants me out the game and I don't know why.'

'Sounds like bad news,' said Silver. 'One particular person or a gang?'

'A gang, east European.'

'Shit, not been muscling in on their interests, have you?'

'I almost wish I had, then at least I'd know what it's all about,' said Steven.

Silver was examining the underside of the Honda with a powerful torch, using the fingers of his left hand to rub away dirt. 'Well, well, what have we here?' he said, pulling something from the offside rear wheel arch and handing it to Steven. 'Problem solved.'

Steven looked at the tracking device for a few seconds in silence. 'I didn't tell anyone about the Honda,' he said. 'No one knew I had it.'

'Someone must have seen you driving it.'

'I tend not to drive at all in London.'

'Well, I'll leave it to you to work it out,' said Silver. 'Maybe you should leave that with me,' he added, nodding to the tracker.

Steven handed over the device. 'What will you do with it?'

'I pass a transport caff on the way home. I'll stick it on one of the sixteen-wheelers heading for the Channel ports. That should keep the buggers amused for a while.'

Steven thanked Silver and headed for his flat. He felt better for having discovered how his attacker had known where he was but was still left wondering how the opposition knew about the car in the first place. He had deliberately opted not to use a pool car and had made a point of not telling anyone what he was using and yet someone had still managed to find and tag it. His blood ran cold when he considered that it could have been an explosive device instead of a magnetic tracker.

Steven was still thinking about this in the bath with a gin and tonic in his hand when the phone rang. Cursing the fact – or was it his imagination? – that it always did when he forgot to take it into the bathroom with him and thinking that it might be Tally – although he had said he would phone her – he got out the bath and padded through to fetch it.

'Dr Dunbar? It's Linda Haldane in Edinburgh.'

'Oh, hello,' said Steven, remembering with a slight frisson of excitement that he'd asked her to phone him if she recalled anything at all that might throw light on what had angered her late husband so much. 'How are you?'

'Well, thank you,' replied Linda automatically. 'The children and I are moving out tomorrow. We've spent the day packing.'

'I'm sorry,' said Steven, remembering that she and the children couldn't afford to stay on in the house because of the financial problems raised by Scott's death being treated as suicide.

'You said that I should contact you if I came across anything, no matter how small . . .'

'Yes, I remember.'

'Scott taped something to the underside of his desk. I found it this morning when I was clearing away his things and dropped something on the floor. I had to crawl under to get it.'

'What was it?' asked Steven, aware that his pulse rate had risen sharply.

'An envelope with two cards in it.'

'Cards?'

'Record cards like the ones he used in his file index. I suppose he didn't want anyone to find these ones.'

'Like the burglars who came to call,' said Steven thoughtfully.

'The police said they were looking for drugs,' said Linda.

'Maybe,' said Steven, suddenly seeing things in a different light. 'What's on the cards?'

'Some sort of code. There are letters and numbers, not telephone numbers. They don't make a lot of sense to me I'm afraid.'

Steven, who was still dripping wet, wiped his hands on the towel he'd hastily tied round his waist and grabbed pen and paper from his desk before asking for details. He copied down the information as it was read out.

'First one, C-O-L-E space N-A-T space 4-0-9 space 1-0-0-7 hyphen 1-0-1-1 space 2-0-0-1.'

Steven read it back to her.

'Second card reads, N-R-G space 2 space 2-3-7 space 2-0-0-1. That's it, nothing else I'm afraid.'

Once again Steven read the letters and numbers back to her.

'Do you think it could be significant?' asked Linda. 'I mean, does it mean anything to you?'

'Not right now but if your husband went to the trouble of hiding these cards, there has to be a good reason,' said Steven.

'Something that will help prove Scott didn't take his own life?'

'I hope so,' said Steven. 'Keep in touch. Let me know where you are.'

The bath water had gone cold. Steven dried himself and got dressed. His whole demeanour had changed because of the phone-call. At last he had got a break. It might not make sense right now but he felt he had something to kick-start an investigation that had been threatening to hit the buffers. He called Tally and told her about the call.

'You deserve a break.'

'All I have to do now . . . is decipher it,' said Steven.

'I have confidence in you.'

TWENTY

Next morning Steven asked Sci-Med for an update on the green sticker children. It was emailed to him within the hour. Eight more children had been referred to clinics and hospitals with skin complaints varying in seriousness from simple rashes to actual skin degeneration and loss of sensation.

He shook his head as he read through the list but then started to feel puzzled. All the children had been exposed to the contaminating agent at exactly the same time and yet they were developing symptoms at widely varying times. This was not normal for poisoning. Poisons were not subject to the vagaries of individual immune systems as infections were. If the production manager, Dutton, was to be believed, the line used for vaccine distribution had never been used for the toxic compound so the toxin must have already been in the reservoir of vaccine when it was attached. That meant all the kids had been given the same dose, so a variation in body weight should have been the only factor in play. The kids weighing least should have come off worst as they would have received a higher dose of poison per unit body weight.

Steven had the relevant information to hand. He checked up on the records he had on his laptop and compared body weight to dates of referral for medical treatment. There was no correlation at all. In fact, the smallest and lightest child in the group had been the last to develop symptoms.

'What the hell's going on?' he murmured as he searched for any other relevant factors among the sick children. He drew a blank but the appearance of Trish Lyons in the list reminded him that he should have checked up on her condition. He'd been avoiding doing this for fear that he would hear nothing good. He called the hospital in Edinburgh.

'We had to remove her arm,' said Fielding. 'But I think you already knew we were going to have to do that?'

'Yes,' agreed Steven. 'Has that stopped the tissue damage?'

'I'm afraid not,' came the measured reply. 'She's lost sensation in her feet . . . she's wasting away before our eyes.'

'Jesus,' murmured Steven. 'Her poor mother must be going through hell.'

'She is,' agreed Fielding. 'Actually she's fallen ill herself.'

'I'm not surprised,' said Steven. 'She's been under such stress for so long. She's a strong-willed woman but . . .'

'No, I didn't mean that,' interrupted Fielding. 'We think it may be the same problem that Trish has.'

'What?' exclaimed Steve, feeling as if he'd just been hit between the eyes. 'How can that be?'

'I quite agree, it's a bit of a puzzle but she's developed a large white patch on her arm and she's been feeling very unwell . . . She's been admitted to the Western General for tests.'

Steven put down the phone. How could Trish Lyons' mother have been exposed to the toxin? Poisons weren't infectious or contagious like bacteria or viruses. You couldn't catch a poison . . . His gaze went back to the green sticker records showing on his laptop. These were solely the records of the children who'd been given the vaccine. There was no information in them about their families. He called Sci-Med and asked for an urgent check on all the families of green sticker children.

'What are we looking for?' asked the duty officer.

'Anyone who has had cause to go to their GP since their children were put on the green sticker list.'

'You mean, boils on the bum, cut fingers, verrucas . . .'

'Everything,' snapped Steven and put the phone down. He was edgy. His nerves were strung to breaking point. He had the awful feeling that he was on the brink of uncovering a nightmare.

He knew he'd have to wait some time for the information he'd asked for so he got out the codes he'd been given by Linda Haldane and started playing around with them to see if he could make any sense out of what appeared to be a random collection of letters and numbers but obviously wasn't if Haldane had gone to the trouble of hiding them. There was a very real possibility that the knowledge contained in the codes was the reason Scott Haldane had ended up in woodland with his wrists slashed.

Steven looked for anagrams and acronyms among the letters and for jumbled up phone numbers or dates among the numbers but without success. Apart from anything else, he was having difficulty concentrating when his mind kept straying to what Virginia Lyons' illness was telling him. He was making coffee when the duty man at Sci-Med called back.

'Four of us have been working on it non-stop,' said the man. 'Turns out quite a few have been to see their doctor. Want the report emailed?'

Steven said that he did and thanked him. He tapped the end of his pen anxiously on the desk until the little envelope icon appeared in the taskbar signifying the arrival of the report. He activated the Sci-Med decoder and started to read through the unscrambled document as it scrolled up on the screen. Ignoring the everyday complaints that were the staple of GPs' surgeries, Steven was left with a list of twenty-eight close family members of green sticker children who had consulted their doctors about skin problems or loss of sensation in one or more limbs. His fears had been realised. There was now no doubt in his mind. He called Tally.

'Steven? I've only got a moment. I'm in the middle of a ward round.'

'They've been lying.'

'Who's been lying?'

'Any or all of them,' replied Steven. 'The toxin in the vaccine story is rubbish. The kids weren't poisoned at all, they've been infected. We're dealing with an infectious agent here.' He told her about the family members who'd fallen ill.

'My God,' gasped Tally. 'This just gets worse and worse.'

'The vaccine itself is the problem,' said Steven. 'The contamination story was a blind.'

'Steven, this is truly awful.'

'Infectious disease in children is your specialty. Can we meet? I need to pick your brains.'

'Of course. Look, I'll get someone to cover for me this afternoon. Do you want to come up here?'

'Let's not take any more risks. I don't want your Special Branch minders knowing about the meeting. Do you think you can give them the slip?'

'I don't know ... I suppose so ...' said a startled Tally. 'They're not expecting me to try to avoid them. After all, they're on my side. I make a point of saying hello to them.'

'Give them the slip; drive south on the M1. I'll meet you in the main restaurant at Watford Gap services at 3 p.m.?'

'All right. Take care.'

'You too. Keep looking in your mirror. Make sure you're not being followed.'

'And if I am?'

'Find somewhere to stop and call me.'

Tally put the phone down without saying anything more and Steven knew what she must be thinking. He hated involving her but she was an expert in infectious diseases and that was exactly what he was going to need if he was to make any sense of this latest twist. A wave of frustration washed over him as he recognised that he still couldn't see motive in any of this. A group of children had been given a supposed vaccine that had infected them with some undetermined microbial agent that was eating away at their flesh and was now being passed on to their families. Who in their right mind would want to cover this up and pretend that nothing had happened? The biotech company who had designed the vaccine? The government officials who had been colluding with them? Or was it conceivable that some other faction was involved? His hand went unconsciously to the holster under his left arm. The odds seemed stacked against him.

'Who designed this place?' growled Tally as they entered the restaurant. 'Hieronymus Bosch?'

'His sort of style,' agreed Steven as they walked towards the serving area, thinking that a motorway service station was not an experience to make the human spirit rejoice. The sound of electronic games machines, the smell of fried food and the clatter of dirty plates being collected did little to provide a reassuring ambience.

'You weren't followed?' Steven asked.

Tally shook her head and said, 'I felt guilty sneaking away but no, I don't think I was followed.'

'I need your input. If an infectious agent is involved, as I'm sure it is, why can't any of the labs grow it?'

'It's possibly viral. Many viruses are difficult to grow. You often have to rely on serological tests showing antibodies in the patient's serum to indicate an underlying infection by a specific virus or group of viruses.'

'Serology tests were all negative,' said Steven.

'Then I'm at a loss,' said Tally.

'Why would children respond differently in terms of time to an infectious agent?'

'Some might be more immune than others, depending on what they've been exposed to in the past, or it could be that the agent grows very slowly and victims succumb at different rates.'

'What sort of agents are we talking about here?'

'If we're considering everything, we'd have to include prion diseases like new variant CJD, they can take a very long time to develop, and many viruses can remain in latent form for undetermined periods of time. In the case of bacterial infections, TB can take a couple of months to grow in culture.'

'I suppose TB would still be the thing to go for here,' said Steven. 'After all that's what the vaccine was made from and is designed to combat but none of the labs managed to grow it . . .'

'Because it's not a live vaccine,' completed Tally.

'Suppose it was? They could have been mistaken about that too.'

'Possible I suppose but from what you've told me the symptoms exhibited by the victims are nothing like TB. Tuberculosis is primarily a disease of the lungs, a chest infection.'

'You're right,' sighed Steven.

They sat in silence for a few moments before Steven offered to get Tally more coffee.

'I'd rather not,' she said. 'Have you made any progress with the codes Linda Haldane found?'

Steven shook his head. 'Not yet.' He brought out a copy and handed it to Tally.

'I see what you mean,' she said. 'Not exactly obvious . . . By the way, there was one thing I meant to mention to you. On the two occasions you've been attacked your assailants picked you up at my place.'

'I was aware of that.'

'On both occasions you had just paid a visit to St Clair Genomics.'

Steven gave this some thought. 'The first time I was driving the Porsche. I signed in at Reception and entered my registration number in the visitor book . . . The second time was on a Saturday morning when St Clair was the only person there. He was expecting me: I'd called the day before. I didn't sign in but the Honda was the only car in the car park apart from St Clair's. Someone could have bugged it while I was inside talking to him . . .'

'Just a thought,' said Tally.

'And a good one. So why would St Clair Genomics want me dead?' mused Steven. 'I only know what they and the government told me.'

'Maybe they thought you might find out what you've just told me about the infectious nature of the agent,' suggested Tally. 'That they were lying about problems on the production line and that there really is an issue with the vaccine itself. It has the capacity to kill people?'

'And they of course would stand to lose millions from cancelled government contracts,' completed Steven. 'That makes sense but why did they think I would find out?'

Steven slapped his palm against his forehead as the answer came to him. 'Because of my interest in Scott Haldane,' he exclaimed. 'I asked St Clair twice if the name Scott Haldane meant anything to him and he said no. He was lying. Rumours of what Haldane was saying must have got back to the company.'

'St Clair must have thought you were getting too close to finding out what Haldane knew,' said Tally.

Steven nodded. 'That's why they killed him. A GP, working in an ordinary practice in Edinburgh, figured out there was a major problem with the vaccine the kids had been given and maybe even what it was. He'd been told the kids had been given BCG but somehow he suspected different . . .'

'I guess it'll become clear when we crack the code,' said Tally.

'If Scott Haldane worked out what was wrong with the green sticker children then it's odds on that Alan Nichol, the designer of the vaccine, must have worked it out too. He must have wanted to blow the whistle but his employer didn't agree.'

'So they came up with the toxin story to hide the real truth and murdered him when he wouldn't go along with it.'

'It's just a question now of how many snouts are in the trough,' said Steven thoughtfully.

'You can't think the government people knew about this?' exclaimed Tally. 'Now we know that it's all about money.'

'I'd like to think not,' agreed Steven. 'But we know there are individuals who at the very least collaborated in giving an untested vaccine to schoolchildren and finished up giving them an infectious disease which is now spreading to their families. That's quite a skeleton to have in your cupboard.'

'I'm certainly glad it isn't in mine,' said Tally. 'I don't know how they're going to live with themselves.'

Steven took a moment to reflect and then said, 'Of course, if they really still believe the toxin story that St Clair came up with and don't know about the infectious nature of the vaccine, they won't think they've done anything wrong. They'll believe that their far-sightedness has led to the development of a new vaccine against TB which will shortly be going into production to protect the people. They'll be expecting knighthoods and rounds of applause from a grateful nation.'

'But the vaccine is infectious and dangerous,' Tally protested.

'We know that but we can't prove it,' said Steven. 'The vaccine has been tested by umpteen labs and no infectious agent has ever been found in it. We know that Scott Haldane and Alan Nichol were murdered and we know why but we haven't got the slightest shred of evidence.'

'But the circumstantial evidence is overwhelming,' said Tally.

'People won't hear what they don't want to hear.'

'But surely no one in their right mind could let vaccination go ahead when you tell them what you know,' said Tally.

'St Clair will stick to their story of a rogue toxin and those with reputations on the line will want to believe them.'

'But you must stop them,' exclaimed Tally. 'Sci-Med must stop them. You have to make them believe what you say is true. John Macmillan will believe you surely?'

'I think he will,' agreed Steven. 'But he'll need conclusive proof too before he can do anything. No one on the government side is going to want to listen even if they think it might be true. They'll play for time so that they can melt away into the background and become the anonymous faces of yesterday's government machine, men spending more time with their families or growing grapes in France or writing biographies of past politicians in the autumn sunshine of Umbria. New faces will be left to deal with new emergencies. It's always the way. One man starts a war, another has to finish it.'

'My God, do you really believe that?' asked Tally.

The look on Steven's face gave her the answer.

'Then you'll have to crack Scott Haldane's code and give them proof they can't ignore.'

Steven's response was to hurl himself across the table and topple Tally off her chair to bring both of them crashing to the ground.

TWENTY-ONE

Tally let out a scream but the sound was drowned out by the windows beside them shattering in a hail of automatic gunfire. Steven's arm held her pinned to the floor, keeping them both huddled behind the brickwork along the base of the windows which stretched the entire length of the wall. The air was full of flying glass and splintered woodwork as bullets ripped into the serving areas. Trolleys jerked and bounced and overturned, display cases exploded and people cowered everywhere, seeking what cover they could, horror etched in their faces. Some screamed constantly, seeming only to pause for breath, others were struck dumb, their faces white as snow.

Everyone in the restaurant assumed that the service area was under terrorist attack but Steven knew differently. He had noticed two men enter the restaurant a few minutes before and look around casually as if seeking a missing colleague. The fact that one had examined only the right side of the restaurant while the other covered the left suggested to him that this had been agreed previously and that they just might be professionals looking for a target. The fact that Steven noticed one give the other an almost imperceptible nudge after making momentary eye contact with him confirmed it. He had carried on his conversation with Tally but had watched them leave and walk over to their car some fifty metres away to open the boot. When they both started to head back to the restaurant carrying overcoats over their arms he knew at once what they were concealing and that he and Tally were in big trouble. As soon as the first man dropped his raincoat to the ground to reveal the muzzle of an automatic assault weapon, Steven had dived across the table to bring both himself and Tally into the lee of the brick wall supporting the windows as the glass above them shattered.

Steven indicated to Tally that she should crawl away from him, keeping close to the shelter of the wall. She started making for the far end of the room, using her elbows to propel herself along while he turned over on to his back, drew his gun and waited. There was a chance that his attackers would make good their escape but there was also a possibility that they would check to see if they had achieved their objective.

There was an eerie quiet about the place, broken only by the sound of sobbing somewhere in the room and shouting coming from far away. It was the kind of silence that follows the mayhem of a high-speed rail crash when the almost unimaginable momentum and energy bound up in the accident, the force which creates such a screaming hell of tortured metal and splintering wood, is suddenly spent, leaving nothing but an eerie quiet.

Steven did not blink. He steeled himself to continue waiting – even when he saw the muzzle of one of the guns appear above the wall – but, as soon as the second appeared, he sprang into action, swivelling round on the floor to put both feet firmly against the brickwork and push himself out from the wall. Holding the Glock firmly in both hands he fired two shots in quick succession – one into each of the two figures standing there. He went for body shots, the biggest target: he couldn't take the chance of missing with a head shot. Both men slumped to the ground but Steven was well aware that the Glock wasn't the most powerful handgun in the world.

With the words of a training sergeant from long ago echoing in his head, *Never take chances; if they go down, make sure they stay down*, Steven scrambled to his feet and holding his gun out in front of him, looked cautiously over the wall. One of the men, although badly wounded, tried one-handedly to bring his weapon round to bear on him. Steven shot him twice more and he lay still. The other man was lying motionless as if already dead but Steven saw that his finger was still curled round the trigger of his weapon. *Never take chances*. He shot him too without checking further.

Then he turned and hurried towards Tally who was cowering against the far wall with her knees held under her chin and her expression a mixture of horror and disbelief.

'Are you all right?' he asked gently, squatting down beside her.

Tally looked at him in silence for a moment before saying slowly and deliberately, 'They really don't like you, do they?'

It was such a ridiculous thing to come out with that Steven couldn't help but smile. Tally couldn't quite manage one but she put her head against Steven's chest and patted him with the palm of her hand. 'You're something else, mister.'

The noise level was rising as the whole place started to come to life again. People were running; people were shouting; the sound of emergency service vehicles in the distance grew ever louder.

'Let's get out of here,' said Steven, realising that the response to the incident was about to become organised. 'While we have the chance.'

He grabbed Tally's hand and together they stepped over the retaining wall and out through the gap where the windows had been into the car park. They got into the Honda, which was nearer than Tally's car, and drove off down the southbound slip road just as barriers were about to be pulled into place.

'They'll close the motorway,' said Steven as he gunned the Honda out on to the main carriageway with the rev counter on the red line in each gear. 'We'll try to make it to the first exit.'

Once again they were just in the nick of time as police were in the process of closing the exit road. One officer was about to raise his hand when he realised how fast the Honda was travelling and changed his mind, stepping smartly out of the way to let it past. Steven braked hard at the top of the exit road and saw in his mirror that it had now been closed off with two police vehicles straddling it.

'What now?' asked Tally, rubbing her shoulder where the seat belt had bruised her.

'Somewhere quiet and anonymous,' said Steven. 'We need time to let the dust settle. I don't want to risk going back to my flat right now in case it was me they followed and they know where I live.

'Steven, the M1 is closed, a motorway service area has been shot to pieces and there are two dead men lying back there . . . just how long is it going to take for the dust to settle? I mean, are we both going to live that long?'

'I'll get Sci-Med to dress it up as a gangland feud.'

'I know I don't understand too much about any of this,' said Tally. 'But I can't see your . . . what is it they call it when you need a way of getting out of a bad situation?'

'An exit strategy?' suggested Steven.

'That's it, an exit strategy. Do you have one?'

'We have to crack the code,' said Steven. 'Once we know the full facts and pass them on there's no point in killing me.'

'Are you sure the other side know that?'

'Rules of the game.'

'Game?' exclaimed Tally. 'You call this a game?' She looked and sounded angry.

'Sorry,' said Steven. 'That was male bravado talking. I'm as scared as you are, believe me.'

'You couldn't be,' sighed Tally. 'You just couldn't be. I keep praying I'm going to wake up and find this has all been a nightmare and I never met anyone called Steven Dunbar.'

Steven gave her a sideways look and she squeezed his knee in apology.

They lapsed into silence until Steven said, 'How about here?' He slowed as they came to a large, blue sign advertising Radleigh House Country Hotel.

'As long as it has hot water and gin,' said Tally. 'God, we've no luggage,' she added as an afterthought. Steven brought the car to a halt in the gravel car park fronting the hotel.

'I've got a bag in the back. It's just got odds and ends in it but it'll get us past the front desk. We'll get ourselves cleaned up, call room service and have a bit of a breather before deciding where we go from here.'

'Will you call Sci-Med?' asked Tally.

Steven nodded.

Tally was in the bath and Steven had just tipped the room service waiter who had delivered two large gin and tonics and a plate of smoked salmon sandwiches when his phone rang. It was John Macmillan.

'The business at Watford Gap services . . . Anything I should know?' asked Macmillan.

'Another attempt on my life,' said Steven. 'Dr Simmons was with me at the time.'

'Russians?'

'I didn't get the chance to ask,' replied Steven acidly.

'How many and what was the outcome?'

'Two, both dead.'

'Any danger of you being identified?'

'I don't think so. They opened proceedings with a Kalashnikov overture played on the windows. There was widespread panic, people under seats, that sort of thing. It should be possible to pass it off as a gangland feud.'

'Right. I'll tell that to the Home Secretary. Where are you?'

'In the country.'

Macmillan waited, expecting more, but nothing was forthcoming. 'Quite right,' he said. 'You must feel you can't trust anyone.' He cut short the ensuing silence by saying, 'But we've made progress in establishing the Russians' interest in all this.'

'Really?' asked Steven, suddenly feeling that he might not be so alone after all.

'You asked about the funding behind Redmond Medical and St Clair Genomics. It turns out they have a common source; a company called European Venture Capital is the principal backer in both cases. It's a concern that has been attracting the attention of our security services for some time, especially their front man. He's an Englishman named Marcus Rose. They think he's the old Etonian front for Russian Mafia money coming into the country.'

'So the Russian Mafia bankrolled the Nichol vaccine?' said Steven as if almost unwilling to believe what he was saying.

'And stand to make millions out of it. Funny old world.'

'The vaccine's lethal,' said Steven.

'What?' exclaimed Macmillan.

Steven told him what he'd deduced.

'But if you're saying this thing is infectious, why couldn't the lab people grow anything?' protested Macmillan. 'They all drew blanks.'

'I'm trying to find that out,' said Steven.

'You're going to need proof,' said Macmillan. 'The government is hailing the Nichol vaccine as a major step forward in protecting our people. On the other hand it would explain why those who'll benefit from the vaccine hitting the shelves want you dead.'

'It's my connection with Scott Haldane, the GP in Edinburgh who was treating Trish Lyons, that's making them think I'm a threat,' said Steven. 'I think Haldane figured out what was going on and that's why they killed him, but his wife has come up with something that might help find out what it was.' Steven told Macmillan about the hidden envelope and its contents. 'I'll be back in touch when I've made progress.'

'Right, I'll get to work on preparing a feast of gangland outrage for the newspapers to breakfast on.'

Steven took her gin through to Tally who was luxuriating in a bath filled with Molton Brown bubbles, courtesy of the hotel. She opened her eyes when Steven put the glass down within reach.

'Life has just taken a turn for the better,' she purred. 'Albeit a very temporary one . . . What did your boss have to say?'

'The Russian Mafia are behind the Nichol vaccine.'

Tally's eyes opened like saucers. 'How on earth did that happen?'

'The West is awash with dodgy Russian cash looking for respectable outlets to launder it through – property, real estate, football clubs. It turns out that one of them is the venture capital company which backed St Clair Genomics and their development of the Nichol vaccine. Nichol's "success" means a big return on their investment.'

'And withdrawal of the vaccine would mean a big loss?'

'You got it.'

'At least, it begins to make sense now,' said Tally. 'Mind you, I'm not sure if that's a good or a bad thing.'

'I think our aim should be to make it a thing of the past,' said Steven. 'And to do that, we have to figure out the meaning of the codes on Haldane's cards.'

Tally looked up at him from the bubbles. 'Bring them through . . . and your drink . . . and get in.'

Steven joined Tally in the bath, letting out a sigh of appreciation as the warm water lapped up over him. Tally smiled and said, 'Funny where life can take you when you're least expecting it . . . Where are we exactly?'

'Not sure.'

Tally gave a little giggle that told Steven the gin was going straight to her head. 'Cheers,' she said.

'Cheers,' said Steven, raising his glass in response.

'Right, I'm ready,' said Tally, leaning back and closing her eyes again. 'Let's have my starter for ten . . . no conferring.'

Steven smiled and read out the series of letters and numbers from the first card.

Tally tried to interpret. 'Cole . . . Nat . . . colenat . . . colenate . . . No, let's have the second.'

Steven read out the second.

'N-R-G . . . Energy? . . . No.'

'They both end in the same four numbers,' said Steven. 'Two, zero, zero, one.'

'A date, two thousand and one?' suggested Tally.

'Could be . . . Maybe a reference to something that happened several years ago?'

Tally's eyes shot open in response to Steven's use of the word 'reference'. 'Read them out again,' she said.

'C-O-L-E space N-A-T . . .'

'Cole . . . Nature,' she said. 'They're not codes at all: they're references. They're shorthand references to papers in scientific journals! Cole is the author's name, *Nature* is the journal. What were the numbers?'

Seeing immediately that she was right, Steven completed the decoding. 'Volume 409, pages 1007 to 1011. Two thousand and one. Brilliant.'

'And the other?' asked Tally.

'N-R-G. Can't say it rings a bell . . .'

Tally gave it a few moments' thought. '*Nature Reviews Genetics*,' she announced. 'We're there!'

'Volume 2, page 37, two thousand and one,' completed Steven.

'Now we just have to find out what they say and why they're relevant,' said Tally, pulling the plug and stepping out of the bath.

'We need to find a medical library,' said Steven.

'I would suggest going straight to my hospital but that's probably a bad idea in the circumstances?'

'It is,' agreed Steven. 'Special Branch will be looking for you and they're possibly not the only ones.'

They dressed hurriedly, snatching mouthfuls of sandwich as they did so. 'Mmm, they're good,' mumbled Tally. 'Wish we had more time. You know, you could always hand over the references to Sci-Med and let them check it out?'

'No,' said Steven. 'We've come this far. Let's see it through.'

'If you say so,' conceded Tally reluctantly. 'Thinking about where we left the motorway, I reckon the med school at Warwick University in Coventry is probably the nearest.'

'D'you know it?' asked Steven.

'I do,' said Tally. 'Leicester and Warwick universities have strong links and my hospital's a teaching hospital. I know Warwick well. I can take you right to the library.'

'Just what I wanted to hear,' said Steven.

Steven paid for one night with his credit card and ignored the looks that passed between staff on the desk.

'What would my mother say . . .' murmured Tally as they left.

'I reckon we'll just drive until we pick up a road sign,' said Steven as they hurried across to the Honda.

'Keeping well away from the motorway,' added Tally.

They followed country lanes in a vaguely north-west direction until, with a joint sigh of relief, they came to a junction with the A35, signposted Coventry. This was quickly followed by frustration when they found themselves stuck behind a tractor for what seemed an eternity until it turned off and they picked up speed again.

'Any guesses what we're going to find?' asked Tally.

Steven shook his head. 'None at all. You?'

'I can't imagine,' said Tally. She gave Steven directions as they entered the Warwick campus with both of them feeling nervous.

The plan was to walk straight into the medical library and head for the reference section but a severe-looking librarian looked up from her desk when they entered and the fact that she didn't smile or divert her gaze made Tally feel guilty. She walked over to the woman and showed her hospital staff card. Steven followed up with his ID which was examined in detail.

'How can I help?' the woman asked.

'It's all right,' replied Tally. 'I know my way around.'

Steven winked at the woman and got a stony stare for his trouble.

'I bet New Year at her house is a barrel of laughs,' he murmured as they walked towards the reference section.

'Ssh.'

Tally ran her finger lightly over the alphabetic labelling at the end of each row of shelves as they passed, getting ever nearer to the back wall where the atmosphere was heavy with the smell of old books and dust. 'Here we are, N for *Nature*.'

'You get the genetics journal; I'll get the other one,' whispered Steven.

A quick search of the shelves to his left and Steven found the bound copies of *Nature* journals from the year 2001. He removed the one containing volume 409 and took it over to an unoccupied table where he sat and waited for Tally to join him. His mouth was beginning to dry with excitement as he whispered, 'You read that one and I'll read this. Then we'll talk.'

Tally complied with a nod and they both opened their volumes to begin reading.

Although he didn't expect to feel encouraged by what he found, Steven had not anticipated the wave of horror that swept over him as he read the abstract of the relevant paper and slowly started to realise what must have happened at the St Clair Genomics lab. Even the reason for Scott Haldane working out what the problem might be became clear when Steven remembered that Haldane had worked for a long time in Africa. Haldane hadn't known anything about the Nichol vaccine at all: he had recognised the symptoms of a disease in Trish Lyons that he couldn't quite bring himself to believe or mention to anyone at the time.

Steven slowly raised his eyes and saw that Tally had been filled with the same sense of horror. She mouthed the one word, 'Leprosy?' and he nodded as if subconsciously unwilling to confirm it. 'This paper reports the work of a group at Cambridge who sequenced the leprosy genome,' he said. 'They found it to be a cut down version of the TB genome, as if at some time back on the evolutionary path, leprosy had discarded all the genes it could do without. TB has four thousand genes, leprosy only sixteen hundred.'

'And that's the reason they can't grow it in the lab,' said Tally. 'The leprosy bacillus has to grow inside cells in the body, stealing nutrients from them and evading the immune system until it can infect the Schwann nerve cells. This in turn leads to sensory loss – the reason leprosy sufferers have such horrible disfigurement. They don't feel it when they burn or cut themselves which leads to mutilation and continual infections.'

Steven thought of Trish Lyons and the accident with boiling water. Trish had suffered horrible injuries but she was also shocked by the fact she didn't feel pain. That's what she had been trying to tell her mother and now Virginia Lyons was beginning to experience the same loss of sensation in the patches that were breaking out on her skin. Steven closed his eyes for a moment against the full implications of the nightmare.

'But how could it happen?' asked Tally, looking bemused.

'Alan Nichol,' said Steven but Tally's eyes still asked the question.

'He made his vaccine the "modern" way. He used the techniques of molecular biology to cut down the size of the TB genome in the lab until it was – he thought – no longer infectious only he had created a new version of the leprosy bacillus by accident. It stimulated antibody production against the genus that TB and leprosy belong to – Mycobacteria – but the strain didn't grow in the lab so he thought he had made an effective non-live vaccine . . . to the applause and go-ahead from a grateful government.'

'Oh God,' sighed Tally, shaking her head. 'What an absolute disaster.'

'Judging by the way the infection raced through Keith Taylor, this strain may actually be worse than real leprosy itself,' said Steven.

Tally nodded. 'It sounds like it can grow faster,' she said. 'Maybe it has a few more genes.'

'On the other hand, it's not progressing particularly quickly in the others,' said Tally. 'So maybe the human immune system is working better against this strain than it does against real leprosy?'

'God, I hope so,' said Steven. 'Any idea what the treatment is for leprosy these days?'

'I seem to remember reading in a journal recently that the World Health Organisation was recommending multi-drug therapy in their bid to stamp out the disease. Dapsone, rifampicin and clofazimine if I'm not mistaken. It's not a disease I've ever come across.'

'I guess that goes for all the other physicians and skin clinic people who missed the signs too,' said Steven.

Tally made an apologetic face. 'I suppose so . . .'

'If there is a god, he's making it bloody hard for us agnostics to recognise the fact,' said Steven.

'What now?'

'I'll tell John Macmillan everything, get him to pull the plug on the vaccine, get treatment organised for the green sticker kids and their families and start the crucifixion scene in Whitehall.'

'You don't really think anyone there knew the whole truth, do you?' asked Tally.

'Not that it was leprosy in the vials,' said Steven. 'But, ultimately, these people were responsible for being taken in by a bunch of Russian gangsters and damned nearly licensing a vaccine that would have given kids all over the country leprosy. Given the opportunity, I personally will bang in the nails.'

Steven brought out his phone and was about to call Sci-Med when one of the library staff appeared at his side. 'I'm sorry, that's against the rules,' she said.

Steven gave a half smile. 'Of course,' he said with a sideways glance at Tally. 'We must stick to the rules . . . otherwise we'll get in a right mess . . .' He took the phone outside and called Macmillan.

Tally waited for a few minutes inside and then went out to join Steven just as he was finishing the conversation. 'All right?' she asked.

'All done,' said Steven. 'The dogs have been let loose.'

'Do you think the government will fall?'

'Right now, I neither know nor care. John Macmillan said that Downing Street will be calling in the leaders of the other parties to "keep everyone in the loop and chart the way ahead".'

'And us? What do we do?'

'We lie low for a couple of days until Marcus Rose and Phillip St Clair are banged up and their Russian pals know the game's over.'

'My God,' said Tally as if suddenly realising something. 'The hospital must be wondering where I am and my car is still in the car park at Watford Gap and I haven't phoned . . .'

Steven put a finger on her lips. 'It's all being taken care of,' he said. 'Macmillan has been in touch with the hospital. You are currently providing invaluable assistance to HMG and will be officially on leave until such time as your services are no longer required. Your car will be returned to your home.'

'But I have the keys . . .' said Tally.

Steven smiled.

'I suppose that was silly,' she said, getting a nod in response. 'Just how long are my *services* going to be required?'

'Let's see now,' said Steven. 'We'll lie low for a couple of days and then we're going up to Scotland for a short break: there's someone there I'd like you to meet.'

'I love it when you're masterful,' said Tally.

Steven smiled.

'Just don't get too masterful . . . or I'll cut them off . . .'

AUTHOR'S NOTE

The scientific papers cited in this work of fiction are real and listed below. Readers may be interested to know that, in a study conducted by Lockwood and Reid and reported in the *Oxford Journal of Medicine* in 2001, the median time taken between the onset of symptoms and the diagnosis of leprosy in the United Kingdom was found to be 1.8 years. Delay in diagnosis occurred in 82% of cases. Misdiagnoses as dermatological and neurological conditions were important causes of delay and 68% of patients finally diagnosed with the disease had already suffered nerve damage leading to disability.

Cole et al, *Nature* 2001: **409**: 1007–1011
C. Dennis, *Nature Reviews Genetics* 2001: **2**: 237
D.N.J. Lockwood and A.J.C. Reid, *Oxford Journal of Medicine* 2001: **94**: 207–212